## Praise for WAVES

*... a remarkable novel ...*
PHILIP P[...]

*Sharon Dogar is a writer to watch.*
MEG ROSOFF

*... fabulously atmospheric and only the most hard-hearted reader
could fail to be moved by the ending.*
SUNDAY TELEGRAPH

*... a compelling story that mixes tense, erotic descriptions of first love
and first sex with overtones of the supernatural thriller.*
OBSERVER

*Sharon Dogar seizes the season with her own particular brand
of probing, looming, sensual enquiry ...*
GUARDIAN

*... an atmospheric, suspenseful tale ...*
SUNDAY TIMES

*... a mystery, the unravelling of which is handled with skill and elegance.*
IRISH TIMES

*Haunting, well-written and deeply into adolescent psychological turmoil,
this novel provides a gripping reading experience ...*
CAROUSEL

*Broodingly sinister, compelling and painfully beautiful by turns.*
BOOKSELLER

*The story sucks you into its undertow and beaches
you, gasping, 345 pages later ...*
OXFORD TIMES

# From the Chicken House

Can love really change everything? Can it wipe out memories, family guilt, present-day hate? Or do we have to *do* something first – pay a price? Sharon Dogar's astonishing second novel is electric, taut, exposed, violent, romantic, heart-breaking and life-affirming. Everything that love is.

Barry Cunningham
Publisher

# Falling

## SHARON DOGAR

Chicken House

2 Palmer Street, Frome, Somerset BA11 1DS

Text © Sharon Dogar 2009
Cover illustration © Georgina Hounsome
Illustration © George Fiddes
First published in Great Britain in 2009
The Chicken House
2 Palmer Street
Frome, Somerset BA11 1DS
United Kingdom
www.doublecluck.com

Sharon Dogar has asserted her rights under the Copyright, Designs and Patents Act,
1988, to be identified as the author of this work.

Cover design by Steve Wells
Interior design by Steve Wells
Typeset by Dorchester Typesetting Group Ltd
Printed in UK by CPI Bookmarque, Croydon, CRO 4TD
The paper used in this Chicken House book is made from wood grown
in sustainable forests.

1 3 5 7 9 10 8 6 4 2

British Library Cataloguing in Publication data available.

ISBN 978 1 905294 69 5

Though nothing can bring back the hour
Of splendour in the grass, of glory in the flower;
We will grieve not, rather find
Strength in what remains behind . . .

Thanks to the human heart by which we live,
Thanks to its tenderness, its joys and fears,
To me the meanest flower that blows can give
Thoughts that do often lie too deep for tears.

*William Wordsworth*

For my mum and dad: Miraj Din Dogar and Anne Dogar

And for my sisters: Janice, Yasmin and Parveen

With love and thanks for being nothing like the characters in this book.

*'Because that's what families do, isn't it, they survive!'*

# Prologue

I saw a picture once.

A picture of a deep blue-green tropical sea; a picture of where the land stopped and the sea began. Only the land didn't give up straight away; it kept on trying to surface, reappearing in little green islands, small stranded bumps in the sea. Like a necklace, a chain of deep-green pearls, each one separated by the blue, blue water.

I still think of that picture sometimes.

I wonder if that's what special moments in a lifetime are like – that they stand out in a sea of sea.

Or maybe it's what whole lifetimes are like. I know

that's what Sammy might think, that the struggling green islands are like lifetimes, each one of them separate and all of them different, yet somehow still connected.

But me, I think the islands are like moments. Single moments in time, saved and held on to – just waiting to be put together to make sense, to make a story.

Like memories.

Or choices.

And then there are the decisions.

Each one can leave you in the sea, drowning; each one can connect you back to land.

They can change everything, or nothing.

Sometimes you have to hold on.

And sometimes you have to let go.

Sometimes you have to remember.

And sometimes you think you'll go crazy if you don't forget.

And then there's forgiveness. What's that about?

It's a word, that's all, and after everything that's happened to Sammy and me, I think I know a better one. A word that comes out of all the moments we've had, together and alone.

Me and Sammy.

I think the word we're looking for here is understand-ing. But that's us. Me and Sammy.

Maybe you're different?

I know I was . . .

# Part One

# Neesh

*'Useless!'* That's what the new teacher's eyes are saying to me. Saying it so loud that I can't hear the actual words coming out of his mouth. I mean, I can hear the words moving in my ears – but they aren't in tune with his lips somehow. It's like his mouth's moving faster than my ears or something. I try to blink the words straight.

Blink. Blink, blink.

And slowly the words come clear.

'Take your coat off.' That's what his words are saying. Their meaning lands in me, echoes.

Blink. Blink, blink.

'She's weird, sir, she don't never take it off.'

*Yeah, that's right,* I think, *listen to Gita.* But the teacher doesn't, he just goes right on like he's sure he knows best.

'I'm talking to *you*, Nushreela, not the rest of the class!' he says, and he bends down low towards me, trying to look into my eyes, to see me. I drop my head further down. Down and down, until all my eyes are filled with is the floor. A little, tiny, dirty square patch of it. *Why don't you know?* I'm thinking. *Everybody else knows. Didn't anyone tell you I don't talk? Stop making them all look at me.*

And then I see my speech therapist's face in the dirty patch of floor. 'Not *can't* speak, technically she can,' she always says to anyone who asks. 'There's often an emotional element to becoming mute . . . a trauma, maybe . . .' I usually stop listening at this point. The colours above her head are as lifeless and bored as I am at having to make shapes with my mouth. *Why* I won't talk is what she never asks me, but it's what she wonders. Well, *sorry*, I think, but I thought you were the one who was meant to have the answers.

I shake her out of my head.

'Is that a no, then?' asks the teacher. I don't look at him. I put my hands over my knees, snuggle them deep into the warm silky pockets of my coat, hold on to it tight.

Cold.

I'm so cold.

I can't take my coat off, ever; it would be like taking off my skin.

Can't ever.

Blink. Blink, blink.

'Are you being deliberately difficult?' the teacher asks, and I steal a quick glance at his blue, blue eyes, over in a flash. I can see his confusion, it floats above his head. It's grey, grey and woollen, like the long old-fashioned socks Jammi wears to his private school. The new teacher doesn't know what to do with me.

Neither do I.

I drop my head even lower, so that my hair and dupatta (that's veil in your language) fall across my face, hiding me from his eyes. Perhaps if he can't see me he might go away.

'Really, don't worry about her, sir!' says Gita, but what she really means is *Look at me instead. Notice me.* Everyone wants to look at Gita. I dart a glance at her through my hair.

Dart. Blink, blink. Gita's gorgeous. Lips the colour of brinjal (that's aubergine) and eyes that glitter.

Not like me.

'It's just her thing, like, innit, sir,' she goes on, 'having her coat on. Going on at her about it's just cruel, like teasing an animal.'

Everyone laughs and I bite the inside of my lip hard. The blood tastes clean and salt, the pain of it is sudden and real like the insult. I'm not an animal.

I draw my coat even closer, hold it on tight. Beneath the warm black wool I'm beginning to sweat, armpits prickling, everyone's looking at me. No one can make me take it off. *He can't make me, can't make me take it off,* I whisper in my head.

Can he?

I'm frightened, though. What if he can? My finger pokes right through the lining of the coat. Oh no! I'll have to sew it up again.

'Can you take it off?' he asks.

Question: Can I take my coat off? Can I speak? Can I do anything right?

Answer: No.

The teacher doesn't sound angry, only polite and determined. I don't know what will happen next; this is new. Most of the time I just get thrown out of class. I can sit in the annexe where it's warm. I can read. Nobody asks me any questions, nobody sounds like they can even see me. I like it like that.

I like it.

*Go-away-go-away-go-away,* I think at him.

Q: If I think it hard enough, will he do it?

*Go-away-away-away.*

A: No.

I shake my head again but he's still here.

Blink. Blink, blink.

He's still standing here, looking at me, and the class begins to chant, 'Off, off, off, off!'

'That's enough!' he shouts.

*Go away, go away, I can't see you,* I think. But he only drops his own head lower, even closer to mine.

Oh no! My hair's all greasy-dirty-filthy-disgusting. Greasy-dirty-filthy-disgusting, like the floor I'm staring at. I want to reach up and cover my head, BUT I CAN'T, I'd have to let go of my coat – and then what would happen?

'You'll boil, Nushreela!' he says. 'Even the radiators are overheating!' But he's wrong, I'm cold. I'm always cold, even when I'm sweating I'm still freezing, like I'm wrapped in ice and packed at the bottom of the world where nothing can ever warm me.

Q: Is it a Paki thing, always being cold?

'Perhaps she's cold, sir!' someone says. 'And she's not being insolent, she can't talk!' His voice is sky blue and calming. His voice makes my heart jump and pound at the bars of my ribs.

His name is Sammy.

*Let me out, let me out!* my heart shouts at me, crashing against my bones.

Q: Is that why it's called a ribcage?

I close my eyes. I blink so fast I can't see at all any more. The world's a blur. I can't see Sammy's lovely long dark hair and puzzled face, staring at me. Can't see that thing in his eyes . . . can't see the shape of his body . . . or hear the sound of his singing . . . all the things that make me . . . that make me want to . . .

Blink. Blink, blink.

But it's no good blinking because I can see the whole of him so clearly inside my head. I can always see his face. When I first met him it was like I was meeting a picture that was already outlined against the backs of my eyes and just waiting for him to come along and fit into it. We've been friends forever, but if that's the case then . . .

Q: What is it that I feel inside me every time I look at Sammy?

A: Nothing, nothing, nothing. Don't look, Neesh, don't see.

Danger.

I shiver.

'Are you *really* cold?' asks the tall white teacher with his dark hair and blue eyes. I nod, and at long, long last, he sighs, stands up and walks away.

Given up at last. Jesus, Mary and Mohammed (peace be upon them), what took you so long?

I heave a sigh and sink back into my coat. I pull up my dupatta and cover my hair.

'Useless . . . hopeless . . . can't do a thing with her.' That's what the teacher's back says to me, and the colours above his head change and turn in the air like clothes on a washing line. He's going further and further away from me. He's going so far away that perhaps he'll walk right through the wall. Yeah? That would be funny. What if he just walked right through the wall without stopping, where would he be then? Lost, that's where.

Lost.

Like me.

'OK everybody,' he says, 'excitement over! Carry on with your stories.'

I bend back over the clean white paper and begin to write. I always write the same story, because it's what I've always seen inside me. I'll write it next week, and the week after as well. None of the teachers bother to stop me any more. It's like a dream, a film that's always running inside my head, only the weird thing is, I don't know if it's a beginning or an ending. I only know that it's always stuck in the same place. It goes like this . . .

*I'm standing on something that moves beneath me, rocks me. Far in the distance on a shining lake, there's a boat. Only you can't really see the boat because it's so buried in flowers, so heavy with them that the whole thing's sinking, leaving only a flowery boat-shape, an echo of a boat, floating low in the water.*

*There's a man standing at the back of the boat with a pole.*

*A stick man, with stick-thin arms, punting all the flowers slowly through the water.*

*And he's so far away that it looks like they're hardly moving.*

*Behind and above him the mountains make themselves out of the sky.*

*Below him the same mountains hang motionless in the clear water. Reflected, suspended upside down.*

*The whole world is pale. Pale-blue sky and snow-capped mountains.*

*The water takes on the colours of everything around it.*

*Only the man and the boat are bright, because the flowers are red and gold and orange.*

*And the man is a deep chestnut-brown.*

*They look like they're stuck on to the scene, like collage. And they cut the sky and lake in two, marking the difference between where sky starts and the earth ends.*

The picture rocks against the backs of my eyes. I see it again and again, and however hard I try, I can't ever make it go backwards or forwards.

Sometimes I think if I can only describe each piece of it minutely, perfectly, then maybe, maybe everything will change and it will move forward. Sometimes I imagine being on the boat myself. I imagine I can sink my arms into all those flowers, lie down in them, roll in them, throw them in the air and feel them land all over me then . . . and then . . .

Q: Then what?

A: Then the picture fades, and if I try too hard to make

it move all I feel is that I'm falling, falling, and the next thing I know I've blacked out.

I write and write the words that show the picture in my head. And when I've finished I go right back to the beginning and start all over again.

'Hello!' says the teacher. 'Anybody home?' And I see his hand waving in front of my eyes, like he's rubbing the picture out. Everybody laughs, except me.

Except me and Sammy.

Q: Where does it come from, the picture? Why doesn't it ever fade, and what's it waiting for?

A: A shiver. I don't know the answer. I'm not sure I want to know, and then I think that maybe it's not just the picture that's stuck, it's me too.

Stuck in my life.

Stuck in my old coat.

Stuck in my house with my sicko brother and freaked-out mum, and I wish I was someone else, anyone else but me.

And then I hear Sammy begin to hum. He's sitting right behind me and humming under his breath, singing an old nonsense song that we made up years ago. We used to sing it to each other in silly accents to the tune of Dad's old Bollywood records.

'Ip-in-ee-pin-ah-terri-terri-sutta!' The sound of his voice holds me up, and I see us both the way we used to be when we were just kids.

We're six and we sing the nonsense words over and over

– 'Ip-in-ee-pin-ah-terri-terri-sutta!' – until we're laughing so much we have to hold on to each other as we fall over.

Sometimes it feels like we've known each other for ever.


## Sammy

*Oh, come on Neesh,* I'm thinking, *just do what the teacher says and take your coat off! I mean, what would happen if you did, would the world cave in?* But she doesn't, she just holds her curled-up left hand in her lap and goes off into one of her daydreams – and it does something to me when she does that. It always has. I hate it, and you know why? Because her daydreams don't have me in them.

She did it the very first time we met.

I can still remember the first time I ever saw her. I think she was five and I was about six. Our families have always been connected – it's something to do with the time Grandpa spent in India during the war.

'We arrived just in time to watch the empire fall apart!' he laughs. 'Grandstand seats!'

'It was the ruin of you, that place!' says Mum, but Grandpa doesn't look ruined at all to me, or if he does it's only in the way that lovely old buildings are when you know that their foundations will go on forever.

'How did India ruin you?' I used to ask.

'It was there I found the light in my soul and had it extinguished!' he'd say. Or, 'Through the fine art of religious bigotry and personal prejudice!' And sometimes he'd smile. He wasn't really finding it funny, I did know that – but what I never knew was why not. I know Grandpa was only about my age when he was sent out to India to stay with his uncle, and that something happened when he was out there, but I've given up asking for the details. When I do, he just says things like that; things that kind of make sense but still manage not to tell you anything. And then, sometimes, he looks so sad when I ask him about India that it's me who wants to stop asking questions.

But he was happy about Neesh and her family coming to England.

'Hi!' said Mum. 'Nushreela, isn't it? Well, this is Sammy!' I looked up and there Neesh was, looking me straight in the eyes. No one had ever looked at me like that before. She just stood there and stared, and then she blinked, like her eyes were taking me right in.

Blink. Blink, blink.

And I couldn't take my eyes off her. She was so golden and bright and shining. She was Rapunzel and Princess Jasmine and every story I'd ever had read to me, and she was every Moghul miniature painting that Grandpa used to spend hours staring at in the British Museum while I tore around the gallery, waiting for him to get to the Egyptian rooms.

I watched her right back as her eyes closed. They shut so slowly, like she was closing a door somewhere deep inside her, *click*, and I would always be on the outside. I didn't want to be on the outside. I wanted to be on the inside, wherever she was behind her dreaming eyes. I felt this feeling rise up inside of me as she began to sway and fall. A fear that I had to catch her, and even though I was only six I reached out for her as she fell, sure that only *my* hands could catch her and make her safe. Our hands grazed, just a touch, and then I drew back as our palms sparked.

'That's what comes of wearing polyester!' whispered Mum sharply, meanly, backing away from the falling Neesh, and pulling me with her.

'Oops-a-daisy!' said Neesh's dad, as he swooped her up and held her in his arms, where she blinked, and opened her eyes wide, looking at him.

Blink. Blink, blink.

And she looked around, not happy (at least that's what I thought) until her eyes rested on me again. And then she laughed and she was the Neesh I came to know, the one that used the bobbles on the end of her plaits as weapons of mass destruction and made up nonsense words with me to her dad's old records.

'Ip-in-ee-pin-ah-terri-terri-sutta!'

I hum the words now under my breath, hoping she'll hear me, hoping they'll wake her up, bring her out of her daydream and connect her back to the real world. I hate it when she blanks out. I feel like maybe one day she might never, ever come back. Where does she go, and what does she see? Back in the days when she would talk, before her dad left home, she used to tease me. She used to tell me stories of where she went when she blacked out. She swam under the sea and she flew down low over the ocean. She sat on top of mountains, and she had tea with Rajahs while sitting on her elephant.

'No you never!' I'd shout, but I was just jealous, jealous that I was never, ever with her, not in a single story. And once I was so angry about it that I ignored her and played with Jammi, her brother (who I hate), for three whole weeks instead. She didn't say anything at all. She just grew sadder and sadder, until in the end I couldn't bear it any more, and so I said sorry.

And she said, 'I don't go anywhere, Sammy. Sometimes I see a boat on a lake and then it all just goes black, and there's nothing. No stories, no elephants, just nothing.'

And she looked at the floor, and my heart tipped over and I was scared. I didn't know until then that there *could* be nothing.

We never spoke about it again. We tried to pretend it never happened. And I wished I'd never asked, because that's when she stopped telling me stories and we began to grow up.

We grew up, and Neesh's dad left, and she stopped talking, and I found other ways of blanking out the fear I always feel inside me. How? I keep manically busy. Cricket, science, singing, acting, you name it, I do it. I'm your everyday all-rounder, and the secret of my success is this: that sometimes, just sometimes, if I do things fast enough or hard enough, and for long enough, I can forget the fear. The fear that maybe there's this place, this great big black hole inside of me, called nothing.

'Slow down, child!' Mum says, and then she laughs. 'Take a chill pill! You've got your whole life to get through!'

Yeah right, Mum.

Anyway, Neesh is the only person in the world who's ever been able to put the fear inside me to sleep. She doesn't even have to do anything, just exist, which is why I hate it when she blanks out like that.

'What's wrong with Neesh, Mum – why does she do that?' I used to ask.

Mum would sigh. 'Now that's a long story. Let's just say it runs in the family, and Neesh . . . well, Sammy, she isn't, well, stable.' And her face would close up, and I knew there was no point asking any more questions 'cos I wouldn't get any answers.

I look at Neesh.

Blink. Blink, blink.

She's staring at the teacher but she's miles away, and the flick of her long eyelashes reminds me of a bird's wings flitting across her cheeks.

I wish she'd turn and look at me, or maybe even acknowledge the fact that I exist. Because recently, it just seems so harsh we don't meet up any more. And the worst thing is that my mum actually agreed with Neesh's mum that we shouldn't be friends. And Grandpa was no help at all, that was the real surprise; he just muttered something about not really having the right to 'intervene', while Mum went on talking total crap . . .

'Sammy, it could . . . well let's just say, if you and Neesh . . . well, if your feelings for each other changed, well then it could be very, very awkward, to say the least!'

'MUM!' I mean, I was only eleven for chrissake, and she was my best, best friend. My blood bro, the pink Power Ranger to my Tommy, and now we couldn't even meet!

We got over it. I mean, we say hi at school, or did when she would talk. Now we just smile at each other and I look out for her. Whenever I can.

Know what? I still love looking at her face. The proportions of it are perfect − 1.618 to 1 all the way − and I'm amazed no one else can see beyond her hunched shoulders and hanging hair. Because for me it's like she makes a pattern. A pattern that only her face can make. The shape of it just skips my eyes and goes straight for the centre of my brain. I can't explain it, not even to myself, don't want to most of the time, because it scares me. It's like I just want to look and look and look at her for ever, without stopping, because I'm scared that if I do take my eyes off her, when I look back she'll be gone. And where she was standing there'll be nothing but air. An empty space.

And that's when I think that maybe I *do* know what Grandpa means by his light being extinguished, because when I see Neesh these days it's like she lights me up. And is that good or bad? Is it right or wrong? And is it really anyone else's business but mine anyway?

I shake my head. I'm really not helping myself, even *beginning* to think like this is crazy.

I mean crazy. We're friends, right, we've known each other forever. I wouldn't give that up for anything.

Not for anything.


# Neesh

The playground's cold and grey. Grey concrete, grey sky, grey groups of kids in grey clothes. Nothing's stuck on or bright, like flowers. I hate it. Even the colours above the kids' heads are all in shades of grey. Damp and depressed.

The air's heavy and cold, even though it's already nearly May.

I hold my coat on tight, I hold my coat around me like it could keep the cold out, but nothing ever does. I'm always freezing.

'OK?' asks Sammy as he walks past me, and smiles. I nod. The air above the heads of all the girls turns green. They don't get it, how come Sammy even notices me?

'Hey!' shouts Gita. 'I'm sixteen today, oh Sammio! Sixteen and legal!'

Sammy laughs.

'Over here Geet!' yells Terry. 'On me head!'

'Wrong part of your anatomy!' yells Sean, and they all laugh.

Last year when Leah Dunhill was sixteen, all the boys set up a page on the net, a clock that counted down the days and minutes and hours till she was sixteen. Tick. Tock. It was funny; all the numbers on the clock were marked with cherries. I laugh. I imagine Leah's body springing open as the clock strikes twelve. I imagine all the boys lining up like clockwork soldiers.

Then I shiver. Suddenly it doesn't feel funny any more. It feels dangerous, like the sun suddenly dropping out of the sky. Like a light going out. Like when Dad left and everything changed, and my voice fell out of my body because it had nothing left to say any more.

But now sometimes, when I look at Sammy, it feels like the light's beginning to flicker again. On, off, on, off, like I'm trying to come back to life, only I'm not sure I want to.

I know no one else wants me to.

I hug my coat. Dad bought it for me before he left. It tries to keep me warm now that he's not here. I stand in the freezing playground and remember Dad. I see him the way he used to be at home, he's talking . . .

'The girl's cold,' he says to Mum. 'She's freezing, why haven't you bought her a coat?'

And then they shout at each other.

'She is not eating food,' shouts Mum. 'No, that girl eats money, all girls do, nothing but dowries and paying for them, and what for? Why is she at school anyway? At her age I was making the atta and cooking for my brothers.'

I didn't say anything, but that didn't stop me thinking things. I thought, *yeah Mum, I go to school and make the atta* (that's flour for chapattis) *for my brother as well. What about that?*

'What did we come here for if it wasn't education?' Dad says back. He never shouts, and his head flicks sideways like a bird's. That's what Dad looked like when he did that, like a bird in a tree that was asking you to come its way, just to try it, just to see – but I don't think Mum wanted to, and in the end neither did he, much, because he went away.

He did tell me he was going, sort of. He sat on the end of my bed. It was night.

'Hello uppi,' he said, but I didn't say anything. I could already see the dark, dark clouds above his head, sense the words forming in his mouth. He said them quickly, as though that could make it any better.

'Your mother's not a bad woman,' he said, and I stared at him. She seemed pretty awful to me. I think he was just trying to make himself feel better because he was about to leave me with her. 'You know, I was lucky she married me! If her aunt hadn't been a daa'in (that's witch or healer) she would never have had me!' He laughs, even though he knows it's not funny, and then he waits, waits for me to say something, anything, just to help him along. But I can't. I can't speak, I know what's coming, I can already see him getting further and further away from me, until he's just a dot in the distance, a hole in my world. He's leaving me.

'I've seen her picture, Neeshi, your mother's aunt,' he says. 'You are so like her, and that's the problem, eh? It is that every time your ummi looks at you she sees her very own auntie.' He stops and sighs; I can see the sharp black lines of pain stabbing the air above him.

'What happened to your great-aunt, it was a very terrible tragedy. She lost her life, you know, and your mother is very frightened, my uppi, that it will happen to you too!'

*Take me with you, then*, my eyes say, *take me with you*, but he looks away. He looks at the floor. He looks at anything and everything except me.

'Neesh, what you have, it's . . .' and then he does look at me, looks at me as though he's almost scared, 'it's a gift, as well as a curse, never forget that. Your mother, she can only see the curse. If we were back home, they would say you were a witch, hah! But here all is modern, modern, and what you have is intuition and healing only! Nothing to worry about, is it?'

But he doesn't sound convinced. We're both silent and I think, *he'll say it now, he'll say it,* and my heart beats so hard it hurts, but he doesn't, he just says, 'You know already, don't you?' And I feel angry then, so angry that he can't even say the words himself. *I'm leaving you, leaving you with nothing but a bunch of words.* I don't want words. I want him.

'It's not you, Neeshi,' he says. 'It's this world here; in this place there is no sunshine at all!'

And after he's gone there's no sunshine for me either. I can't speak. I'm scared that if I open my mouth I might scream. And Mum gets even crazier without Dad here.

'Your father, always giving you guriya ideas. Education, hanh! What good will that do you when you're screaming for a child to come out, hanh? You tell me that?' And she laughs. I don't.

'What can you see?' she says, and her face is sharp and suspicious, but I only shake my head and mouth the word *nothing* back at her. But it's not true; if anything, the things I can see got far worse after Dad left. The colours of people's feelings intensified over their heads until sometimes they glowed so hard I couldn't look.

Blink. Blink, blink.

Mum stares at me, suspicious. 'Are you sure you are not seeing things any more?' I can never see Mum's colours and that really scares me; it means I never know what she's going to do next. She looks at my left hand; it's still bent and curled where she used to tie it up to stop me using it. I write with my right hand now. Badly.

'We will never change you,' she says, and she shakes her head, 'but at least we can stop it with you. No more witches. No boys for you, no children, no marriage, no more daa'ini in our family!' And she sighs. 'At least we have Jammi to carry on our line!' And she looks at me. 'Do you hear me?' I nod. 'Go! Go, go, go.' And she flaps her hands at me like I'm a stray goose let loose in the village. 'Out of my way, I don't want to see you!'

I go into my room, and sometimes it's OK, but sometimes the old lady who used to live here is in there. She fell down the stairs and died. No one else wanted to live in her house. That's how come *we* got it. It's a pain though, because she's the nan of the biggest bastard in the school, and she's always asking after him.

'*How's my Kef?*' she says. '*Will you tell him, love? Will you tell him we never would have left him, not if we'd had a choice?*' I try to block my ears, because whenever she says that it reminds me that Dad's gone.

The only thing he left behind was his razor blades. He left them in the bathroom, each one wrapped in a small packet of carefully folded wax paper, layered one on top of the other in a tiny plastic box. I take them everywhere, and sometimes when it gets too bad I uncurl my bad left hand and . . .

'Feckin' weirdo!' yells Kef. It takes me a while to re-focus, to get myself back to where I really am, which is in the playground. *What?* I feel my mouth moving silently into the shape of the word, but no sound comes out.

Q: What am I doing?

A: I'm standing still in the middle of the playground. My arms are held out from my sides and I'm twisting them over from the wrists, palms up, palms down, over and over, so that I can feel my arms move in the tiny space that's left between me and the coat my dad bought me. I want to remember when it was too big for me, when it felt like I had forever to grow into it. But now it's tight, as tight as snake's skin, a skin that's fighting to be shed.

'Out of the way, wanker!' yells Kef, and then a ball hits my shoulder. 'Stupid bloody Paki,' he says. 'Move it, I told you, MOVE IT!'

Kef's voice chills me, scares me, paralyses me. I stare at

the colours above his head. They're the colour of hate, green streaked with yellow, like bad shit.

'Feckin' weirdo!' says Kef, again. 'You got a problem with lookin' at my face?'

*Be careful, Kef, you've your dad in you!* The words whistle through me, sharp as a blade slicing my brain. They're so sudden and surprising they nearly manage to make it out of my mouth.

*BE CAREFUL, KEF,* says his nan's voice inside me, *you've your dad in you!*

She's trying to warn him! But I know I'm dead if the words make it out of my mouth. I gasp and hold my hands to my mouth to catch them, hold the words in the palm of my hands. She wants me to tell Kef something so badly, but I can't, I can't let the words out, he'd kill me.

'What you doin'?' Kef hisses at me, looking at my hands holding my mouth. '*You're* the one makes *me* feel sick!'

I stumble away from him, away from his shit-streaked hatred. But the old lady's voice comes with me, plaintive and complaining.

*Tell him, someone has to warn him . . .*

'Do it your friggin' self,' I say silently to the voice, because I don't want to see things no one else sees; I don't want to know what's wrong with people, or how they feel. I want everyone's thoughts and feelings to stay right where they belong, in their own skin, and keep the hell away from mine.

Someone touches me.

Don't!

'Neesh,' whispers Sammy. 'Move! Now! Get out of Kef's way.' And he begins to drag me across the playground.

'Paki lover!' shouts Kef at Sammy. Kef's always been a bastard, but recently he's graduated, moved right up a notch into being a totally screwed-up shit head. Every one's noticed it, no one knows why. Everyone stays away, no one answers him back. Everyone does exactly what he says, and quickly. Everyone that is, except Sammy.

'Right,' Sammy shouts back at him. 'And why would I want to change that?' And he lets go of me and holds his hands out to the world, palms open wide like he's spinning in oxygen, taking on so much air that the rest of us would just drown if we even tried it. He laughs, and everyone laughs with him, and I think the air above me must be orange, a deep orange that shimmers with longing for him, and I thank Allah himself (peace be upon him) that no one but me can see the way I feel.

I walk away but a part of my body stays with Sammy, right there where he touched me. My arm zings, the little patch of skin beneath my coat is tingling and warm and longing to undress itself. I can feel the nerves of it dancing like light on water.

*Touch me,* they cry, *hold me.* But he doesn't, does he? Course not! We're just friends, aren't we, old friends. And that's the way it has to stay. A phrase runs through my head, I don't know if I read it somewhere or made it up, but it just keeps on saying itself: a witch should never wed nor bed. A witch should never wed nor bed.

OK, but I can look, can't I?

So I watch Sammy as he picks up the ball that hit me. He holds it in the air. 'Ready?' he shouts, and everyone looks up at him as he turns, ready to run in. Everyone knows about Sammy: this year the county, next year who knows, maybe England.

Clever, good-at-everything, perfect Sammy. He runs in a long wide curve. He lopes up in long strides, and then he's heading straight for the batsman . . . his arm whips back . . . his whole body leaves the ground, and it's like we're all willing him up into the air, his body's leaning right back at an impossible angle . . . defying time, defying gravity . . . and then his foot hits the ground and his whole body rockets forwards and the ball flies straight and true out of his hand . . .

. . . and before I know it I'm imagining standing in that boat full of flowers. I'm right in it, and the air is full of flower-heads raining down on me. Softly, so softly, like the touch of Sammy's fingers landing on my skin . . . and my body begins to beat to the tune of its longing before I can cut it off.

'HOWZAT!' Sammy yells. His arms are up, fingers pointing to heaven.

'Sammy!' Terry gives him a high five, sucks through his teeth. 'Magic man!'

And I smile.

'Take your eyes off him, bitch!' say the girls next to me.

I look away.

'That's right, keep your freaky eyes off of him, he's mine,' says one of them.

'And mine when you're finished!' laughs the other, like he was a spliff being passed around.

I walk away but the feelings stay with me, the feel of his hand on my arm, of his eyes watching me, warm like sunlight on a brown stream. Mostly, these days, all I do when I see Sammy is try to hold back the feelings rising inside me like leaves unfurling, like a skin waiting to be shed. But . . .

Q: How do you stop a feeling?

A: You can't, can you? You just have to be patient and wait for it to leave.

I hold out my hands to the air, hold out my hands as though this feeling was something I could catch and hold and keep safe in my hands for ever. As though it was something I was allowed to have.

'Weirdo!' shouts one of the girls, and she's right, isn't she? I must be, because it is weird, isn't it, to be standing here, holding out my hands and waiting to catch something that can only ever exist inside me?

# Kefin

Kef's angry. She makes him angry, that Neesh. I mean, why does she exist, why do any of them? Feckin' hell, the way she stands there, staring at feck all. She's in his way, always in his way. It's not like he didn't tell her to move, dumb-ass Paki. She should stop starin' at him. He draws an imaginary mark across her face, four lines, cross hairs that join at her nose. He pulls the trigger. Bam. She's finished.

Only one problem, she's still here, ent she? Her and her kind, takin' over the world. That's what Dad says, one day we'll all be feckin' beige, or taupe. Feckin' taupe, like a sofa. What the feck kind of gay colour is that?

'MOVE!'

Kef yells at her. He's only centimetres from her face, his spit and hatred flying. But she still doesn't move, she just stands there gagging into her hands. It makes no sense to him, none at all. Maybe it's that she makes herself sick. Yep, that'd explain it.

And then it happens, the thing he hates Neesh for more than anything, the thing that always happens when he's around her, the bitch. He begins to hear his nan's voice in his head.

'*BE CAREFUL, KEF!*' says his nan, but she's dead, isn't she, so how can she be talking to him? He doesn't answer, that would be mad, wouldn't it? So he answers Neesh instead.

*No,* he shouts in his mind, *NO! I think you've got it wrong there, Paki, you're the one who needs to be feckin' careful – of me!* But it doesn't make any difference; the words inside him don't go away. They get worse, they echo through his head, just like his nan was right in there and talking.

'*Be careful, Kef, you've your dad in you!*'

Kef sniggers. Well, she's wrong there, isn't she? Dad's nowhere, because Dad's dead too now. Kef should know, it was Kef that killed him. Only Kef's not sure whether he's *really* dead, because it would be just like Dad, wouldn't it, to *pretend* to be dead, just so he could frighten the shit out of Kef when he saw him move. Anyway, it was an accident, wasn't it? Only Kef's not sure about that either; I mean when you've *wanted* to kill someone that much, and for that long, how do you know whether or not you *meant* to do it?

There's no one left now, no Mum, no Dad and no Nan, just Kef, and he knows why, don't think he doesn't, it's all her doing. That Paki-slut Neesh. She moved into Nan's house after Nan died, and that's when it all went wrong, isn't it? Bloody Pakis. And he gets that strange feeling that he gets whenever he looks at Neesh, like she's stolen everything he ever had, including himself. But it all started with her takin' his nan's house. That was the first time he ever saw her.

'Dressed up like a fuckin' ice-cream sundae!' said Dad, as they walk past. She's stepping out of a white van, and her socks are white and lacy too, ending in black shiny patent-leather shoes. And she has long black hair tied in two plaits with red shiny ribbons. Kef is transfixed. He wants to look and look at her. He stops his scooter on the pavement just to stare. She's the most beautiful thing he's ever seen, like sunlight landing on the pavement.

'Kef!' His dad slaps his back. 'Keep movin'.' And Kef

does exactly what his dad says. He pushes his foot against the pavement but somehow his head can't turn away, his head stays facing her, searching for the extraordinary colour of her – golden, like sunshine. She turns to look at him, and smiles. A wide-open, happy smile, and she lifts one end of her plait, and waves at him with it. And before he knows what he's doing Kef's hand begins to lift in response . . .

THWACK! He's on the ground, the concrete hard against his face.

'That was your nan's house!' Dad is saying as he drags him upright, not bothering to wipe the blood from his nose. 'And those are Pakis moving in, and don't you forget it!'

Kef stares at Dad. He doesn't understand, but he does understand this: the girl is standing in the doorway of his nan's house, and somehow this means it's her fault that Nan's dead.

The girl is still staring; she sucks the end of one plait and stares wordlessly at the air above his head. He hates that, it makes him feel like he doesn't exist. He wants her to look at *him*.

'Fuck off, the lot of ya!' shouts Dad, and the girl's dad stops at the gate with a tissue in his hand, that he was bringing for Kef's bloody nose. The girl stares, not smiling now. Her father lifts her away from Kef and they disappear into Nan's house. The door closes softly like a light blown out.

'Pakis in our nan's house! She'd've turned in her grave,'

says Dad. Kef shivers. Is that what Nan does deep under the ground, does she turn and turn in that little box, not able to get out?

'Go back to your own country!' yells Dad, but no one answers, no one comes back out. The door stays shut. And Kef understands something. He can't ever go into the house again, because Nan's dead. She's gone now, like Mum. And now there's only Dad left, but Dad's not nice, Dad's scary.

Kef looks at Neesh in the playground.

*Well*, he thinks, *Dad's gone now, hasn't he, and no one can stop me.* For a brief second Kef almost remembers that before the hate, there was another feeling, a feeling like sunshine landing on pavements, but he locks it down. He's the dad now, and he's gonna do Neesh if she doesn't get out of his way. But when he looks up he sees Sammy already pulling her across the playground. He watches Sammy as the school door shuts behind them, locking him out.

But no doors can stop him now.

He can have her any time he likes.

Kef smiles.


# Neesh

I hang around the playground for a bit after school and pretend I'm not listening to Gita and her gang. They're outside the main gates of the school, swinging their bags at each other.

'That's sick!' says Nell.

'C'mon, 'fess up, which one d'you think's really fit?' asks Gemma.

'None of them, it's, like, a law of physics or something, innit, teachers can't be fit!'

'Boll-ocks!' laughs Gita.

'You're well fucked!' says Nell.

'So's your mum!' giggles Gita, and they all fall about.

'I reckon you're too busy eyeing Sammy to notice any-one else!' shouts Nell.

'Talkin' about yourself again, Nell!'

'As if!'

'As if what?'

'As if anyone wouldn't pull him, given half a chance!'

'And then what?' smiles Gita, and Nell smiles too.

'Mmm,' she says, 'well now, what would I do with Sammy Colthurst-Jones given half a chance . . .'

'Or even a whole night?' giggles Gita.

'Maybe I'd let *him* decide!' laughs Nell.

Gita gyrates her snaky hips. 'I wanna have his babies!' she sings, and they all laugh, all join in, swinging their hips together as Gita sings, and their colours sway above their heads, merging, joining together, and I know that I'm alone and separate.

I hate it when they talk about Sammy. *You don't know him*, I think. *You don't have a clue about how far away from all this he could be, if his mum let him.* All Sammy has to do is wait to inherit his grandpa's house, the house he never talks to anyone about (including me), the house his mum says will make him rich and cut him off from the rest of the world one day, so he'd better get used to how the world really is, right now. That's how come he's at school in a dump like this.

'A whole night!' laughs Leah. 'You won't need that long!'

And the rhythm of the group changes as they turn to stare at her. They don't say anything, just look, and I can see the air above them pulsing red and orange with fascination; but Leah just chews her gum and keeps them waiting.

'How would you know?' asks Gita.

'I wouldn't, would I,' she says, 'anyways not about babies – made him wear a rubber, didn't I?'

And all the colours begin to bend and sway her way, but Gita doesn't give up that easily.

'Who with, then?' she asks. The colours of the group hover between the two girls like flies, buzzing and wondering where to land next.

'That's for me to know . . .' sings Leah.

'You're lying! Lying!' says Gita, and she takes out a fag, and all the colours in the air lean towards her.

'Ask Damian if you don't believe me!' says Leah.

'Uh, Le-ah, bit desperate innit, with Damian!' and the colours all shift and land over Gita, who smiles as a few of the girls start making gagging actions behind Leah's back.

'Fuck off!' says Leah, without even turning round.

'Anyways, how would you know?' she goes on. 'For all you know he's brilliant!'

'Well, was it? Is he?' asks Gita. She says it like she wants to know; they all do.

I do too. Was it? Is he?

Leah gives a weird sound, like a snort that thinks it's a gasp.

'And what's that supposed to mean?' asks Gita, and Leah begins to run her fingers through her hair, only she can't because it's all stiff with gel. Her eyes are dark where the black pencil has all smudged, and it looks a bit like Allah (peace be upon him) forgot to draw her eyes in properly.

She starts to twiddle the ring in her nose, turning it round and round. No one says anything, everyone waits – and then she laughs. 'Like I said,' she says, 'it certainly doesn't take a whole night!' She says it like it's funny, like she's passed some horrible, horrible test and she's out on the other side of the river, way beyond us. But the air around her doesn't look too good; it looks as though it feels a bit pale yellow.

'I'm saving myself!' says Gita, and everyone laughs, but they can't see the suddenly blue blue air above her head, not wavering at all but absolutely certain. She laughs too.

'Saving yourself, who for, what for?' asks Leah in her world-weary voice. 'Get it over with, and get used to it!'

Gita smiles at her, and Leah should watch out really, because she doesn't seem to know they only put up with her because of her parties and her money. She can't see the air turn shark-grey above Gita's head as she moves in for the kill.

'For something better than being some geek's friggin' blow-up-doll, that's what for!' Gita smiles. Leah pushes herself off the wall then and stares at her.

Face-off.

'You just haven't got the nerve to do it!' says Leah.

'And you just ain't got the style not to, blud!' says Gita, like she was some gangsta's girl!

Leah stares at her.

'Do you really think, I mean really truly and seriously think, that Sammy Colthurst-Jones would ever even look at you once, let alone twice?' she says, and there's something about her voice, she's dropped the street act and it's so posh it makes everything she says feel real and true and certain. For just a sec Gita actually looks shaky.

'He'd look at me way before he'd look at a guriya like you!'

'What does that mean?' asks Leah. 'Take it back!'

'It means white trash!' says Sani, and my own colour crosses the divide and joins the others, because whatever I am I'm not white; and even though Leah can't see the colours, she senses something's changed and it makes her notice me. She stares at me and I feel cold, colder than ever. My colours try to disappear, to freeze themselves out.

'Oh Gita, Gita, Gita!' Leah says, and I know then that she's sounding just like her mum, even though I've never met her. 'You may have the loveliest eyes, my dear, but you are as blind as a bat. There's only one girl Sammy Colthurst-Jones's got eyes for, and she's sitting right over there, looking like she's waiting to be recycled.'

They all turn and stare at me, and then they do laugh.

'What? Little Miss Blink-blink?' they say, and they begin to blink their eyes and turn in circles, bumping into each other, pretending they can't see. *But I can see,* I want to shout at them, and that's the problem. I can see too much. Gita stops and looks at me.

'No way!' she mutters, but her colours shift above her, don't look certain.

'Like I said,' says Leah, 'you can't see it, but if she let her hair down and held her head up she'd look just like that girl in that old film we had to watch in English, the one who was having it off with Romeo when she was playing Juliet!'

I look away. I stare into the distance, but inside my heart's thumping. She thinks I could look like Olivia Hussey! Somewhere up above me I reckon my colours must be shining like a rainbow.

'Well, Sammy can see it,' Leah says to Gita. 'Bet you your Mulberry you can't pull him!'

Gita holds on to her bag with both hands; it's her most precious possession, she's told everyone a billion times it's the real thing, she must have saved for ever to get it. She gives me a good long stare. And by the look in her eyes, and the colours above her head, she's not seeing me as Olivia Hussey with her long dark hair and green eyes and skin like a peach, playing Juliet.

'Deal!' she says, and they all start laughing, and Leah holds up her hand, and they high five, and then they all walk away together, hips swinging and their colours floating above their heads. Separating and merging, flashing, moving and shifting, but always in touch with each other. Always together.

They've already forgotten I exist.

I begin the walk home. It's going to snow. I know things like that, always have.

What if I could hold my head up and keep my shoulders down like Leah said, would it really work, and would Sammy see me differently then, see me like Romeo sees Juliet? . . . I shiver. Maybe not like that, not like Juliet . . . she had to die, didn't she?

I stop and lean against the big silver birch in the park. I always come here on the way home, it's the place where I stop to draw breath. Trees and plants don't have colours, they just are. They're not like us, always trying to become something else.

The tree is full of small leaf buds. I put my arms around it; I wonder if the warmth of my arms will strike up a memory somewhere deep inside it, like a flicker of summer. I close my eyes and imagine what would happen if the tree suddenly burst into life all green and golden.

Q: What about me? What about if Sammy put his arms around me? Would I burst into life, all green and golden?

A: I laugh. I imagine my arms bursting into branches and breaking out of my coat. I laugh and I lean against the tree with my eyes closed and pretend that it's Sammy I'm resting against.

'Weirdo!'

I know it's Kef straight away. I don't move. The bark of the tree feels rough like his voice. I wish I could peel it off and wrap myself in it. I wish I could disappear – but I can't.

'Hey! I'm talking to you, weirdo!'

I keep my eyes closed, like if I don't see him maybe he isn't here. But he is here, and even the tree seems to shiver beneath my fingers at the sound of his slow, hate-filled voice, and I hold on to it tight, but the poor tree goes right on trembling like its leaves are being whipped away from it by a cruel breeze. I listen to the sound of Kef's footsteps coming nearer, sliding on the dead leaves and mud and—

'Shit!' he says. 'Stupid feckin' tree.'

I open my eyes.

Blink. Blink, blink.

We stare at each other. There's a thin red streak across one of his cheeks, just under his left eye, where the tree's branches caught him, whipped him; the bruise beneath it is already growing and swelling, but he doesn't notice. He can't notice. That's his problem. He doesn't see anything. Beneath all the hate and excitement his eyes look empty.

'All alone, weirdo?' he says. He's not asking or anything, he already knows I am.

Blink. Blink, blink.

His colours clash above his head, flashing like birds fighting in mid-air, wings beating, changing from black and grey and shit-streaked yellow to red and orange. I blink again; he's full of fear, of terror and hate, and something else that frightens me even more. He's full of desire and longing.

I'm wondering what he'll do next, but in my head his nan's voice is going wild inside me, chatting away to him as if I wasn't even here!

*'What've you done, child?'* it says. *'What good could possibly come of it?'*

Blink. Blink, blink.

I try to concentrate on one thing at a time; I try to focus on Kef. I can feel the excitement inside him; it comes with a sharp picture of him peeling my skin off like the bark of the tree, just to see if it's white underneath. I try to hide behind the tree; I wrap my arms around its solid safe trunk, as though it could save me.

'You should try hugging something human!' Kef says, and now he steps closer, right up close, as though he thinks he is that human thing I should be hugging.

*'What've you done, what are you doing?'* shouts his nan inside me. *'Oh lord, child, will you help him?'* pleads the old woman's voice.

And I laugh out loud at that, *me*, help *Kef*? How?

Can Kef hear her? No, he can only hear me laughing.

'Fuck you!' he whispers, and he steps even closer. As close as his whisper, so close I can feel his angry blood beating like goose wings, and I can feel his desire, but it's like the two feelings are all mixed up with something else, with a terror that's twisted deep inside him, and the sorrow and fear and . . .

No! I try to pull back, to back out of his eyes and head, but I can feel him pulling at me, drawing me in, wanting me. And it's what his nan's voice wants too. It's like I've got Kef on one side and his nan on the other, '*Help him, child, oh, help him,*' and there's only me stuck in the middle: the filling in a sandwich about to get eaten.

And then it happens, the thing I always try not to do, the thing that made Dad leave and makes Mum hate me. The thing that means I'm weird and different.

I look inside Kef. Right inside him, and for me it's like breathing or walking, or all the other things that we can do without even thinking about it. There's a picture inside him, a picture he wants to get rid of . . . and I hear his nan's voice, asking him a question . . . over and over . . .

'*Why did you do it, Kef?*'

And at the sound of her voice the picture inside him sharpens at its edges, begins to come clear. I can see Kef standing, and then suddenly, violently, his feet are off the floor and he's being shaken like a doll. Kef pushes at the man's chest and he drops him. There are words, I can't hear them, but I can feel what they do to Kef; they drive him wild. They drive him up from his feet, and he picks something up and swings it, hard. It's satisfying, the crack of wood against bone. And then Kef's standing, looking

41

down, and on the floor is a . . . a body . . . a twisted head, a neck, a . . .

'*Why, Kef! Why did you do it?*' wails the voice inside me, but I manage to draw back, press my lips close and tight, hold my hands over them, trying to keep the voice in. If he doesn't want to listen to it I do not want to be the one who makes him.

'What?' he says, suddenly, and he's so close that I can smell his breath; it's foul like skin-shrivelled dead things that lie in dark corners, decaying. I step back, keeping the tree between us.

He smiles.

'Nowhere to go!' he says. 'Enjoy living in my nan's house, do you?'

I can't answer, but the voice inside me has got no problem at all. '*Kef! No!*' it shouts.

'Only me here, baby!' Kef laughs.

If only that was true, I think. I wish.

He reaches into his pocket slowly. His eyes are cold and crazy. I can't concentrate on everything at once. I'm slipping on my own guts.

Outside, I can feel the tree, can see Kef standing with his knife in his hand.

Inside me, his nan won't stop, her voice goes right on as though I didn't exist: '*Kef . . . oh, Kef . . . what have you done . . . what are you doing?*' And then the voice begins to shout. I see her old mouth, all wrinkled at the corners with seeped lipstick running in the wrinkles. '*Help him!*' says

Kef's nan, just like she's always said, ever since I moved into her house, but now her urgency twists and pulls at me. *'Save him!'*

And I know right then that I can't hold out, and I don't, I just give in and let her speak. Her voice comes flying out of me. It's so old and sad and lonely, an old lady's voice, and I don't want to know it. I don't want anything to do with what it's saying or why, but her words come right out of me anyway.

*'What have you done, Kef?'* she says.

And at the sound of her voice, Kef stops. Stops dead.

I'd stop too if I was him. I mean, it's his nan's voice coming out of my mouth, her voice exactly, not an imitation, or a copy, but her. Imagine it – what would you do?

'What did you say?' he asks, and I shake my head. 'How did you do that?' he says again.

*'Two wrongs don't make a right, young man!'* says his nan, before I can stop her.

Kef flinches, takes a step back.

'So what have I done?' he asks me.

I shake my head. I wish I could say I don't know. I wish I could say I don't care. I wish I could say leave me the fuck alone forever, but I'm too busy trying to hold his nan's voice inside me and save myself.

'No problem,' he says, and he shrugs, 'it's not as if you're gonna get the chance to tell anyone, anyway, is it? I mean . . .' and he looks me up and down.

He steps forward, his knife balanced in his right hand, his

eyes on mine. They sweep over my body as if they're looking for exactly the right place to land. I wonder if it will
hurt. I wonder if my dad will ever find out I'm gone. I'm
so terrified I forget all about his nan until I hear her words
come screaming out of my mouth: *'Kef! No!'*

He leaps away from me and I take my chance and run. I
run and I don't stop to hug any trees along the way.

My heart's still beating fast when I get home. *Jesus, Gandhi,
Mary and Mohammed (peace be upon them) help me.* I look in
the fridge to calm myself down. Just the sight of all the
food in the fridge does that for me, calms me right down.
Dad used to laugh, used to say I was feeling all the hunger
he felt as a child when he was in the village. At least, I think
to myself, I don't know what it's like to starve. But maybe
I do? There are different types of starving, aren't there? It's
not just about food.

'Hey! What's for sups?' asks Jammi (but you can think of
him as Jammy, as in Jammy Bastard, if you like – I do). He's
sitting with his big feet on the sofa, the one I'll have to
clean after he's gone out with his mates. He's playing with
his Wii, listening to his iPod – my fat brother, who eats all
my food then farts and never cooks a thing.

I don't answer. I look in the fridge, look at all the con-
tainers I've put in rows, neat rows, like I wish my life could
be put into. I'm still shaking and scared, but nobody
notices. I don't want to go up to my room. What if she's up
there, Kef's nan? What if she's waiting for me?

Brinjal (aubergine), okra (lady's finger), dhaniya (coriander), channa daal (chickpeas) and atta (flour).

I don't look at the meat. I don't like it. It reminds me of what we really are: blood and bones and muscle. Edible, in bits. I take out the green and gold tin of ghee (butter without milk solids) and flick on the gas flame. The ghee melts in the pan and I put on an apron (over my coat) and begin to breathe. It's all right, everything's all right.

Slice the onions, gold and red. The skin falls off like tough little rose petals. I heap them up. Peel the garlic and ginger. Put it in the pestle with rock salt. Bash, tip it in to the bubbling onions. Slice up chillies, inhale their strength and drop them in, the smell rises.

Breathe it in. Breathe.

I choose the spices, watch them pop in the dry pan, crush them up still hot in the pestle, warm smell like crunchy sand. Lower the heat, stir them in.

I watch my fingers, slim and brown.

Sure and safe and good.

It's all right; it's all going to be OK. I can't hear any voices. Kef isn't at the door and no one is going to blow the house down.

Good magic this is, just cooking. No voices, no weirdness. I'm fine.

Slice and salt the brinjal (like I said, that's aubergine). It cries tears when you salt it, whatever you call it.

'Smells good, Neesh,' yells Jammi. And I almost smile before I remember that I hate him. Pour in the tin of tomatoes and up the flame. Stir. Sizzle till it smells like honey. At last all the ingredients begin to sing together, sing like a full choir rising in crescendo – and the ghee escapes from the liquid, bubbling all around the brim. Bang – trap the goodness in – lid on.

Yes! I'm beginning to feel fine.

'What's this?' Her voice cuts through me like lemon in oil and my stomach heaves; the knife slips, I cut my finger.

'Clumsy!' she shouts.

*Clumsy,* my mouth mirrors hers.

She lifts the lid of the pan and sniffs the food; suddenly the smell is wrong, all wrong and bad, bad, bad like me. Not fine at all.

'Where's the meat?' she asks. 'I told you before . . .'

*Told you,* I mirror with my mouth, nodding.

'Are you a girl or a fish?' she shouts, and she opens the fridge. 'What's meat doing in the fridge? Hanh? You think we are mice? You think we are cows maybe?' And she laughs, 'Grass curry!' She picks up the shredded spinach in her strong fingers, crushes it between them and drops it.

'Get the meat.'

I stand still.

'Get it out,' she says.

*Get it out,* her words make shapes with my lips. I pick up the paper package; it smells of dead blood, of muscles still tight with fear, it trembles in my hands.

'Cook it! Men need meat, not grass.' She stares at me.

I empty the meat on to the board, it wobbles. Muscles,

bones, tendons; I can see where they should all join up and live. I can see where they can be cracked and broken. My own muscles shake, my own bones tremble. What if it was me? What if it was me on the board, all broken up into little bits?

Perhaps it is.

I feel my bones begin to shriek inside me and my hands start to shake. I think of Mr Fell, the science teacher, saying we are ninety-eight per cent animal. Does that mean it's nearly all of me on the board?

'Cut it up,' she says.

My heart kicks against my ribs. I touch the meat, it's so cold and dead . . . I stop . . . I try again . . . I stop . . . I can't . . . she's smiling. *Cut it up*, I mirror the words, hoping they'll make it happen, but they don't . . . and the wind whistles by my face. Her hand lands, hard and stinging . . .

'Useless!' she says. 'Useless, useless, useless . . .'

I watch her then, as she cracks the bones between her strong fingers. She doesn't hear them shiver and shake and shriek like chalk across a board. She is big and strong and brave and fearless.

'Sometimes I think my first feelings about you were right, Neesha,' she says. 'I should have left you on a hillside and starved you. I knew you were a daa'in from the very first moment you came out. Not a single cry from you, just your big eyes looking all about! Now Jammi, he screamed like a murder! But you, only looking all around you, recognising. Been born before, even that daa'ini midwife dropped you fast as she could! Bloody problem is, no hills in this place to leave you on. What would I do, put you on a roof, hanh?' And she laughs. 'And look at you, can't even cut a piece of meat. What man would want you anyway?'

She seems almost happy now, and I stand quiet, waiting. Don't make me go upstairs, please, just don't make me go upstairs.

'Go on, then!' she shouts after a while. 'Cook your grass.' And I reach for the spinach. 'You are not like me,' she says. 'When I was your age I was prize to be won. When I went to dig up the turnips all the boys took the cows out!'

I listen to her . . . I imagine the bright afternoon light in the village back home, the yellow earth, the village pond and the field. I see her big and strong and swishing the threshing machine, taking the tops off turnips. I can see it as she speaks, and I know she's right, all the boys did come out, but suddenly as I look at the picture I know this too: that they looked at her with suspicion. That they looked – but they were frightened to touch. And I know why: because of her aunt, who was a healer, a daa'in who could make people better just by touching them – a witch just like me. And no one will ever want to touch me either.

No one except a weirdo like Kef.

'And who did I get in the end?' Mum goes on. 'Your father . . . why him? Allah (peace be upon him) tell me!' And she means Dad, my dad. 'I could have had that Sanjay, look at him now, twenty houses all over the place and money . . . money . . . money . . . so much money it looks like he has to hide it in his guts!'

She looks at me. I'm smiling, because that is exactly what Sanjay looks like – like he's hiding money in his guts and it's giving him a pain! She laughs too and I flit around her bright, bright light, like a shadow. Like a moth that's longing even to be burnt, if only the light that is my mum could just see me.

'Go to your room!' She says it suddenly. I swallow, stand there.

*Why? Why?* I want to ask, but I don't have to, I already know. Sometimes she just doesn't even want to look at me. Especially now I'm older, especially now I really do look like that picture of her aunt. I walk up the stairs as slowly as I can.

Sometimes, when I was a child, she used to follow me up later. 'You know we have to help you,' she would say as she tied up my left hand. The pain of it was terrible, it was purple and blue and a deep, deep grey, and once as she did it she told me why. 'One day you will thank me,' she said, and I nodded, because I knew she believed it. I believed it too. How else could she be so horrible?

'I will save you. Your father, he is a weak man,' she told me, 'he thinks women have choices. Hanh, my aunt thought that! It is always what you daa'ini think. Because you can see things you think you can do as you please. You think you can choose? Oh, yes! Well, look what happened to her. All I ever saw is her picture, but everyone remembered – all except your father, and his dunder is full of only milk, not man-ness!'

Q: *How did he make me, then*? But I kept the question silent.

'So! Our family bears witches but we will stop it here. For you there will be no marriage, and then you cannot throw yourself away, can you?'

By now the pain was so bad I thought I might faint. The deep, deep purple-grey flashed with black. I could barely hear her, but the odd word still connected with something inside me that began to make pictures as she spoke.

'Hah, boats and flowers! What nonsense is that? Could he buy her a future? Or even furniture? No, so what was he doing with her, answer me that? Didn't he know what his playing would cost? Oh yes, it is easy for them, isn't it, the English, always a home to return to. But she was already in her home and there was nowhere else for her!' Mum wailed this last bit, tightening the cord around my hand so hard that the purple finally turned black and I began to fall. I was falling off a boat into a bottomless darkness . . .

I sit on my mattress on the floor. I don't want to think about any of it. Not Kef and his nan, not my mum, not my dad, not Sammy . . . I dig into my school bag (plastic, Tesco's) for the packet of razor blades. I look at my hand, my left hand. I know how to stop all the badness in me – Mum taught me.

Slowly I pick up the blade. There aren't many left now. Dad used to untwist his razor and fit the blade in. He used to whistle old tunes, Bollywood tunes and English musicals: 'If you were the only girl in the world . . .'

I draw it across my palm. I write in blood along my lifeline and all the way down to my wrist. I watch the blood drip and then I lie back on the bed. It's all going, disappearing. Kef, his nan, Mum, the fear. Everything's gone except the lovely slow drip of the blood trickling down my raised arm.

I blink and close my eyes.

The picture is there, as it always is. I try to zoom in on the boat full of flowers. I imagine them in red and gold. And I let myself fall, fall backwards into the heap. I feel them raining down on me, landing on me, and I wonder who is throwing them into the air.

And I know who I long for it to be.


When I wake up there's a cold, hard, white-bright light shining in through the curtain-less window. It's morning and the muffled, noise-deadening sound tells me it snowed in the night.

'Neesha! Where are you? Jammi has to get to school, you know! Breakfast doesn't make itself!' shouts Mum.

I look around me, clear up the razor mess and get downstairs fast.

'Do I have to wait all day?' asks Mum, and I give her the tea. She likes it milky, all milky, sugary and white. Not like her, then.

I laugh out loud at the thought and they both sigh at each other.

Q: What is there to laugh at?

A: Nothing.

Weird Neesh. Hungry Jammi. Angry Mum. Some things never change. I wish Dad was here, that hasn't changed either.

Jammi pinches the skin under my arm. 'Make some more shamis,' (spicy small burgers) he says. 'I'm short of dosh!' I always have a plate of them ready in the fridge. Jammi enjoys asking me to do things that'll make me late for school.

I fry some up, he sells them at school. I don't like it. It makes me think of his friends eating me, like meat without bones. I wrap them up and hand them over, and then I wait until he's way up the road before leaving.

I walk fast, head down, eyes on the scraped-clean pavements; that way I don't get caught up in the colours, in all the things happening inside the people walking past.

'Hey, Neesh!'

I jump, I'd know that voice anywhere, but I don't want to see him, can't look at him. It's Sammy. I feel my heart pumping heat into my face; the colours around me must be fizzing!

My eyes go blink. Blink, blink.

'Hey!' He's right beside me, touching my arm. His colours are green with glitters of gold, and I'm so excited that my feet get carried away and just zoom on ahead of us. 'Hey! Hang on a minute!' he laughs, then he's beside me again and we walk along together, saying nothing, leaving our dark footprints on the frosty crushed-diamond pavement.

'Hello?' he asks, and his voice is . . . it's so calm, that's the word. Calm, like the water of the lake in my mind. It's deep and mellow and warm, like fresh toffee just before it sets.

'What's going on with Kef, Neesh?' he asks. 'He was down the Anchor last night telling everyone that he was after you.'

And as he talks his colours begin to seep into each other and turn sludgy and scared, but he keeps his voice calm, like he doesn't want to scare me. I don't answer, I can't. I can't really explain what's going on. Even if I could talk, how could I explain what I am, or what happens? I mean, imagine it . . .

*Well, you see, Sammy, Kef's nan's worried about him, even though she's dead. He's done something bad. I think maybe he's hurt someone, or killed them. Every time I see Kef I hear his nan's voice. I've always known her. When I was little I thought everyone had someone who lived in their bedroom walls. It's a nightmare. Sometimes the only thing that makes it all go away is cutting the palm of my hand and rubbing myself out, all the way along my lifeline.*

I shrug. I don't even want to begin to think about it, not even with Sammy.

'Mmm,' he says to himself, and then he whistles for a bit,

sings some weird tune, and I know that he's singing to help the fear inside him. I can feel it still buried deep in his bones, written across them like it always has been, ever since I first met him. I know he does all sorts of things to keep it away from him. Like right now, he's trying to sing his worries to sleep. The words come out crisp on the cold air.

'If my complaints could passions move,

Or make love see wherein I suffer wrong . . .'

Only he strings the sounds of the words out so they're all separate, like this: *pass-i-ons moo-ve.* I move the words too, feel the shape of them on my lips.

*Pass-i-ons moo-ve.*

*Or make love see—*

Sammy breaks off.

'Kef's changed, Neesh. I mean, he's always been a nasty feckwit, but now it's . . . I dunno . . . it's more than that. He was saying all kinds of weird shit, Neesh, like that you think you know what he's done – that you were winding him up and pretending to be his dead nan. He says you *spoke* to him, Neesh!'

*No!* I want to say. *No, I didn't, it was his nan speaking to him out of my mouth, not me. If I could speak, I'd speak to you. To you, Sammy.* That's what I want to say, but all that comes out is this.

Silence.

And I realise this. I realise I've tried so hard to keep all the voices inside of me so quiet that there's no voice of my

54

own left at all. It shocks me.

'It's crap though, isn't it?' Sammy goes on. 'I mean, you can't speak, and if you could, you'd . . .' and then he runs out of words. He can't say it, can't say, *you'd talk to me*.

*But it's true!* I want to yell at him, and we stop and stare at each other, and you'd think, wouldn't you, that all the things I feel when I look at him would have words attached to them, only they don't, they've dried right up in my throat. Only his song-words are going round and round in my head.

*Pass-i-ons moo-ve . . . or make love see . . . wherein I suffer wrong . . .*

Q: How? How do passions move?

A: Like they do when you look at him, Neesh. Like that.

Q: And what does it mean, *wherein I suffer wrong*? Wrong like me and Sammy being together, is that what the love can see? Why is it wrong? Why? And I get the answer straight away, in Mum's voice.

A: '*Too many questions, too many whys and wherefores, you are a witch completely, will all your questions bring you happiness?*'

I bat her away. I stop and look at Sammy. It's quiet in the snow, the traffic hums. And he's lovely. He's like a volcano that looks all soothing in the distance, its surface so calm with wisps of smoke rising, but inside he fizzes red-hot with fear and energy.

He looks at me. Our eyes connect like a latch lifting or

a door opening, and I reach out to touch him, and then I remember I can't do that. *'No boys, no marrying!'* says Mum. I always thought that made me lucky. I mean, who wants to marry some arsehole like Jammi anyway? But I don't feel lucky now.

My hand drops. He looks at it and a shadow crosses his face, then his own hand moves towards mine, but somehow before it arrives it leaves again.

'Don't you get it, Neesh?' he says. 'Kef's raging round the place telling everyone he's gonna kill you! Kef's looking for you, and he doesn't want to be friends.'

I start to laugh; I don't know why because not a single thing about my life is funny, but sometimes it just happens to me.

'Neesh! For chrissake!' He's angry, and I stop laughing.

And pass-i-ons moo-ve.

I can feel them, moving, inside me.

And Sammy looks at me and smiles. And it feels . . . it feels right, so right, just like the snow that's falling and landing upon us, soft as flower-heads.

I wish he could see the silver line that grows as he smiles. It lies floating in the air between us, not quite touching him, not quite touching me.

I smile at it. But he can't see it, so he doesn't know why I'm smiling.

'Sometimes, Neesh,' he says quietly, shaking his head at me, 'sometimes I don't understand why I bother.' But it's weird because the meaning I hear is completely different; the words I hear inside him are these: *I'll always bother, forever, whenever, whatever.* I stare at him. I don't know if I heard those words *really* moving inside him, or whether I just *want* to hear them so badly that I made them up.

I feel like I've known him forever, and just like he can read my mind he starts singing our song, the song we always used to sing to cheer each other up, when one of us was sulking, or angry, or sad or worried: 'Ip-in-ee-pin-ah-terri-terri-sutta!'

But I don't want us to sing that song any more. I want a new song.

'Pass-i-ons moo-ve,' I whisper.

The words come out so slowly that they grate in my unused throat. They don't sound like music at all, but at least the voice is mine. It's not a tree voice, or an old lady voice, or any other of the voices I sometimes hear. It's my own voice, and at the sound of it Sammy smiles, and the air around him is lit up in blue and gold, and I can feel his blood suddenly begin to dance inside him, as happy as a warm spring wind. His hand reaches for my cheek, his thumb brushes my lips.

'Neesh!' he says. 'You're speaking!'

'S . . . s . . .' The sound slips under my teeth, but I hold on to it, like I want to hold on to Sammy and to this moment. I try again.

'Ss . . . sing it,' I say.

And he lifts his voice up and sings out loud into the cold,

clean air:

> 'If my complaints could passions move,
> Or make love see wherein I suffer wrong,
> My love it was enow to prove,
> That my despair hath governed me too long . . .
> That I do live, it is thy power,
> That I do breathe is thy desire . . .'

His voice rings out, and the words seem to hang on the air before they dissolve and fade away. His voice wakes me up. It makes my heart feel like it's holding on to the tail of a kite, a kite that will lift me high into the air and carry me away, fly away with me forever. But I know I can't fly. I know that the real world will still be waiting for us somewhere. Spread out below us and waiting for us to fall.

I stare at him. He stares at me. And neither of us needs words now.

'Neesh?' And maybe it's the way he says it, maybe it's the look in his eyes or maybe it's that I forgot to eat breakfast. I dunno. All I know is that it's happening again, that feeling. The one I had the very first time I saw him. It's like he's spinning past my eyes to a place deep inside me where we fit, and my whole body's trembling to an echo of itself. And then I'm falling . . . sudden, unexpected, the world tipping beneath my feet.

I slip on the ice and I feel the lurch in my stomach, the sudden leap of fear from my gut to my brain, the rush of adrenalin through my body as I realise I *am* falling. Really falling, expecting the ground to come up and hit me, hard. When suddenly, unexpectedly, wonderfully, something is beneath me, holding me up. Sammy's hands catch me, hold me and steady me. I feel them let my body drop a few centimetres to break my fall and then take my weight. I feel my fingers fly out and grasp his wrists, and in the freezing cold I feel our skin spark, like static.

I open my eyes just in time to see our books scatter over the ice, and then he begins to lift me up until our faces are just centimetres apart. And the earth seems to rock beneath our feet, to be disturbed like a boat steadying itself on the waves of our sudden movement . . . and Sammy's shaking his head.

*What?* I ask him, mouthing the word, feeling the warmth of my own breath blown back at me from his cheek.

'I don't know,' he says, shaking his head, 'it's like I've forgotten something. I've . . . ' And he looks around him as though he wished he could catch a breeze that's already blown right through him and long gone. Slowly he helps me stand up. We can't look at each other. We're frightened of what we might see. We step apart, not knowing what to do or say.

'Watch out for Kef, Neesh,' Sammy says in the end. 'Keep your eyes on him, not in the air, or anywhere else when he's around. Stay out of his way . . . he's not just fed up, or sick of school like the others, he's a total psycho!'

And then we're at the school gates.

'Don't go out of those without me, promise?' he says, and

he still looks a bit shell-shocked, like a bit of him has gone missing in action somewhere.

'Hey! Sammy!' Someone throws him a tennis ball, wide out to his left. An impossible just-out-of-reach catch, waist-high and whizzing. By the time his head has turned to see it, his arms are already out there, throwing him sideways, fingers stretching. And I see the line drawn in the air between him and the ball. I see the beautiful deep white cloud of energy and concentration that surrounds him, as he flings his palm out and, *smack*, him and the ball connect.

Perfect.

The staff room window opens. 'Catch!' yells a teacher.

The colours around Sammy are golden and glowing with satisfaction as he raises the ball in his hand. 'Howzat!'

Sandra and Sonia are right next to him. 'Sammy! Sammy! He's our man!' they yell, and they do this weird little dance together, that makes them look like frogs. But he ignores them. He holds the ball up in my direction and looks straight at me, and he smiles. Our eyes meet and I see our longing and desire zinging on the air; it flies between us in a bright golden spark, darting on the air like the Quidditch snitch, linking us together as though the space between us didn't even exist.

'Eyes off, you friggin' witch!' whispers Sonia, and it's like the air has gathered itself up into a fist and thumped itself all the way through my body. I double over. When I can look up again Sammy's staring at me. His hand holding the ball has fallen to his side, and his colours shift on the cold air, back into a deep and troubled purple, like a bruised cloud hanging over him.

The girls all turn to look at me like they've finally noticed I exist. They don't like what they see. The look in their eyes feels like stones, a hail of them falling, landing all around me. I stare back at them.

'You got a problem?' asks Leah.

And I wish I could say *Yeah, big one! Huge, massive, life-threatening mega problem − and the least of it, Leah, is the fact that you don't like me.* But I can't. I see Sammy notice that something's going on and begin to run towards me, but I walk away, fast.

'Neesh!' he shouts at me. I turn and catch his look; a look like the last glance of sunlight on water before the night falls.

Q: What's happening, Sammy?

Q: What do we think we're doing?

## Sammy

I catch the ball, an impossible catch. I hold it up and I laugh. I hold it high in the air for her to see. *I caught it,* I'm saying to her, *just like I caught you!* I'm so happy we're back in touch. I know she'll know what I mean, and she does. The memory flies between us and I feel my hands reacting as she fell, moving quickly and surely beyond me, without me. I feel the weight of Neesh's body as she sank into my arms. I can still hear her small gasp of fear, feel the touch of her fingers grasping my wrists, and that's when I remember.

I remember the leap of electricity between us. I remember it happened when we first met, and I remember something Grandpa once said to me: 'You know, Sammio, love's a spark! It's a real thing, and once you've felt it love is no longer just a thought, or a possibility, it's a reality. A reality that once it's born can never be denied, only lived with.'

And suddenly his words make perfect sense to me. I'm stunned. I stand in the emptying playground and I know it's ridiculous, crazy and mad not to have seen it before, but I didn't. I just didn't. And now I have, it feels like everyone else has seen it too, because I've just shown them, haven't I?

All the girls are staring at her and I don't know what's happening, I only know that she's walking away from me, fast, and that all the joy of that fantastic impossible catch is gone – and the ball feels like a rock, immovable in my hands.

'Neesh!' I shout, but she just glances back at me and then away, and is gone.

*No!* The word just forms inside me. *No!* But she's gone.

'Catch me any time you like,' whispers Gita as she skims past. Her perfume smothers me, makes me want to choke.

I stare at the door Neesh has just disappeared through as the playground empties around me.

Me and Neesh?

Me and Neesh?

And I feel her falling into my arms, like cards falling into place to make a perfect deck. It makes such sense that I can't believe I've been so blind. But I have.

*I'm in love.*

# Grandpa: Kashmir

I'm old. That's what I finally understand as I sit here under the same blazing sun that I first saw so long ago. I realise that these days my bones ache, and it is only this, the fearless heat of the Kashmiri sun, that can reach right into them and loosen them. It pushes back time . . . pushes it back and back, until I'm right back where I left myself nearly sixty years ago . . . and I can feel everything that happened then beginning to come alive again. I can feel the story beginning to unfold itself within me, reaching out its tendrils and searching for something to cling to, hardly able to believe that finally I'm ready to listen.

But I am. Let me tell you.

Let me tell you of all the things I've left unsaid.

Let me tell you an untold story.

Not in how or when or why, or what happened next, but in moments.

Moments that when we look back we can see changed our lives forever.

That first moment:

I was seventeen. Mum had dragged me along to the club. I was bored. There were only wives and servants around; everyone else was at work or fighting. The only other English boys were camping out by the lake, and Mum was always trying to get me to link up with them, but I didn't like them.

'Jake!' said Mum. 'I'm meant to be on the houseboat to pick up some mumbo-jumbo medicine your uncle swears will do wonders for my back. Do it for me, will you?'

I could have said no; I could have had an arrangement to play tennis that morning. If I had, my whole life would have been different. Or would it? Was it all bound to happen anyway?

I got up and went. It was hot and I was glad to be away from the lonely women and girls, all busy pretending not to sweat. I grabbed a rickshaw and headed for the lake, with no sense of the future rising up to greet me – but there it was, waiting for me anyway.

She's standing on the roof of the houseboat. Standing as still as stone, but her veil and kameez flutter in the slight breeze, press themselves against her cheeks and briefly reveal the shape of her face and body before billowing out again.

I get closer and watch her looking out across the lake. I feel strange. I feel like I'm trespassing, watching a wild bird that has no knowledge of me. It feels wrong, and so I step up the ladder and cough.

'Ahem.'

She's startled. She turns, and before either of us know it she's falling. Without thinking I reach out . . . reach out and feel the sudden weight of her land in my hands, where the blades of her shoulder bones fit perfectly into each of my palms as I steady her. Her fingers fly through the air in fear and alight on my wrists.

Our skin sparks, lights up the air with our longing.

I lower her to the ground. She sits with her back to me, her fingers still resting on my wrists as I kneel behind her.

Neither of us can move for long, long seconds.

We don't want to. We're frightened of what we might see.

We've *touched* each other. We turn and glance into each other's eyes and away again. What's happened can't be real. I can't feel like this and neither can she.

Because she's from here. India.

And I'm from there. England.

She drops her hands from my wrists and I lift her to her feet. I try to steady us, but it's too late. It's too late; the world will never feel steady beneath our feet again.

We step apart.

To do anything different would mean breaking a lifetime's training. To do anything different would mean breaking barriers built over centuries. To do anything different would mean that we weren't stuck between two truths – that we can never be together and that we can never be apart.

We know all this instantly, just as instantly as we know we want each other.

She hands me the package for my mother. I hand her some coins.

We turn and leave.

Neither of us speaks, not in words. The world we live in has no words with a meaning for this moment; it only has insults.

# Neesh

'Whoa Gita, get a load of that!' Leah whoops. 'Sammy definitely showed her his ball! Better hang on to your handbag, Geet, no way you'll pull him now!'

And they both turn to stare at me, and my cheeks burn and I look away, keep my head down.

Blink. Blink, blink.

'Perhaps he likes the silent type!' Leah laughs. 'You could always try having your lips stitched, Gita!'

And they all laugh, but for once Gita doesn't join in, she just stares at me. I don't like it. I throw up a wall inside me, but her feelings are too strong and they break through. She'd wipe me off the face of the earth if she could. She's black, cold, hard granite.

'Well, well, well,' she says, 'boys arriving like buses! First Kef's after you, now Sammy. What've *you* been doing behind the bike sheds?'

They all stare at me then. I keep my head down, grateful Sammy's not in this lesson.

Blink. Blink, blink.

'My mum's always said boys aren't into conversation!' says Nell.

'Yeah,' says Gita, 'even so!'

They'd have to be desperate to look at me, is what she's thinking; she might as well say it.

'Anything you want to share with us all, Gita?' the teacher asks.

'Discussing human psychology!' Gita shoots back.

'Well, I hate to have to remind you, Miss Syal, but this is a maths lesson!' he tells her.

'Ah, sir,' she laughs, 'call me Gita again! You know how much I love it when you talk dirty to me!'

There's a silence, she's gone too far, and at last no one's looking at me.

'Perhaps you need some time alone in the annexe,' suggests the teacher, 'to think over appropriate social boundaries.'

With a huge sigh Gita stands up and gathers her books. Everyone waits; she's had it now so she'll land him a one-liner. Even the teacher knows it. Gita waits till she gets to the door. 'Sir?' she asks, but he doesn't even look up. 'Did anyone ever tell you talking like a dictionary just doesn't do it for a girl?' And she leaves the room, closing the door quickly.

'All right?' he asks me.

I nod.

He sighs.

Nell leans over to me. 'Kef says he's gonna kill you – bad night, was it?' and she smiles. She thinks it's a joke; lucky her. If my life carries on this way Kef might not be the only one who wants to kill me, my whole family might join in.

The bell goes, and I stay in my seat as long as I can. I'm scared, it feels like I've taken a stone out of a pile, and if I'm not very, very careful the whole lot's about to cave in and crush me.

*I told you!* Mum whispers with satisfaction inside me. *No daa'in should ever marry!*

*I don't want to marry him!* I think back at her, *I just . . . just* what?

I want to touch him again, feel his wrists beneath my fingers. Feel that spark leap between us, like the fingers on that ceiling somewhere in Italy.

*And then, hanh?* asks Mum inside me. *You think it will stop there? You think boys are lights that you can switch on and off each time you fancy?*

Q: How would I know?

A: I wouldn't.

I wait until the classroom's empty and the corridor's clear, and then I run. I'll be late for the next lesson, everyone'll stare at me and then the whispers'll begin.

*What? Sammy and Neesha, no way!*

*Is that why Kef's gonna kill her?*

*Nah, that's cos she's a Paki, innit!*

More laughter.

I can see it all, hear it all about to happen. I stop running.

Q: What am I running to, anyway?

A: Nothing but the next lesson.

Nothing.

I've got nothing to run to. Other girls want to be celebs, brain surgeons or hairdressers, or just to pull someone. But me, I've got nothing to run to and everything to run away from. I just haven't seen it quite that way before.

Slowly I turn around and head the other way. I start walking out of the school. I walk out of the corridor. I walk out of the buildings and across the playground, and then I walk into the street. I can't believe I'm doing it, but I am! My feet are walking away and I'm going with them. Into the park and under the trees, where I stop, sit down and start to laugh. It was so easy!

Easy–peasy–paki–pleasy!

I laugh some more, lean back against the tree and close my eyes . . . and inside me I feel Sammy's arms catch me over and over, feel the sudden safeness of his hands, feel the way they let my body drop a few centimetres before steadying me and helping me up. I remember the feel of his wrists beneath my fingers, can still feel the spark . . . and then . . . and then . . . the surprise, the look of recognition in our eyes . . .

This can't happen.

It can't happen.

But it's happening anyway, right inside me. The feeling that leaps between us is real, only it doesn't fill me with joy or hope or any of the things it should do, it fills me with fear. I don't know what to do. So I do what I always do in the end, I go back to the place I call home.

I'm cooking when the doorbell goes; I pretend I haven't heard it.

'Shotgun!' yells Jammi, as though he ever answered the door anyway. I go on measuring out the lentils, watching them pour from the jar like rough sand. Boil them up with the spices. Concentrate on the food, the chopping, cutting, boiling.

The bell goes again.

'Ding, dong! You're unbelievable!' it sings. I hate it. Mum bought it at a car boot sale, and no one ever knows what it's going to sing next.

I start to fry the onions and garlic slowly, watch them turn transparent in the butter, add the red flecks of chilli, wash my hands. I can't hear it, but I can feel my heart still thumping, and I picture Sammy outside the door, his finger on the bell.

'Ding, dong. One day I'll fly away,' the doorbell sings.

I wish I could fly away. Someone's flipping at the letter flap now. Flip. Flip, flap.

'Ding, dong. I should be so lucky, lucky, lucky, lucky!'

Sometimes I think that doorbell can read minds.

'Neesh! Someone's banging on that door like bloody head-metal!' yells Mum.

'Neesh!' says a voice through the letter box. 'Neesh!'

And at the sound of his voice I turn everything off. The bubbling dies away, the smell of onions is cut short, drifts on the air.

'Hey, Neesh, it's me, Sammy! Open up!'

Sammy. I'm not imagining it, it really is him, but he can't be here, he can't be.

I stand very still and feel my heart beating.

*Don't!* says Mum's voice inside me. *Don't throw yourself away.* And I wonder what she means. Slowly I go towards the door. I open it and there he is, standing there, his hand still in mid-air, about to bang on the door again.

'Oh! Neesh . . .' he says suddenly. 'I . . .'

'Hi.' The word comes out slowly, unsurely, but he smiles at me. He smiles at me as if I've said a whole sentence, or maybe even a paragraph.

'You're all right!' he says, and he grins. 'I was worried!' I think he must be mad, to be standing at my door as though it's the most normal thing in the world, smiling at me.

I nod, and we stand there, staring at each other.

'Where've you been, Neesh?' he's saying. 'I thought . . . I thought Kef had found you!'

I shake my head.

'Why's he looking for you?'

I shrug my shoulders.

And then he does something so surprising it wipes my mind completely clean. He touches me. He reaches out and touches my shoulder. Not because he has to, and not because I'm falling and his instinct takes over – but because he wants to.

'We need to talk,' he says. I open my eyes wide and point to myself. *Me? Talk?* I mouth.

He laughs. 'Well, maybe you need to listen. We've got a problem.'

'Come on,' he says, 'you look like you need air.'

I imagine it. Air, sweet air. I imagine stepping outside and following the glowing line that he offers me. I can see it shimmering in the air between us. I see two steps floating beneath my feet, steps up towards him . . .

'Nushreee-ee-la! There's a damn gale going through this

72

house!' Mum yells. I know I should shut the door. No, that I *must* shut the door. I'm whispering it in my mind, *shut it, shut it, shut it, shut him out.* But my body won't obey me.

Because it's wonderful, the way he doesn't jump, or flinch, or look scared by the sound of my mum's voice. He just laughs! He thinks what she's said is funny . . . and his laugh is like . . . it's like church bells, church bells ringing on top of a rumble of summery thunder, fearless and true. I stare at him and he laughs again and, without waiting for an answer, he pulls me gently through the door, closing it softly behind us.

'Just as well you've always got your coat on,' he laughs, and for a moment we're up close. Frighteningly, terrifyingly, wonderfully close.

'Race you, Neesh,' he says, 'race you to the end of the street.' And his eyes gleam at me just like they did when we were six and I had my hair in plaits. Long black plaits that I flicked him with. I don't know what's happening any more. I only know that pass-i-ons moo-ve. No, they don't just move, they dance, and suddenly my heels have wings, wings that are taking me down the road in the softly falling snow, being chased by his laughter – and then he catches me by the elbow and we're running, running through the grey streets that are swiftly turning white. And he's still laughing, and I hear a noise come out of me, cracking and sudden on the cold night air, sounding something like laughter.

Q: Where are we going?

A: We don't know.

All I know is the feel of his hand on my arm and that it feels like escape, like hope, like a promise that there might suddenly be something more than the cold, grey streets, the half-empty house – and the life that I live in them.

It feels like we could run for ever. But we can't. We stop. We stand, gasping for breath in the falling snow; the flakes are falling fast now, covering the world in white, wiping everything out. He reaches for my hand and together we tip our heads back and taste the falling snow.

Laughing.

There are no words. Only pass-i-ons moo-ving. Just him and me and the snow. And then we sit in the deserted bus shelter together.

'Neesh,' he asks, 'have you got a computer?' I laugh, shake my head, wish I could say, *Jesus, Gandhi and Mohammed (peace be upon them), all I've got is a mattress on the floor! But Jammi's got a desktop and a laptop.*

'Well,' and he blushes, the air around him turns a deep, deep red like a sunset longing for the night to cover it, 'well, there are loads of places on the net, it's like meeting friends in a café, kind of leaving notes for them and stuff, only in cyberspace. Anyway, the other thing is, you can play games, do questionnaires, things you just answer and, well, the thing is . . .'

I smile. I don't understand any of it but I can see his colours tangling furiously above his head and longing to be sorted, so I nod just to help him along. He takes a deep breath.

'Listen, Gita and her gang played a trick when we were all in the computer room, they sent me a questionnaire, and I thought it was like a pop-up, something no one would ever see or know about. It was stupid of me, Neesh. What they wanted was to find out, well, they wanted to know . . . oh, shit!' he says in the end, and he shoves a piece of paper into my hand. 'Just look at this when you get home, and Neesh?'

'Yeah?'

'Leah sent it to me; it was a trick, OK OK, a way of finding out whether or not I fancied you.'

*What?* I mouth, and his fingers reach up and trace the shape of my lips.

'I love it when you do that,' he says, so I do it again.

*What?*

'I love it when you do that,' he says again.

My fingers reach up, reach up to do the same to him but before I'm even halfway there my hand loses all its courage. He catches it before it drops and holds it to his mouth. His lips are warm and red, and as surprising as berries on a tree in winter. The warmth from them spreads right through my body. I close my eyes, feel his thumb resting on the corner of my mouth, his breath on my palm, and a picture flits across my mind . . .

*The girl and boy stare at each other across the flowers. Their eyes burn, their breath rasps as though they've been running. Their eyes connect over the rising smell of the flowers that lie like a river between them. The distance between them is huge, is nothing, is uncrossable, is perfectly possible . . .*

I open my eyes and look into Sammy's. There's only the snow falling outside the shelter and the look in our eyes as we stare at each other, and the distance between us is nothing, is everything. Slowly we take our hands away from each other's faces.

'It's true, isn't it?' he asks. 'I mean, I didn't really realise it until today, but I . . .'

*What?* my mouth asks.

'You and me, Neesh. I've only just seen it and . . . anyway, it's all there on the paper.'

I fold it up and put it carefully in my pocket.

We walk back slowly. And he knows somehow, knows that I can't speak, that I need to watch all the colours of his feelings shifting and turning all around him. There are so many, each colour fading and then flashing. Shining for just a moment in absolute certainty before hesitating, fading and giving way to another. He stops us just around the corner from home and reaches up, traces my lips with his thumb as though he wants to imprint the memory of my mouth on his mind – and for the briefest second, as his skin connects with mine, all the colours in the air come clear around him, are transparent, and I know I will hold this moment to me like treasure, hold it tight against the fear of being me.

His hand drops, and he shakes his head and laughs his fearless laugh. Suddenly I wonder if he knows anything at all. Does he even know the world's a dangerous place?

'Bye then,' he says.

*Bye,* I mouth back.

'Bye,' he says again, but neither of us moves.

*See you*, I mouth.

'See you,' he says.

But somehow we're still standing here, stock-still in the falling snow, and I'm not looking at his colours now. I'm looking at him. At his brows that are so dark and straight, like they have to protect his eyes from themselves. At his eyes that are wide and open, and his nose that is so straight and probably a bit too long – but somehow his face just fits itself so well that I could look at it for ever.

'If we stay here long enough we'll turn into snow-people,' he says, and I wave and turn to go, but he catches my hand, he smiles – and he leans towards me, and for a moment . . . I think . . . I feel . . . that maybe he's going to kiss me . . . and I almost lean forwards, almost, but then I see the eyes of Mum and Jammi, and Gita and Nell and Leah and Kef. And strangest of all, I see my own eyes too, feel that bit of me that sees the world in colour-whispers and that can heal, whisper to me, *give him up, give him up,* and I know that I should, but the fingers of my right hand don't listen, they curl around the bit of paper in my pocket and hold on to it tight.

'Ss . . . see you,' I manage to stutter and he smiles his

bright, radiant smile, and then he waves and disappears into the whirling flakes.

'Bye!'

And there's only the sound of his laughter left on the air echoing in the snow. I feel suddenly empty, as though all the colours in the world have faded to a dull, dull English grey. I watch the falling snow, I hear him singing as he walks away: 'If my complaints could pass-i-ons moo-ve, or make love see . . . wherein I suffer wrong . . .' I imagine the soft fat flakes of snow are flowers. Flowers that are bright and orange, like longing. Flowers that fall all around me, touching me like a promise, a promise of something to come. I hold on to the piece of paper in my pocket and slowly walk home.

'And what you smiling at?' shouts Mum. 'Door open, lights on, food cold before it's cooked and you think it is smiling matter?' She's standing in the kitchen next to the congealing daal, with Jammi smiling right beside her.

Fat bastard.

'You were with boy?' she says, and I drop my head, hoping she can't see the gleam in my eyes or feel the leap in my heart every time I remember Sammy's thumb tracing the shape of my lips, hear his laughter like church bells.

'Well?' shouts Mum. 'Jammi says you were with a boy! Hanh! There's only one thing any boy would want you for! Watch out, Nushreela! You know what will happen! Then you will be spoilt goods. You will lose your energy if you go with boy! And then we will have to find you a husband! Hanh!'

'Yeah,' slides in Jammi, 'and we ent got the money for the plastic surgery!'

Is she joking? Would she really marry me off even after everything she's said? Could she, without Dad here? I don't know. I can't tell. I only know it isn't funny.

'No more going with boys! I told you!' she says, and she has. She's told me healers are always in danger. Danger from the secrets that people feel they know; danger because no one likes the person who heals them. Who else can they blame when it doesn't work – the world, for being too random? No, they blame the person who should have made them better, and that's me. I don't really know if Mum's right about people like me never marrying, but I know this: I know it suits her to think so. I mean, if I left here what would she live on? I make most of the money we've got. Without me and my healing there wouldn't be any food, and that's really why she doesn't want me to marry, isn't it? What I want to know is, how does she think I can do one thing without the other? How does she think I can see people's fears and illnesses without seeing the colours and the visions as well? It's like . . . it's like wanting the jam in the middle of a sponge without the cake to hold it in. It isn't possible.

I sigh.

I pick up the coriander and begin again, chopping and cooking, but this time it's different. This time I'm not alone. I'm imagining Sammy walking through the snow on his way home, singing, humming. The knife slips suddenly across my hand, a line of blood rises in dark dots across my thumb. I lift it to my lips, where it mixes with my spit.

Metallic taste.

Q: What does it taste like, a kiss?

A: I don't know.

I feel the letter crackle in my coat pocket and suddenly I can't bear it any more. I run upstairs, sit on my mattress and take out the piece of paper Sammy gave me. I unfold it, smooth the crumpled corners. It's still warm, from my skin, from his. At first I don't get it, it's like a questionnaire, a quiz or something, there are two questions.

**Have you ever been in love, are you now, and if so, who with?**

And underneath it says my name, over and over again. Neesh. Neesh. Neesh. Like he can't believe it.

**Neesh.**

And underneath there's another question.

**But who would you spend just one night with?**

And then the paper's torn off. At first that worries me, and for some reason I think of Gita. I think of how cold and angry she feels, but then I see my name again and I hold the piece of the paper against my cheek, crushed and warm. 'What?' I whisper to it. 'What?' And even the words sound warm against the paper; I breathe them in because I don't really need to ask the question, I know what it means. I've known it forever, haven't I? And it comes again – that feeling like a latch lifting and a door opening, and everything that should be in place being in place. And I whisper a question, whisper it out loud.

Q: How could anything that feels so right be wrong?

The answer comes startlingly clearly. It arrives in my mind complete. In words that feel like they've been spoken before.

A: Because of the world around us.

And suddenly it feels as though all the things I hold in my hands, the memory of his touch on my mouth, the words on the page I'm holding, are nothing, are already water that runs through my fingers even as I try to catch it.


# Kefin

'*What've you done, Kef?*' Kef hears the words inside him in his nan's voice.

They make him shiver.

'*Kef! No!*' The voice is so clear that he looks up expecting to see her, to see Nan, but all that's there is the tree. Neesh has gone again, disappeared. He hates that. That's what everyone does. Mum, Nan, everyone leaves him. Kef groans. How does Nan know what he's done? *What* does she know? He's gonna kill Neesh if she's told Nan.

Feck! Nan's dead, for chrissake! She doesn't know anything! It's just a great big Paki con trick, innit? Neesh's trying to trick him into *admitting* it, ent she! But then how does *she* know?

He shivers.

He doesn't want to go back to the flat but he has to, there's nowhere else for him to go. Slowly he walks up the concrete stairs; the lifts never work. The stairway smells of piss and chip fat. On a good weekend it smells of puke and beer *and* piss and chip fat.

Kef's footsteps slow as he gets closer to the door of the flat. He goes softly, lightly, silently.

He stops at the door. He puts his ear to it slowly and waits. He waits a long, long time. He is completely still. He is completely silent. After a while he puts his key in the lock and turns it. Even then he doesn't actually go in; he just pushes the door all the way open, right back to the wall, and waits. He listens again and then finally steps over the threshold. He walks into the sitting room. On the floor by the fire is a hump covered by a duvet. He stands well back and stretches out a toe, touches it gingerly. Kef backs away from the hump, keeping his eyes firmly fixed right on it. He walks backwards all the way into the kitchen.

He shuts the kitchen door, puts a chair behind it, and only then does he sit down. Dad's a crafty fucker; he could play dead for years.

Kef sits at the small table and stares out of the window, waiting. Neesh'll have to come out of her house soon. He can see Nan's house from here. She used to come out the front and look up, wave. And Kef would wave right back. Sometimes she came out with a tin, and waved it in the air. That meant cakes.

'*What've you done, Kef?*'

Jesus! It sounded just like Nan, just like her. He doesn't want Nan to know, not never. *It wasn't . . . it wasn't . . . I mean, it was an accident . . .* His eyes flick rapidly towards the door and away again, fast.

Shit! What's he gonna do? He looks out the window. Neesh appears in the snow with Sammy. They're laughing. What've they got to laugh about? What's so funny about being an ugly Paki-weirdo?

*'What've you done, Kef?'*

That question. It keeps on coming. He keeps on hearing it, over and over. He wants it to stop. It's got to stop. He looks at Neesh. It's her, she's the one that made the question come, it wasn't there before, was it?

'I ent done nothin'!' he whispers to himself.

*'So what's that on the floor in the sitting room then,'* comes the next whisper, *'fairy cakes?'*

'Shut up!' shouts Kef, as though it wasn't him talking, and he looks down and sees with surprise that the knife is in his hand. He looks at it.

'Dead meat,' he whispers, 'that's all Neesh is.'

He hears the words in his head.

*Dead meat.*

She won't laugh when she sees this in her face, will she? He lifts the knife to his eyes, turns it and watches its blade glint. He likes the feel of it in his hands. It's not Dad's any more. It's his, Kef's, he's earned it.

'See this knife?' he whispers to himself. 'See this knife, Paki? It's got your name written all over it!'

Kef strokes the blade. He doesn't seem to notice it cut across his fingers.

'*What've you done, Kef?*'

The words feel like metal scraping metal in his guts. Absently, he sucks his bleeding fingers.

'*What've you done, Kef?*'

It sounds like Nan's voice, it *is* Nan's voice, but it can't be. She's dead. Kef shivers; perhaps she can see him, perhaps she's watching him, right now.

But she's dead. Everyone dies.

Except Dad.

'Mmmm,' says a voice inside him, 'but we *changed that*, didn't we?' and then it giggles. Kef looks at the knife. Whose voice is it he can hear? He slowly runs the blade of the knife under the kitchen tap. He wipes it clean. It was Dad's knife. He strokes it; he feels better when he does that, stronger and more in control.

He goes back to the window just in time to see Neesh shut the door and Sammy walk off singing into the snow.

He spreads his fingers against the windowpane as though he could reach out and touch her, and then he sees his fingers bleeding and he wonders – how come? How did that happen?

# Grandpa: Kashmir

Kashmir is still here . . . as I always hoped it would be.

If I was ever strong enough to return.

Some people believe there are parallel universes, places where all possibilities, all the things that could (and maybe should) have happened, become probable or real. I hope so.

And if there is a parallel universe, then maybe there's a place where the divisions between us – white, brown, priest or imam – are not just cracks for our hate to breed in, but spaces. Spaces where we can think and feel, and learn to make our choices. There I go again, hoping, dreaming. Have I learned nothing in all these years? Sometimes I wonder!

There'll always be hate, I do know that. But then again there'll always be love, too. And when I looked at her, my girl, all I could see was love. All I could see was her. She cut out the rest of the world from underneath me.

Blinded me.

And now I'm back, back in Kashmir where we began. Back to confront the picture of her that haunts my memory and runs through my mind over and over, repetitively, inescapably.

*I'm running to meet her, my feet pounding and my heart bursting. It's dawn, the sky a faint pale breath of rose. I break through the trees surrounding the lake and see her. She's standing on the roof of the houseboat. I stop, full of relief that she's OK; that she's still here. I take huge breaths of the cool air, and watch as she takes a slow step up on to the low railings. She balances for a moment. She shimmers, dressed all in white like a slim column of air, and then her veil falls back and even from here I can see, with a shock, that her hair has been cut off.*

*I start to run, but even as my feet move, she steps off the railings. She doesn't look down or up or back. She just looks straight ahead, to where, in the distance, a man is poling a boat full of flowers straight across the horizon.*

*'No!' I hear my own voice shout. I feel my arms stretch out, as though even from this impossible distance of time and space I could still catch her.*

This is how I wake from my nightmares, with my eyes wide shut and my arms out ready and waiting in the darkness, still hoping after all these years I can catch her.

'Goodness gracious, he's beginning to speak Urdu like a native!' says Mum.

'Mmm,' mutters my uncle – as though he knows that's not the only language I was learning.

We met on the boat. She taught me words. She taught me more than that. She taught me a whole new language.

It's like this.

We know each bit of each other even though we've hardly touched. Our eyes alight, lift, turn and fly across each other's bodies. I know the turn of her wrist where her sleeve falls back, the arch of her neck where her veil lifts. At night I imagine kissing the narrow bone of her ankle. You see, that was all we had back then: a glimpse, a promise, the lust of imagining a run of unbroken skin. Perhaps it's not so different now?

But I digress. The moment:

It's hot. We are surrounded by the heat and we are always waiting. Not just for the rains to break and fall, but for our longing to do the same. Sometimes I feel like a ticking clock about to explode, its insides flung open and springs all burst about. Whatever I do alone at night – and I do it often – it still doesn't stop the longing whenever I see her. It is always there like the heat all around us, ever-present and building.

Our eyes touch. *Ping*, and then away from each other again, trying to find a place to rest. I look out through the window to where a boat full of flowers punts its endless way past the window. I don't think. I run outside and I shout,

'Arjah!'

The boat turns, and heads towards me.

'How many?' says the boat-man, pointing at the flowers.

'All of them!' I say and his smile splits his face apart. Together we throw the flowers from boat to boat. They fly through the air to land on the small prow of the veranda, where they spill like a gleaming river through the shadowy doorway of the boat.

When we've finished I have to wade through them to

get back inside. My eyes are blinded by the transition from light and flowers to the cool inside of the boat. I blink and wait.

Blink. Blink, blink.

And as my eyes clear she takes shape before me. She's standing beside the doorway with her hand covering the smile on her face. She has rolled her shalwar all the way up above her knees, is paddling in a river of flowers. Her eyes shine above her fingers.

For an ageless moment we stand and stare at each other. We know it is not only flowers that stand between us, it's whole worlds. We don't move.

This is the moment.

The moment she stares at me, eyes shining, and I at her.

'Farida.' I say her name.

'Jake.' She says mine.


But I swear to you. I swear that even though I longed for what came next, I didn't move first. I swear with every bone, each drop of my blood and all my muscle and sinew that I would never have taken that step, not one step, if she hadn't first.

In that one moment, with one movement, she broke every barrier the world had placed between us.


She steps towards me. I still don't move. She steps closer and I feel my hand lift; I feel my thumb trace the reality of my longing all the way across her bow-strung lips. I feel my heart stop and then start again as she does the same to me.

We stand there, our thumbs resting against the corners of each other's lips, and then she stands back, rolls up her sleeves, slips her long brown arms deep beneath the flower-heads and throws an armful of them into the air. We throw flowers into the air until they fall like the longed-for rain, all over us. They fall on our faces and into our open mouths. We fall back and let the flowers catch us.

We dive under them.

We roll in them.

We tunnel through flowers, searching until we find a strand of hair, a laugh, a stretch of unbroken skin that under the touch of our fingers becomes an arm, a leg, face, a breast.

Until we finally find the shape of each other.

The relief is tremendous.

The release is exhausting.

We fall asleep on the wooden floor amongst the flowers.

When I wake up the sun is fading. There's a strange hum in the air and when I open my eyes I see the odd bee is hovering over us in the late sun, feeding in the fallen petals. I look at her. I close my eyes, open them again. I blink, but she's still here, still real. An orange marigold rests in the dip between her collarbone and shoulder. Across the lake somewhere I hear the bray and call of English voices, the crash of water breaking as they throw themselves in. I turn away.

Her skin is brushed to glittering by pollen and burnished golden by the low dying sun flowing through the doorway.

She opens her eyes and smiles at me.

'Good God, marry me,' I say both to her and to the ache in my chest. 'Please, marry me.'

That moment.

I see it over and over. In my mind's eye this is where I have tried to keep us for all eternity, locked in that moment forever: where we are whole and golden and buried in flowers – and each other.

But time kept on going.

'Impossible,' she whispers, and then she laughs. 'A boat full of flowers, my niquat!'

'Niquat?'

'Bride-price!' She smiles and lifts a finger to my lips. I do the same to her.

'Marry me, then!'

And she comes closer to me but her eyes no longer shine. They are dark and full of something suddenly forbidding. She presses her finger against my lips.

'Never,' she whispers to me, 'never tell anyone!'

And for a moment I can't take it in. I can't manage the difference between her soft whispering mouth with its warm breath, and the fear and terror in her words.

'But what could be wrong with this?' I whisper back.

'It's not about us,' she hisses, and her face is sharp and anxious, 'it's the world around us.'

But I smile. I smile and grasp her hand. I lift her up and spin her through all the crushed flowers. Slowly she comes with me, until we're both spinning and dancing and crushing the remaining flowers heedlessly beneath our feet.

*See,* I want to shout. *Look at us, just look at us!* And in that moment I believe the spark between us can light up the whole world, defy it. Conquer it.

'Shhh,' she whispers, breathless, 'softly.'

But I didn't know how to tread softly, because no one had ever taught me.

The natives had a story back then, that even the snakes ran away from the white man, but why? Because we didn't know how to slip through the grass, listening. We wore our boots so big and loud even the snakes fled before us.

We didn't listen. We always thought we were right.

I thought I was right too.

But I wasn't. I was wrong.

That's what I must face.

I thought we could change the world. I didn't see that it was the other way round. That the world saw everything – and that it would change us.

# Sammy

I sing all the way home. Not just one thing, a whole medley. Weird how when I'm with Neesh I feel like singing all the songs Dad loved best. Dowland, Taverner, the songs that remind me of being in empty churches with him, or hearing him play the piano.

First up is 'If My Complaints . . .', our song, mine and Neesh's now. We'll have it at our wedding, I think, and then I laugh at myself. Yeah right, and what type of wedding would that be? Christian, Muslim, Pagan? I'm halfway through 'Wonderful World': 'I see skies of blue, and clouds of white, the bright blessed day, the dark sacred night . . .' and the snow's landing on my upturned face, turning my cheeks numb with the cold and making my eyes blink against the dusk. 'I see trees of green, red roses too, I see them bloom, for me and you . . .' when suddenly, and for no particular reason that I can think of, I remember a whole conversation I once had with Grandpa.

Grandpa's on his hunkers in his marigold beds, pointing to the flowers. I'm only about six, and he's saying, 'In India, Sammio, you know you can buy a whole boat full of these.'

'Why?' I ask him. 'Why would you want to?' And he sits back with the earth on his hands and the sun in his face, and he smiles at me.

'They use them as offerings to their gods, and to whoever they worship.'

'Did you ever buy a whole boatload, Grandpa?'

'Yes,' he says, 'yes, I did, laddie.'

'Why? Did you buy it for God in Heaven?' I ask, and he laughs out loud then, laughs all the way across his garden, out over the lake he built, and all the way up into the cloudless blue sky.

'There is no God, Sammio, not for me.'

Sometimes Grandpa's so brave it frightens me; what if God heard him?

'Who did you buy them for then, Grandpa?'

And his eyes slip away from me and I follow them, out to where the sun glints off the lake and shines on the old Kashmiri houseboat that floats on the water, turning its old mellow wood yellow in the light. When I look back at him Grandpa's eyes are dark and cold and sad and angry. They scare me.

'I bought them for a person,' he says, 'a girl. There's a word, Sammy, *niquat*.'

'Yes!' I nod my head, importantly; I know what a kneecap is. 'It's where your knee bone's connected to your thigh bone?' I say.

And Grandpa laughs his laugh, the laugh that's just for me, the one I never hear anywhere else, and I watch him as the tears dash down through the runnels in his face.

'Sammio, you're not just a tonic, you're a cure!' he says, and then he's suddenly serious again.

'No!' he says. '*Niquat* means *bride-price*, it's what you give to the person you wish to marry, it's like a promise.'

'You bought them for *Granny*!' I shout, and then his

face closes up. His eyes go dark and I know that I mustn't ask any more questions. I know I'm in that place where the fear rises inside of me, and the story is too frightening to be finished. I think it must be because Granny is dead.

That night Mum read me *Rapunzel*, but it wasn't the Rapunzel from the book that I saw in the tower, it was Neesh. It was Neesh who stood at the small window high in the tower, letting down her long dark hair for me to climb up. And in my dreams my feet fitted so easily into each tightly woven triangle of her hair that they lifted me all the way up the tower to where she waited for me. But then came the scary bit. Whenever I saw that room, that tower with her in it, letting down her hair and waiting for me, it was always filled with flowers. Bright red and orange and yellow flowers, just like the marigold beds at Grandpa's house.

And now, as the snow lands on my skin, I feel scared, just like I did then, and it doesn't feel like a wonderful world at all. It feels terrifying. I think of my mate Mohammed, and how he was dragged off a bus in Bradford by a crowd of ignoramuses just because he had a big rucksack on his back and some freak thought he was a bomber. Suddenly our safe little world doesn't feel safe at all. First off, it's so big, way too big, and with great big gaps in it that we can fall into. And random – that's the scary thing, totally random, because we never know what's going to happen next, do we?

I hold on to the thought of Neesh. I see her mouth

making the shape of a question, remember the way her lips push themselves forward into a 'wh' so hesitantly and hopefully, as though they wish so much they could make a sound, as though maybe they're hoping to be met halfway, to be kissed. I wonder what I would buy her as a promise, the promise of a future I already know we can't really have, but that I can't stop myself dreaming of. I wish it was summer and I could ravage Grandpa's marigold beds until I had a boatload of flowers for her. And the thought of that gets me all the way home; in fact I'm right at the front door and trying to get my key in the lock when I hear Gita's voice.

'Hi!' and she's right there in front of me, standing in the snow outside my front door.

'Hi!' I say back, but I'm blushing already. She stares at me and bites her lip. I can't work out if she's angry or what. I'm pretty sure she must have seen the questionnaire. I can see it right now:

**If you could have just one night with somebody, who would it be?**

I can see now they all thought that's where I'd put Neesh's name. Leah and Gita had a bet (like Neesh and I were horses or something) and they needed to know if I fancied her; only it wasn't Neesh's name I put down for the 'one-night' slot, it was Gita's, and if I could disappear right now, I would.

Gita's standing there and the snow's melted her make-up and her mascara's run, turning her eyes into weird, wrinkled black starbursts. Has she seen the questionnaire? By the look on her face I'd say yes, she has.

'All right?' I ask, because *I'm* not. I'm wishing I was on a different planet, any planet, so long as it's a million miles away.

'Did you mean it?' she asks. I look away. I don't want to see her face. She looks so sad and angry and humiliated. I feel like shit.

Did I mean it? Yes, OK, so I like the idea of a night with Gita. I imagine she could teach me a few things, and she's fit. Would I really do it? Probably not – at least, definitely not now I know how I feel about Neesh. So what do I say to her right now? I say this.

'Mean what?'

'That I'm only good for a night,' and she doesn't take her eyes off me, not for a second.

'No,' I say. 'I didn't mean that . . . I don't think . . . that. It wasn't . . . it was like a game, Geet, not real!' I finish lamely.

She tosses her head and smiles. I sigh with relief.

'I'm really, really sorry, Gita. I don't think you're only worth that, and . . .' But she doesn't let me finish.

'Reckon you got the names mixed up, eh? I *said* that to Leah! Anyways,' she says, 'it's not like it's a great big deal or anythin', just saw you across the street. I'm on my way to, uh, Leah's. Do you know what number she is?'

*I didn't get the names mixed up, Gita.* The words are in my head, but they don't make it out of my mouth. *I want to be with Neesh, not you,* is what I should say, but what comes out is this: 'Next street along, number 14,' and I don't put her right. What good could it do, I don't want to humiliate her any more, haven't I done that enough already?

'Cool!' she says. 'Let's meet up soon.'

'Uh, yeah. See you, then,' I mutter.

'Yeah, bye.'

And it's just a bit freaky, the way she just stands there till I'm all the way inside, but at that moment I'm just too relieved to get away to notice.

'Who took away your shilling and gave you sixpence?' asks Mum, which is her way of asking me what's up. But I just shake my head.

'Nothin',' I say.

'That's NothinG, thank you,' she says back.

'RighT! SergeanT,' I say, and flop on to the sofa.

'You're soaking, Sammy!' snaps Mum.

'And knackered!' I snap back.

'Bad tempered, too!' smiles Mum.

'Sorry!'

'S'up in the head?' she asks, and I smile.

'It's 'hood, Mum, what's up in the 'hood! As in neighbourhood!'

'I'm not interested in the 'hood, Sammy, it's not the 'hood I'm askinG abouT.'

'I was thinking about Grandpa and his marigolds,' I say, as casually as I can.

'Oh!' Mum doesn't sound keen to talk about it. Her and Grandpa are not the best of mates, never have been, but she's cool with the fact that I think he's the best grandpa on the planet.

'What is it with him and the marigolds, anyway?' I ask.

'As in flowers?' she asks. 'Or has he developed a hidden passion for rubber gloves?' And then, when I don't laugh, she tries to soften her voice. 'Ask him,' she says, which is what she always says – ask him.

'I'm asking *you*, Mum. Whenever I ask Grandpa he . . .'

'He what?' Her voice is sharp, and my own goes deadly calm in response.

'Just seems sad!' I throw off.

'As well he might!' she snaps.

'Mum,' I say, as world-weary as I can make it, 'I don't know if you've noticed, but my balls dropped ages ago and my voice followed not long after, so I think I can take whatever it is that you're both not telling me.'

This is a technique that rarely fails with Mum, shock her with the image and she's so busy trying to be cool with it that the info just drops out of her. Warning, though, only works if used with caution.

Oh, and the truth is my heart's beating away like a bongo. For some reason I'm terrified of hearing her answer.

'He planted them in memory of someone,' she says, and her words are short and jagged, like broken stalks left standing, long after all the flowers've been snapped off.

'Who?' I ask.

'They're something to do with a girl he met in India.'

'What,' I laugh, 'Grandpa and a memsahib? Can't see it myself!'

Mum's not laughing, she's staring at me. 'It wasn't a memsahib, Sammy, it was a local girl, a Kashmiri girl.'

'Oh!'

'Quite!'

My heart's drumming a crescendo now, but my voice is giving nothing away.

'You got a problem with that?' I ask.

She's silent for a long while, and when she does speak her voice is cold and angry.

'It's not necessarily *that* I have a problem with,' she says. 'I have a problem with the fact that your grandpa never loved my mother, whereas she loved him so much she never seemed to mind! That's what I have a problem with!'

'Oh!'

'Quite!'

'Mum?'

'Yes?'

'I'm not sure my balls have dropped enough to want to hear about that, so could you just tell me about the marigolds?'

She laughs.

'I'd much rather you asked him, Sammy, really. It's his story, it's always been his story, and none of us are really sure what happened, we just know that it was bad, very bad. And that he's never really recovered, well, not enough to tell anyone what happened. Sorry, it used to bother me too when I was a kid.'

'Is that why you don't want to inherit the house?' I ask. I know I shouldn't, because she always does the same thing when I do: her skin goes very pink and her lips purse up as tight as a sow's butt.

'I love the house, Sammy, I always will, but that garden, the lake, the houseboat, the trees and flowers and everything in it . . . they're a monument, a monument to whatever it is that's inside him. A monument to a place that he loves remembering more than he loves being with us. And it means he can't . . . well, we're his family, us! Or we should be! Not some dead girl no one's ever met!'

'Dead?' I say, and I feel her clam right up.

'Well, Granny's dead, isn't she?' she snaps. 'They're old!' But I don't think that's what she means.

'Anyway, I can't ask Grandpa, he won't be back for months!' I wail.

'Tough,' she says, and then she softens again. A bit. 'Look, Sammy, this is exactly what I mean. What's he doing off in India, when we're right here?'

'Mum,' I answer, 'I think it's great he travels.'

'But always to the past, Sammy, always to the past, and sometimes, you know, it's nice to have parents that live right where you actually are, in the present! Right where they can see you!'

'Like Dad?' I ask.

'Oh, Sammy!' she breathes. She's right, it's a low blow, but sometimes I can't help myself. We stare at each other.

I stand up and hug her then, because she suddenly looks small and she's my mum, and, well . . . just because.

She sniffs.

'That's how we know Neesh's family,' she says, 'through Grandpa.'

'Oh!' I say.

'You should take out shares in that word,' says Mum. 'Fish pie all right for supper?'

'Fine,' I say, and I nod, but nothing's fine. Inside me everything feels like a kaleidoscope that's been shaken so hard that the colours don't even know what shape to fall into any more.

Later, in bed, I sing some Bach to myself. I sing it slowly and feel the notes begin to rise inside me, emerge, and hold me safe. Is this what Mum hated about Dad's music, that it took him somewhere else? Just like Grandpa's mind is always somewhere else, somewhere she can't reach? Know one of the great things about music, though? It's always the same, each note, so you always know exactly what's coming next. But the sound the notes make when you put them all together, and the feelings they can give you, that changes all the time – just like memories.

Like Grandpa remembering a boatload of flowers.

And me wishing I could give Neesh a present like that.

I can just see the look on her face. The thought makes me smile.

# Neesh

First thing I do when I wake up is reach under the pillow and feel if the piece of paper's still there. It is! I unfold it, read it again and again in case the words have changed. In case somehow I've made a mistake and imagined it. But it's still there in black and white.

**Q: Have you ever been in love, are you now, and if so, who with?**

A: Neesh. Neesh. Neesh.

That's me. Me.

I don't know what I'll do when I next see him, I don't know how to feel. I make breakfast quickly and then I notice Mum staring at me, hard, and when I turn my head I see Jammi looking at me too.

*Wh* . . . my lips shape, and I almost speak.

'You were *humming*,' says Jammi. 'What've you got to sing about, sis?'

I shrug. Jammi stares at me. Sometimes I wonder what I've done to make him hate me so much, but I don't think I did anything except maybe be born. I don't move. He stares.

'Who's the boy you were with?' he asks slowly, threateningly.

'Sammy,' I whisper, and he relaxes.

'Oh, Sammio,' he says, 'he's all right.' I hate the way he calls him that; it's what Sammy's family calls him. And Sammy's never liked Jammi. When we were kids we used to hide from him, take it in turns to dash in to cover whilst the other one distracted him by singing.

'Ip-in-ee-pin-ah-terri-terri-sutta.'

Whenever he caught Sammy he'd try to drag him off to play cricket, but Sammy never went. Whenever Jammi caught me he'd twist my skin on the back of my arms and try to make me scream. I never did, I didn't have to; it was never that long before Sammy got to me. Jammi doesn't think Sammy could ever be interested in me.

*He is! He is!* I wish I could shout. But I don't. I get my schoolbag and try to leave, but Mum's standing in my way, staring into space. She looks like a bomb's hit her, shell-shocked, and as I walk past she does something she hasn't done since I was tiny. She grabs me and hugs me to her, too tight, so that I'm squashed up against her squishy chest and can't breathe.

'No! No!' she whispers. 'Not again!' I pull away and stare at her. 'Neesh!' she calls as I leave, but I start to run. It's not until I'm halfway down the street that it hits me, where do I think I'm going? I can't go to school, Kef's there. I stop. I don't know what to do, and then I see him, Sammy.

He's at the end of the street, standing there, waiting for me – and my heart doesn't race at all, the way it says it does in books – no, it slows right down, it beats slowly and clearly and it fills my whole body with a new feeling, so new that I don't know what to call it. I stop to think about it. It's warm, like getting into a hot bath and the water just holding me up. That's what it's like.

'Hi!' he says. 'All right?' And he looks a bit like he's been up all night. His colours are slow and dark and troubled. I walk fast to get away from the house, and he follows. We don't talk, we just walk for a bit until we're round a few corners, and then slowly I take out the paper and unfold it, hand it back to him. He looks at it, at me.

'Neesh,' he says, 'I'm sorry, I should have told you myself – giving you that piece of paper, it was pathetic. Sorry.'

*What?* I think, *it was great.* I'm not worried about that at all; I'm just worried about where to spend the rest of the day! And I can still feel Mum's arms around me, like she's wrapped invisible bands around me, pressing and squeezing so that I can't breathe freely.

'Neesh,' Sammy's saying, 'I saw Gita last night and I think everyone probably knows what's on that piece of paper. Today's gonna be a bit heavy, so Be Prepared!' He holds his fingers up to his forehead in the Boy Scout sign.

What does he mean? He's laughing, or trying to, but he's not even finding himself funny. The ground doesn't feel right beneath my feet any more, it feels like it's shifting and sliding and I can't keep my balance.

*What?* I mouth.

I stare at him. Everyone knows? The words go through my head. Everyone knows. And I don't feel proud or happy, like I know I should. I'm terrified.

'It's OK, it's OK, Neesh,' he's whispering at me, holding my hands.

But he's wrong, it's not OK. It's not OK. What if Mum finds out, or Jammi's mates, not the ones from his posh school but the ones he hangs out with at night? What if they tell Jammi? What then? What if the uncles hear?

My eyes begin to flicker and the world begins to blur.

'Listen!' he says. 'Think about it, it doesn't say anything about you, does it? Just that I fancy you, not that you fancy me back or anything!'

He must be mad! Can't he see that no one can ever, ever, know about him and me? Ever. It would be – madness.

My body just shuts down at the thought of it. I'm scared I'm going to faint. I feel a flash of remembered pain in my hand, bolt-like and blue, and then I'm falling. Only this time I don't black out, instead it feels like my body's hitting water that shatters into a million fragments before letting me through. I feel the surface close . . . close over me . . . and *then* the blackness comes.

'Neesh!' Somewhere Sammy's shouting my name. 'Neesh, don't!'

## Sammy

She's blacking out again, her eyes flicker and begin to close. Her body begins to sway and fall, and then she's limp in my arms, gone. I'm shouting her name and the fear inside me bursts open and rips through my guts. What if she stays unconscious for ever and never comes back? What if she's dead?

'Neesh! Please!'

She's sliding down my body and I'm trying to hold her

up, but she's slipping through my fingers, right through my fingers . . . like a river joining the sea; I mean, how would you ever find your one and only glass-full in a whole ocean?

I say the first words that come into my head. I say:

'Omigod, Neesh, marry me!'

# Neesh

'Marry me!' The words catch me, hold me. I open my eyes.

We're both shaking and holding on to each other.

'What?'

'Uh, marry me?' he asks again. Only this time like he can't believe he said it either. The colours above his head are so strange, a deep golden orange and red, and they buzz like the sound of late summer. They entrance me so that even Sammy's voice seems far away, and inconsequential. 'I'll ask Grandpa to sort it with your family!' he's saying. 'You know, we'll make niquat.'

What? How does he even know that word?

'Niquat,' he goes on, 'it's, you know, like an offering, a promise, isn't it? Well I can promise to marry you! And in the meantime we can go out, right? I mean, they'll know I'm serious, right?' And the colours swirl above his head, separate into orange and red and deep, deep yellow.

Did he say that? Did he really say that? *Marry me.* Doesn't he know the way my world is, or the word for what he's suggesting?

Impossible.

It's impossible.

'Neesh,' he says, slowly, gently. He holds me by both shoulders and lifts me away from him so he can see my eyes. We stare at each other, hold each other with our eyes the way we want to . . . the way we want to with our bodies, but . . . 'I just want us to be able to be together, that's all,' he says.

Q: But is it that easy, can we really ever just be together?

'Do you?' Sammy's asking. 'Do you know what I mean?'

I nod. I don't want us to be apart either, ever. I rest my head against his chest, the way I realise I've always wanted to, and we stand together in the gently falling flakes, wondering what to do now that the words have been said.

We stand there unable to move, or maybe we're just scared to move because we can't see any direction that it's possible to take. We're lost, not just in each other but in a world that can't make any sense of us.

'Hey Sammy, what you doin'?' yells Sandra.

'Community service!' Sonia shouts back and Sammy flinches away from me. I feel his whole body draw back. I bite my lip; bite it so hard I taste blood.

'My bodywork could do with a bit of a service, Sammy!' says Gita, and she flashes her snaky hips and the colours around her are the deep, deep orange of longing. I stare at them. She notices me staring above her head.

'Something up with my hair?' she asks, and she looks at me and Sammy, standing apart now. 'Good trick, Neesh,' she says. 'I'll remember that one!'

I shake my head, questioning.

'Well,' she says, 'if you let yourself fall over, someone like Sammy's never gonna let you hit the ground, are they?'

'Yeah,' joins in Leah, 'we can all get it if we stoop low enough, and darling, your arse is practically hanging out of Australia!'

'What she do for you, Sammy?' they ask, and then they start blowing air in and out of their mouths in short, sharp puffs.

I stare at them all. I don't know what's happening, I can't understand it. Their colours flash and ride the cold air like storm shadows racing across a hillside. I don't get it. I think maybe they've arrived as a warning, a warning as to what can happen to us, and I want to run. I want to run away as far as I can from Sammy. I don't want him to see this, feel this. I want him to go back to his safe white life, as far away as possible, but he's holding my wrist so hard I can't move.

'Sammy!' I whisper. I try to pull away, but he holds on. His hand's so angry that his fingers twist my bones and his colours are steely rainbow shades of grey.

'Bitch!' shouts Sonia.

The word lands on my body like a stone.

This *is* a warning.

A warning. Blink. Blink, blink.

*Wh . . . ?* I begin to mouth at him.

'What!' they all shout out loud. 'Did you say what? Didn't your mum teach you to say pardon?'

'Pardon? Hard-on, more like!' laughs Leah, and their hatred glows above them.

'Told you, told you, told you!' Leah sings. 'Sammy fancies her!' and she points her fingers at me. Her disgust flies off the tips of them like pale green gob.

Blink. Blink, blink. I try to clear my eyes.

Blink. Blink, blink.

The girls begin blinking too, walking around us with their hands out, bumping into each other again, surrounding us. *Pardon! Hard-on! Catch me, Sammy!* With each insult my skin echoes with bruises. I try to say their names, to remind them of who they are and what they are doing, but only my lips move, no sound comes out. They begin to copy me, gaping like fish. I think my wrist might be about to snap as Sammy tightens his grip.

'Stop it!' He doesn't say it loud, but he's angry. 'For fuck's sake, stop it!'

They only laugh and do it some more, they're circling us now. Some of them blow and puff and some blink and others gape their mouths like fish. Their faces begin to blur, their words sink in and I feel like I'm falling under the blows.

'Gita! Leah! Nell! Sonia!' shouts Sammy. 'What the fuck d'you think you're doing?'

And finally Gita stops and looks at him. They all stop.

'You said!' Gita yells at Sammy, as he holds on to me. 'You told me it was a mistake, that you meant me, not her!' And she turns to the others. 'He did!' she says, and she has tears in her dark eyes.

'I didn't, Gita,' he says gently. 'I didn't say anything, that's just how you took it.'

'Fuck you!' she screams at him. 'Fuck you, Sammy Colthurst fucking Jones!'

'I don't think he's going to let you fuck him!' laughs Leah. I shudder again. Where do they get it from, all the energy that it takes to make the hate that pours out of them like poison? I don't know.

'Neesh,' says Sammy. 'We're leaving, you can't go in there.' He looks at the girls, at the school buildings, and he takes my hand and walks me away, away from the girls and their stunned, frozen colours as they watch us. I feel like my whole life is slipping away from me, sliding out of my hands and into his. It feels dangerous. It feels like the spark between us could set light to the whole world; that we're making flames that are already reaching out towards us, ready to burn.

# Kefin

Kef's cold, but he can't wear a coat. Dad says that coats are for gay-boys.

Knife's never cold. He's always warm, warm in his pocket.

Kef touches the knife. Knife is waiting for Neesh. He's hoping she's late for school; that she'll come running down the road long after everyone else has gone. She'll be alone when he jumps out of the alley. Huh! Dad's not the only one who can spring surprises.

Kef looks at the knife in his hand. His knife now. It can do lots of things. It can slit a fish from lip to belly and gut it till its backbone's clean. Dad does that. Mum and Dad used to go fishing.

*How do you know that?* asks a voice in his head, a frightening voice.

'I don't, I don't know it, I just made it up,' Kef whispers back, and the voice fades.

He holds on tighter to Knife. Knife can frighten people, make them speak. It can find out what Neesh knows. It can *make* her speak, even if she pretends she can't. Knife can get the words out of her. And then he sees her walking towards him and the knife shakes in his hand, shakes so hard that he's barely able to control it.

But she's with someone, she's with Sammy. He holds the knife still and watches. He watches the girls surround Neesh and Sammy. They throw words like knives. Knives that stab and cut her until she nearly falls and Sammy has to hold her up.

She's a dead weight.

Dead meat.

Or she will be, once he can get her alone. Him and Knife, that's all it takes.

Kef steps out of the alleyway. Everyone's gone now, except Gita who's smoking a fag, hiding the tears in her eyes.

'Oi, Geet!' he shouts, puts away the knife. Gita turns and sees him. She's full of shame and humiliation. Fuck knows how she's ever gonna face that down. Sammy Colthurst-Jones preferring Neesha Hussein to Gita Syal. It makes no sense. S'enuff to make you believe in witchcraft, I mean how else could she get her fingers into Sammy?

'Hi,' she says back to Kef, 'you're too late, she's gone off with Sammy.'

'Where?' asks Kef.

'You're keen.' She looks at him, takes a long drag. 'So what is it I'm missing, why are all the dogs after that bitch especially? I mean, is it the perfume she's wearing or what?'

'I said where,' says Kef, 'not why.'

Gita looks at him. She feels her heart beating very hard, it's been doing it ever since she first saw him. She realises she should be frightened. The look in Kef's eyes isn't right. But Gita's got guts and she's angry. She wants to hurt Neesh, make her feel the humiliation. She wants Kef to find her. Serve her right if he does.

'They were heading for the park,' she says, and she watches Kef smile. He doesn't say anything, just smiles and touches something in his pocket and walks right past her.

'Thank you, too!' she shouts after him, but he doesn't even look at her, just carries on walking like she's a used-up tissue he's already dropped on the ground.

Gita's filled with a terrible fear then, a knot that twists in her guts. She wishes she could turn back time and change what she's said, but she can't.

She turns around and heads back to school; she'd rather face her jeering friends than be alone. She needs to be somewhere safe, somewhere like school.

'I didn't mean it,' she whispers.

Safe and warm inside school, she looks out through the window at the steadily falling snow, watching out for Neesh and Sammy, wondering what she's done.


# Sammy

We walk around the park until we find a huge weeping willow. We hide under it. I wrap my arms around her and we stand there. I don't know what to say. I don't know how to say sorry to her for the way people can be. People I thought were fine; people who should know better, people like Gita.

'Are they always like that?' I ask, and she shakes her head, and points at me.

'It's worse because you're with me?' I ask. She nods, and I feel like I'm walking into another world. A world I don't understand. A world where people can change so completely that you don't know who they are any more.

A dangerous world.

'Are you OK?' I ask.

'It felt like,' she whispers, 'it felt like stones landing,' and she reaches for my hands behind her back, touches them lightly — undoes them.

'They're evil, Neesh, stupid, pathetic, don't let it get to you . . .' but she's shaking her head at me, sadly, softly. In a way that's making my heart beat, making me scared.

'What's WRONG with us being together? How could anything that feels this good be wrong?' I hear myself say.

'Nothing,' she whispers, 'and everything.'

'And that's why it feels frightening?' I ask. Because it does, every time I think of the girls' faces, of Kef's face. 'But we can *make* it work, Neesh,' I say, 'we just need to find out how.' And I know she's been asking herself the same question over and over. Both of us are asking, searching, as though there might be an answer.

'We can't. It's not us that's wrong, Sammy, is it? It's what other people think – and what they'll do!' she says.

She starts to shake. It's cold, we're scared.

'It's OK! It's OK!' I say. 'I won't let the zombies get you.'

'Zombies aren't real, Sammy,' she says slowly, hopelessly, 'are they?'

I stare at her. What's she going to do?

'And what if the zombies are out to get you, too?' she asks.

I think of Mohammed again. Mo–ham no–ham we call him sometimes, because he doesn't eat pork. He's so chilled that he thinks it's funny. Or does he? Maybe he doesn't think it's funny, maybe he just puts up with it because he thinks he has to? I've never asked him, have I? I think about the fact that his big sister's in med school and has a Scottish boyfriend. Mo's parents are fine with that, but I know some people give them a hard time. Would people really want to harm us? Could they?

'Sammy!' she says, and before I know it she's dropped my hands and is moving away from me, moving across the snow – running. Not towards me, but away from me.

*No!*

The word rages inside me, rings against my skull.

*No! No! No!*

'Neesh!' I shout out. I reach out for her with my suddenly empty arms and run after her. I hear the words forming in my mind.

*It's not like that! Not in my world. We can make it all right, if only . . .*

She stops to look back at me, and at the look in her eyes I stop dead too. I don't run after her. I can't, because somewhere inside me the fear's broken free and it's twisting and turning, racing through my guts and raging.

I stop dead.

What if she's right?

What if being with me puts her in danger?

And then she's gone. Gone like she was never ever anywhere anyway, except in my imagination.

The trees rustle. The traffic hums. The noise of the world is still going on all around me. I can feel my brain still notating the keys the world operates in, trying to understand. But none of it makes sense, none of it matters any more, does it, if . . . if . . . she's gone.

Already there's an empty sound in my world, a deep silence. A darkness where she's missing. And I hear myself think, is this how Mum felt without Dad? Is this how Dad felt without his music? Is this how I feel without Neesh?

It feels terrible.

# Neesh

I run. I must always keep running, away from that leap, that spark that defies the air and crosses the distance between us. Away from Sammy and his perfect life that I can mess up just by being with him. I remember Mum's words. 'Hanh, you think you have choices, no woman has choices.'

'No!' I shook my head at her.

'You are like your great-auntie, you think you can choose. Don't look me in the eye like that!'

*Like what, like what, Mum?*

'Like you are thinking too much!' she said, even though I didn't say a word out loud.

I run away from Sammy and from the fear of what might happen to us if I stop. I must never stop, never lie down, never let my arms sink into a boat full of flowers and imagine them crushed between our bodies, sticking skin to skin in a heat so strong that the smell of flowers is overpowering, overwhelming.

*Stop! Keep running.*

Now Jammi's words haunt me.

'Shame we can't marry you off, Mr Hamid's wife died last week and he's always wanted a wife who could give him a boy!' He laughed. Mr Hamid's about sixty.

I didn't say anything.

'Witch!' he says. 'You know what happened to that witchy aunt, don't you?'

I don't say anything.

'She didn't just die, you know, there was a reason, a reason why she—'

'Jamid!'

Mum's voice was sharp as a whip-crack, but he just laughed and laughed. I see a light falling faintly on dark water and I feel a fear so bad that I think my body might fly apart and dissolve under it. I hear a chanting, a chanting in my head that sounds something like the words of a prayer.

I see Sammy in the playground again with his arms wide open to the world, spinning in all its oxygen, and I want to leave him there. Somewhere he can breathe. His world.

So I run.

I run as fast as I can, because if I don't run forwards I'll run backwards. Back towards Sammy. Back to where I can lean as close as forever and kiss him anyway.

Q: How could this be wrong?

A: Because it could be the death of us.


'What's on-going?' says Mum.

*Nothing!* I mouth.

'Then why are you home?'

I don't know what to do. If I answer she could get mad, if I don't, same. So I shrug.

'Is it a shaking-shoulders-only matter?' she says. I shake my head.

'Ah, head and shoulders! Is it knees and toes also?' She laughs at her joke, and I try to smile.

'Hanh! You smile like a donkey in water!' and then I really do smile, I can't help it, because I can imagine that's exactly what my smile's like, and she's smiling too . . . and then she lifts her arm and hits me . . .

'What did I say to you?' The back of her hand is hard, her ring grazes the bone in my cheek. 'You think you are going with boys? You think you are the Madonna anyhow?'

'It was just Sammy,' I whisper, because we've always known Sammy.

'You are not child any more. What did I tell you?' and she gets up close, so close that I can smell the fennel seeds on her breath. 'I can only protect you so-so!' she hisses, and I draw back in surprise. Protect me? Mum?

'Your great-auntie, she thinks she can fall in love with who she likes and what happened to her, hanh?'

'She died,' I whisper.

'Don't you know there are worse things than dying?' she asks. I say nothing. We stare at each other and I lower my eyes.

'She thought she could do as she wished,' hisses Mum, 'and when you think like that, what d'you expect?'

I shake my lowered head. I don't know. She grabs my neck and I feel how frail it is, how loosely it's connected to my body. She squeezes. I raise my shoulders to help the pain and try not to make a sound.

She's speaking in Urdu, her words reaching into my ears, probing like long knives. I want to flinch but I'm too scared.

'Listen to me, do you want to be treated so badly that you *want* to die?' she asks suddenly. I look at her and shake my head, too scared to speak. 'Always, always as a child you asked too many questions.'

*Not any more*, I think, *you knocked that out of me.*

'And when the questions don't come out of your mouth they are coming out of your eyes.' I look down so she can't see them, but the question escapes me anyway.

'What happened to her before she died?' I hear myself whisper suddenly, unexpectedly. I need to know and I don't know why she won't tell me. Why does Jammi know and not me?

'She is dead!' she says. 'No point in talking now.'

But villages have long memories. I don't say it out loud but I remember Dad saying it, and how he was the only one who would marry Mum because her dead aunt was a witch, and worse than that, she'd broken the rules, had fallen in love with someone, and done something so terrible that it couldn't be mentioned. Sometimes when I think of the village I can see the women walking, digging, threshing, but the thing I see most are the chains above their heads, all swinging together and linking them, clinking and shining in the bright light. But whenever I imagine my great-aunt, the air above her head is as free and clear and wide as the sky. I wish I could see the picture of her.

'Go to your room,' yells Mum, 'and stay there!'

What happened, what happened to my great-aunt that I look so like, and who has hands like mine? Hands that work best on the left and know how a body feels?

I don't know. I don't know. I only know this: that whatever it is, it's so huge that it makes Mum want to lock me up for ever. And Dad? Maybe that's why Dad ran away — because he knew I'd turn out like her and he didn't want to stick around to see it.

I close my eyes. I don't want to think about Dad.

I hate my hands. I don't know how they work, or why they can feel pain on someone else's body, and sometimes make it better. I only know this: that it makes me different, it makes me a witch like my great-aunt who has nothing great about her — and that we're both bad.

I reach for the needle lying on top of the pile of holey socks waiting to be darned. I pick it up and I prick the soft skin on my left thumb. The blood wells up straight away, easily, a red round globe of it, and I sigh with relief. Better. That feels better. I lie down. Close my eyes.

But the picture of the boat's gone, there's only . . . *thick, black, inky dark, until slowly a chink of light appears like a spear in the distance. Slowly it widens into a pool of light, light shining on dark water, only the light feels forever away, unreachable . . .*

It's like I'm looking through someone else's eyes . . . *holding on to the light in the distance, and I can hear words, whispered words of a prayer, words that are fighting against the darkness and the other words, words from outside, whispered insults . . .*

I sit up. What's happening?

I don't know. I only know I'm scared to close my eyes again. Scared the picture inside me has turned into a black hole, scared of loving Sammy and scared of being trapped at home. But none of that stops the question coming.

'What happened?' I shout it out loud, but for once there's no answer, only silence.

I lift the razor blade and cut along the lifeline of my left hand. It hurts badly; it hasn't had time to heal from the last time yet.

My palm throbs beneath the blade until that's all there is. The pain. The rest of the world is still and silent and empty. I lie back. I hold my breath. I stop breathing until my cheeks pulse and my head spins – until the world tips and there are no pictures any more, no feelings, only nothing.

# Grandpa: Kashmir

Funny, isn't it? How being in love can make you alive to the slightest thing, like the feel of a breeze on your skin turning into the imagined tips of a beloved's fingers . . . but there were bad moments too, like this one.

Mother stands in the light from the window. The sprinkler falls over the garden, keeping the lawn green. I remember the shape of her lifted arm, visible through the light fabric of her dress.

'They've requisitioned White Barn,' she says suddenly, 'imagine!'

And I do. I do see White Barn, but not with soldiers filling it. I see it as it's always been. The long sloping beech woods, the perfect lawns and flowerbeds. The orchard. The walled vegetable garden with its soft fruit hidden under nets tall and wide enough to run beneath.

Startling how I'd forgotten it all, forgotten it was still there waiting for me.

Or for us, maybe? I try to imagine my girl at White Barn, standing in the middle of the lawn, perhaps, under the huge copper beech, looking up into its leaves and wondering where she's landed. Feeling like I did when I first got here – to India – like the heat had slapped me in the face, wrapped itself round me and clung, a hot, wet flannel.

And for the first time I wonder what we're doing.

And I want to know where she lives.

So I go to her village. It's like most villages. The houses

are low and sere and yellow, made of mud. The alleyways are so narrow that two people must breathe in tight to pass each other. Around the village the fields are green with crops; a sandy track runs through the fields. I walk along it.

It feels like at my approach everything falls silent. The wheels stop spinning, the cows stop being milked. It feels as though everything that was alive just a split second earlier has now stopped. Like the last piece of skirt swished through a smartly closed door.

The walls of each haveli has small, round piles of dried mud on top, like mud pies.

Three men come out. 'What do you want?' one of them asks.

'I'm lost,' I say.

'It's best you go that way,' he answers, pointing back along the track to the road.

I stare at the houses, hoping to catch a glimpse of her. I have a wild impulse to shout out her name, to break the oppressive heat and silence with the glorious sound of it.

The men stand there. They don't threaten me, but they make going any further impossible. I turn to go.

As I leave the low shimmering buildings that look like melting sunlight, something lands near my feet. A mud pie! I hear laughter, but when I look back the men have gone, the houses are closed and silent. I pick the thing up and weigh it in my hand. I stare at the tightly packed buildings. She's in there somewhere. I know it, can feel it, along with the invisible eyes staring at me.

Everything is silent. Only the sun beats like a pulse in my eyes. I turn and walk away.

'Not mud pies, dried dung!' my uncle says, when I tell him later. 'They use it for fuel!' He sighs. 'Best not go off the beaten path these days, Jake, that's my advice,' and he gives me a sharp look, 'tempting though it can be!'

The next time I go to the boat, she's not there. I wait. I go back and back, but she's never there.

The boat rocks in the sunlight. Empty.

I thought my heart was broken. I was a child. I didn't know what a broken heart was – not yet.

# Sammy

She's not there. When I wait for her the next day she doesn't come up the road, isn't at school. I knock on the door, but no one answers. I think I can hear her mum somewhere inside the house yelling at her, but only Jammi comes to the door.

'Nah,' he says, 'she ain't in, mate.'

*We used to play together,* I think, *we used to spit on each other's grazes and dare each other to jump off one step higher;* but he just smiles at me and shrugs his shoulders, not even pretending that what he's saying is true.

'For fuck's sake, Jammi, what do you think I'm gonna do to her? Just tell me she's all right!'

He stares at me. 'You're a guy, aren't you, what do you think we think you're gonna do?'

And he laughs, 'Guriya girls not good enough for you, Sammio?'

'Well, they are for you!' I say back, because Jammi has plenty of them and not always one at a time.

He shrugs again. 'Different,' he says, and that's when I realise he really doesn't give a shit and so there's no point talking. I want to tear the front door down, I want to push him aside and run in. I want to find her, escape with her, but I'm too scared of making them angry with her. I walk away.

'Sammio!' he shouts, and I turn around. Jammi beckons me with a finger. I go back.

'A warning,' he whispers, 'go anywhere near her and she

could be in for a very bad time. Understand me?'

I stare at him. 'You belong in the fuckin' ark, Hussein!' I spit back.

'Two by two, fine by me!' and he laughs. 'Got me, Sammio? Believe me, even you wouldn't want her back if certain people got hold of her.'

I walk away, I keep on walking. I walk all the way to the police station, and they do listen (at least at first), and then they say they can't get involved because it's cultural differences, isn't it, and we have to respect them. I feel like punching them and asking them to respect *that*, 'cos that's in a culture too, isn't it, the yob one.

It's agony. Pure agony, not knowing how she is or where she is, or even if she's still in the country, and not knowing whether doing nothing is the best thing I can do.


''Fess up, you got her hidden away somewhere?' says Gita. 'Harem stylee?'

I shake my head, I can't answer, can't tell anyone anything, because if I do what'll happen then? Will they ship her off, marry her to someone else? I wish I did have her locked away somewhere. Somewhere we could both be safe. I don't know where she is, I don't know what's happening any more. I don't recognise the world I'm finding myself in. I can't think, can't eat, can't play music. I can barely talk. I keep seeing her face in that moment, that moment when she turned and looked at me, and I wonder if that was it, the last time I'll ever see her.

I don't know what to do.

'You're pining, mate!' says Sean. 'Perhaps Kef's finally got her!' And he laughs. 'Keeping her in his grotto for later!'

'Is she all right?' asks Gita. 'I mean, Kef *hasn't* got her, has he?' I shake my head, shrug my shoulders, and she tries to make her joke again. 'So where are you keeping her, Sammy?'

'As if he would,' laughs Sean, and I get that they really don't know, the boys think all the stuff on the net was a joke, a wind-up.

I crack a bit; the strain's beginning to show. 'You got a problem with the idea that I might fancy Neesh, Sean?'

He looks up, senses I'm not good and holds up his palms. 'Me, a problem?'

I stare at him. We go back a long, long way, but I'm beginning to wonder, do we really know each other? Are our heads changing as fast as our bodies, our faces, our feelings?

'Pakis are all right!' he laughs. 'It's the love bit that does my head in!' And everyone laughs, I mean even Gita, and then I turn on her.

'What are you laughing about?' I ask. 'Think it's OK to call everyone else a Paki, as long as it's not you? Ha, ha, Gita, it's about as funny as running around and pretending Neesh is blind, or needs to blow guys just to get noticed. Very funny, Gita, fuckin' A-star in how to be a first-class bitch!'

She looks lost suddenly. 'I'm Indian, anyway!' she says.

'Sorry! Sorry, Gita, I'm really sorry!' And I am, because what the hell is Gita meant to do? Take the whole world on?

I need to calm down; I need to go on pretending nothing's happening. I need to work out a way to handle this.

'Yeah, keep your pubes in place, mate!' laughs David.

'Whoever it is, you've got it bad!' says Dan gently.

And Sean holds his hands up again. 'I just think . . . I just think, you know,' he says, 'that you don't wanna get shot in the gonads by some crazy muzzy daddy!'

I shake my head. Maybe he's right. Maybe, sometimes, it's just best to avoid the hassle, only I can't.

'It's not always like that!' I say.

'Your funeral,' he shoots back.

'You're paying!' I say, and that's the cue.

'No, no, no, no, no,' laughs Dan, 'I'll pay!' in his atrocious Irish accent, and we're back on safe ground, acting out our fave scene from Father Ted and moving away from the danger of who we might really be.

Gita stares at us all. Later, when there's no one around, I apologise.

'I shouldn't have said that,' I say, and I'd like to say more, but I can't even explain it to myself yet. It's like I can feel something in the air — almost smell it, a hatred hiding under the laughs. A sickness, not open and visible like Kef's, but hidden like an underground stream running under the streets, ready and waiting to burst its banks and overwhelm Gita, Neesh, her mum and dad and everyone who's different. All it needs is just the slightest bit more pressure on it.

'It's all right, but thanks anyway!' Gita says.

'Thanks for what?' I ask.

'Saying sorry! Sammy?' she asks.

'Yeah?'

'Where is she really, d'you think?'

'I don't know, honest, Gita. I think she's probably just at home.'

She nods. 'Sam?'

'Yeah?'

'What Sean said?' We look at each other and she takes a deep breath. 'It's not, I mean, most dads are cool, like mine, but it does happen, I mean what he said about gonads, it can . . . or it might be her they hurt . . .'

'I know.'

'Right.'

'Thanks!' I say, with brilliant eloquence.

'S'all right, it's just, I know she hasn't got a dad, but her brother's a head case.'

'I've met him, but thanks anyway.'

She doesn't go off, so I wait; obviously still something on her mind. 'The other day,' she goes on, 'Kef was looking for Neesh. I thought, I mean, I was scared that maybe he . . .'

'Found her?'

'Yeah,' she smiles, 'but you really don't think so?'

'No.' I shake my head. 'I think she's at home.' And I smile back. 'Probably got chickenpox!'

'Yeah!' laughs Gita, and we smile with relief at the idea that it could still be like that, that we could still be kids tucked up in bed and all we have to do is wait to be better, but I think we both know it isn't.

'Take care,' says Gita, 'watch your back!'

It takes a few more days of thinking before I get the idea. I'll ring up Neesh's mum but pretend I'm the school. And that's what I do. I sweet-talk the school secretary about an urgent call home, and then I'm in her office and on the phone.

'Mrs Hussein, this is the school. We understand your daughter's been absent for a week now with no explanation.'

Bingo.

'Yes,' she says, 'you have been on the phone already, isn't it, but my daughter is seeing boys and will stay home!'

'That's all very well, Mrs Hussein,' I say, 'and we'll arrange for a meeting in due course, but in the meantime we will be sending her coursework home, and we would like it done and sent back for marking as soon as possible.'

'Do you teach girls how to have babies, Mr Whoever-you-are,' she says, 'or do you think they drop like mangoes from the tree? Is that it?'

I don't say anything. I want to kill her. What's she doing to Neesh, is she even there?

'The work will arrive tomorrow,' I say, 'and we'll expect it back by Thursday at the latest. We'll enclose postage!' I put the phone down quickly before she can argue, or ask to speak to the Head, and I hope like hell it'll work. It's meant to work two ways. One, they'll know the school has its eyes on them, and that Neesh can't just disappear. Two, Neesh will know I'm thinking of her and that I want her out of there.

And now comes the difficult bit. I look at the parcel in my hands. It's in there — black, slim, 80 gigs and holding 15,000 tracks — so far. My whole life is in my hands and on it is a track I've downloaded just for Neesh. Written, played and performed by yours truly. Now I do the hard bit, I leave it in the pile of post waiting to be franked, and walk out.

Walk out trying to look like all I've done is made a quick phone call home, not taken a chance on not only losing the girl I love, but my gorgeous black video iPod too.

What will she do next?

I don't know, and that's the really hard bit.

# Neesh

I'm stuck here. They don't say anything, but every time I head for the door it's deadlocked, or one of them is there, waiting. My key isn't in my bag any more, it's gone.

'That family, they think they can ruin our lives again!' says Mum. 'I would rather see you married!'

I can't breathe; the air in the house feels stale and old. At night she sends me to my room and I can hear the voices downstairs muttering, eating all the food I've cooked, laughing together. She calls me down and I stand in the room.

One of my uncles holds my head up; his fingers are hard under my chin.

'You want to be a good girl, don't you?' I nod.

'We will make sure he's a good man from your father's village,' he says, and Mum laughs, nervous.

'When I came out to thresh the turnips all the boys . . .'

'U-cha!' they laugh.

'But not a man like her father!' Mum says. 'His dunder is full of milk, not man-ness!'

There's a sudden silence. The men don't like it.

'You have made a mistake, Zora,' her brother says, 'she should have been married quickly, it destroys their power! You should have acted sooner!'

Mum gets up and brushes me away as though it was me who made the mistake, not her.

'Better late than never!' she smiles. 'Chai?' They nod and I make them tea, just the way they like it, sweet and sugary with condensed milk.

I'm not even allowed in the garden. Mum makes good use of me, though. Women come for healing all through the day. By the evening my hands want to fall off their wrists and I'm full of clashing colours and pain. The fridge has enough cooked meals in it to feed the whole of Kashmir. It's the only way to stop the pictures and thoughts in my head. I'm trying to piece it together, but so slowly.

Mum hates Sammy's family, but why?

I'm not sure how much longer I can bear it, being locked away. I'm beginning to imagine things. Like climbing on to a roof and jumping, like cutting deeper, and into my wrists this time. Mum can't do this, she can't!

I look out of the window to where the leaves are trying to unfurl in the falling snow. Already the world outside is beginning to feel unreal, like a dream, like something that I only ever *thought* happened.

And then one morning Mum hands me a parcel.

'Working from school!' she says.

My heart leaps up; I know straight away it must be from him, from Sammy. No way would school be sending me work yet, even though Jammi said they'd phoned. I'm glad; it means someone out there knows I exist, that I'm here. Thank God Jammi's out, he'd be on to it at once. I try to stay calm but my heart's thumping at its cage.

'Later,' I whisper to it, and put the parcel down, although really I want to leap on it, tear it apart and see what's in it. I pull out pans, start mixing.

'Ahh,' says Mum, 'burfi, Jammi's favourite. You see, you are so much better without school. School makes girls' blood too rich!'

*Jesus, Mary and Mohammed (peace be upon them), but you talk rubbish!*

I make jalaibi and ladoo, I deep-fry syrupy sugar in long, narrow strands until the smell makes me sick, and then I make him his favourite curry. I cook like an animal paces its cage, dreaming of freedom. I chop the meat, and Mum smiles at me.

'All along I knew I was being right!' she smiles. I smile back, hiding daggers beneath my teeth. I mix in the butter beans, heart thumping, and then the door goes.

*Bang.* 'Isn't it a lovely day, for a walk in the rain . . .' sings the doorbell.

I grit my teeth; Jammi only rings it to annoy me. I look at the parcel sitting on the side, not hidden. Why didn't I take it up to my room? He'll notice. He'll know. *Thump. Thump.*

'Good smells!' is all he says, and he picks the parcel up and flicks it into the air. 'Who's sending you stuff? Better look inside and check it's not lover-boy. Neesh and Sammio, who'd a thought it?' He stares at me. 'He better not have touched you, sis, you know how much that would upset me and the boys.'

I shrug. My heart misses a beat.

'It's just working from school,' says Mum, eating a chocolate. 'Teachers thinking she will forget how to talk!' And that makes them both laugh.

I stir in the tomatoes, watch the fat rise and bubble; I'd like to throw the whole pan at them.

Blink. Blink, blink. The lights in the house flicker in time with my eyes. I think it must be me making it happen. It's been happening all week.

'Damn fuse!' says Jammi, and he throws the jiffy bag down. 'Got the school stamp on it!' he says, and I see he's right, and my heart sinks. I put the lid on the curry, turn it down and take the jiffy bag upstairs.

I hold it in my hands. A parcel. It doesn't look like the kind of thing the school would send. Is it from him? I open it slowly. There's a thick wad of bubbly plastic, and through it is something dark, black.

He's sent me his iPod!

I pick it up and hold it, put the earpieces in, but there's nothing coming out. No sound at all, nothing. And then I see the piece of paper.

*Neesh,* he writes, *look after this with your soul. To work it, flick the switch on the top sideways. Run your thumb over the black circle on the front. See the blue strip moving? Leave it on MUSIC, now press the middle of the circle, and press it again.*

*Listen.*

I do listen, and it's him! It's him! He's in there, in the little sliver of shiny black iPod, singing to me . . .

'This is for you, Neesh,' he says, and he lifts up his voice and sings:

'I want to tell you what I see

When I look at you,

With the backs of my eyes, where your face floats,

In perfect proportion, 1.618 to 1, it's maths not lies,

There where you rest, on the back of my eyes . . .'

And I start to laugh, I can't help it. His voice is beautiful, like watching birds when there's a whole flock of them swooping on the breeze, lifting and snagging on the wind in a great flock before suddenly turning en masse and changing wing-colour. It makes my heart catch . . .

'Turn your face,' he sings, 'so you can see me,

When I look in the mirror, I search for you in my eyes,

Would you? Could you? Should you?

See me too?'

And suddenly, it's not a joke any more, the words, because the sound of his voice is so sad. It's like a wave that can't find the shore, that's just standing on its tip and longing for land, never feeling the joy of rolling over and crashing to the sand, only waiting and longing to feel the earth, solid beneath its feet. His voice is all the colours of the sea.

'See me . . .' he sings.

And his voice is the colour of longing and fear. I have to close my eyes then, because there are so many colours in the music that they merge and blend and glow, like coming from the dark into a bright light. Slowly, as I watch through my lashes, the colours begin to settle and shapes emerge on the air . . .

Blink. Blink, blink.

*A boy and the girl are standing in a stream of flowers. They're looking at each other, staring across a sea of gold and red and orange. They are knee-deep in flowers . . .*

'See me, see me, see me . . .' Sammy chants, and the feel of his words lands in colours and pictures on the backs of my eyes, where . . .

*. . . the boat rocks beneath them. They are standing so close that they breathe the sharp, sweet-sour smell of the marigolds back at each other. The flowers are everywhere. In their hair, reflected in their*

*eyes. The pollen has burnished their skin, brushing them golden.*

*I see that they are frightened to move . . . frightened of the world around them full of hate, and of the spark between them, full of life, burning across the flowers.*

I hold my breath and watch.

*And the girl takes a step . . .*

There's a click, and the music stops, the colours separate and fade. There's a silence. A silence just long enough for my heart to drop right into, before Sammy's voice starts up again.

'Neesh,' he says, 'I don't know where you are and I don't know what to do. I'll be waiting for you in the park, every day, say till five o'clock, under the willow tree.'

Silence.

'Neesh! I know a place we can go, we can be all right. I mean . . . don't stay, not if you don't want to . . . oh fuck, Neesh, I don't know what to say . . . I'll be there, every day, and if you can, let me know you're safe – you can send stuff back in the envelope. There's a video on the iPod!' he says. And then he laughs, his lovely, lovely laugh, like angels landing, and he says, 'Eat this message. Neesh, Neesh, I . . . I think I'm trying to tell you I love you.'

Silence.

'Please, Neesh, just come. I know a place we can go. Or at least find a way to let me know you're OK!'

Silence.

'Bye, then.'

Silence.

'See you?' he says, and his voice is full of hope, hope and fear. Fear that I won't take a single step, away from the world I'm in, and towards him. He's even put a stamped addressed envelope in the package, so I can send everything back to the school.

I don't know what to do, but my body does. I feel it rise up inside of me . . . and I know why that girl took a step through the flowers. She felt like this, like a stalk of grass pushing up blindly through the dark, warm earth towards sunlight, not knowing, but somehow trusting that it's there.

And I know I'm going to get out of here somehow, because now I've got somewhere to go and someone to go to. I realise there are no bars or locks on my bedroom window, I see now that the chains holding me back are invisible, but strong, made of fear. Maybe Allah (peace be upon him) will punish me. Maybe I will forget how to see feelings like colours on the air, and maybe my hands will only be able to love one body and not heal others. Even then, how can this feeling for Sammy be wrong? Didn't Allah or God (peace be upon them), or whatever we call him, make this feeling as well as everything else? And isn't he infinite and wise and compassionate and merciful?

But the only answer I get comes suddenly and swiftly on the air, a memory of Mum's hissed words: 'If you do as you please, then you give the same freedom to others to do as *they* please!' I close my eyes in fear. The picture comes violently fast this time, forms out of a million colours . . .

*The sun is red and sinking behind the girl. The women rip the veil from her hair, and begin to cut. Her hair falls from their hands in long hanks. She doesn't move; only when they stand back and laugh does she finally reach up to feel the surprising air on her naked neck. She turns and looks along the sandy track, as though she thought there might be someone coming, and then the first stone hits her body . . . she blinks, blink, blink, and stares down at her broken skin in surprise . . . and then another stone lands and she backs away towards the trees . . . the stones land like hail, they rain around her fleeing body . . .*

And then the picture's gone. I open my eyes. There's a pain in my body, and when I look down there's a round jagged bruise just above my hip, purple and risen, that even as I stare at it begins to fade. A chill runs through me, right through me like a light going out, or a flame suddenly extinguished.

# Kefin

Kef watches. Kef waits. Kef looks out of the kitchen window, down at his nan's old house, where Neesh lives now, but she doesn't come out. No one does. Not Nan and not Neesh.

Perhaps she's dead.

Perhaps she's gone back to Paki-land.

Perhaps she's hiding from him. Waiting, just waiting for her chance to get out of there and tell everyone.

He goes on watching.

Waiting.

# Sammy

I don't know what she'll do. I don't know what she *can* do. I didn't realise that a lot of the time we think we do know what'll happen next. But I don't, not now, not any more.

Did Neesh even get the iPod? Or is Jammi laughing at me right now as he plays it to himself. Is she under house arrest? Being watched? I don't know, I just turn up and wait in the park like I said I would. It's all I can do. Wait without knowing, and hope that she'll come.

And she does.

She appears through the golden stems of the hanging willows and I think of the words in the film we saw at school, 'but soft, what light through yonder window breaks,' because with her comes a sense of heat and sun, and the hope that everything could still be all right. And relief. Relief that she's still here, still alive.

She's breathing fast like she's been running, and she looks hunted, haunted. She stands like a deer at bay.

'Neesh.'

'Sammy.'

'Hi.'

'Hi.'

She steps towards me. A long-dead leaf drifts down, falling silently between our bodies, marking the distance between us. And she says a whole sentence, very slowly, one word after the other.

'It's weird,' she says, looking all around her as though the world could disappear at any minute. 'I can't believe I've done it!'

And her words make me shiver. She says it like she's coming up for air, coming up from somewhere deep, deep inside of herself; and she's travelling slowly through the water, like a trapped air bubble making its way back up to the surface. Only the surface of the world isn't the same for her as it is for us – it's like it's never still, like it's always slipping out of her grasp, shifting and sliding away from her into something else, into other meanings or feelings that the rest of us can't see.

It makes me want to hold her. Hold her still and safe, so she can breathe at last, and rest.

I hold out my hand. She puts my iPod in it. I put it in my pocket and return my hand. She looks at it, and then she rests her own against it, palm to palm. We stand there. I don't know about her, but for me the space between us just aches, is aching to be arched over and crossed.

'You came!' I say. She gives her head a shake.

'It's like I can't tell what's real any more,' she says.

*Neither can I,* I'm thinking. *Not any more.* We've done something that will change everything. We've switched tracks, set the world in a different motion. Nothing's safe, nothing's certain.

'How long've we got?' I ask her.

'They might know already,' she whispers, and shivers.

We don't even have time to kiss, to take one step closer to each other.

Neesh looks around her as though the trees themselves have ears.

'We should go,' she says. 'Now!'

I nod, she's right, but neither of us moves; it's like we're paralysed, shocked by what we've done. We take another breath together and I watch it drift up into the trees, disappearing. Neither of us notices the snow begin to fall again. Softly. Gently.

'I can't go home,' she whispers, as though it was only saying it that made it true.

'I know, it's OK, I've already thought of somewhere you can stay, at my grandpa's!'

She's shaking with fear and cold. I give her my coat. It's huge, it drowns her. She holds her old coat in her hands. 'My dad bought it . . .' Then she stops and shakes her head and I wonder if we've both got this feeling, like we're in a play, like we're doing and saying things we'd never do in real life – except that, somehow, we are.

'Hey,' I say, and Neesh stops staring through the willows and looks up at me.

I hold out my arms and let myself fall backwards through the willow stems into the deep snow.

'Your turn,' I say.

She turns. I watch her open her arms out, hesitate, and then fall backwards. She lands beside me. I laugh.

I laugh because it feels so amazing to think that out of all the endless billions of molecules, permutations and possibilities in the whole world, she's found me. And I've found her.

But when I look at Neesh she's lying still in the snow with a gentle smile on her face. Lying so still that her lashes are loaded with falling flakes, and slowly she leans up, pushes me down and empties them on to my cheeks.

'Blink. Blink, blink,' she says, and I laugh.

'You're funny!' I say, and then I wonder why it's a surprise, she's always been funny, I'd just forgotten.

'Sammy,' she says.

'Yeah?'

'I'm frightened.'

'Me too.'

She sits up and brushes the snow from her long hair, and listens intently, as though she can hear far-off music.

'Kef's somewhere near,' she says, and she stands up.

I stand up too. 'I'm not sure Kef's our biggest problem right now!' I say. 'Anyway, I can't see anyone!' But she shakes her head at me.

'He is,' she says, 'I can feel him.'

'Good one, Neesh!' I laugh, 'I'm not six now, you know. Anyway, if you can you see into the future, tell me what happens next!'

'Don't!' she says suddenly, and then she grabs my hand and we run.

# Sammy

There's someone out there, behind us in the snow. I can see a dark shadow, a shape in the falling flakes, always the same pace behind, always following. I know exactly who it must be, and the fear in my gut deepens.

It's Kef.

We step up the pace, silently, swiftly, until it almost feels like we're flying. When I look behind us our footprints are disappearing in the snow, gone before they're even made, and this scares me even more, it's like we're being wiped out without even being given a chance to fight back. And then it happens.

I look up and I don't know where we are. I'm lost. All the streets look the same. The cars are covered in snow, the lamp-posts, the street signs; everything's blanked out in white. And I notice how empty the streets are. Somewhere in the distance I can hear children playing, screeching and throwing snowballs, having fun.

They sound a world away.

I look at Neesh. 'Where are we?' But she shakes her head, looks up at a tower block, tries to find her bearings and fails. The world's narrowing down, right down to the space around us. And I'm waiting. I hold my house keys hard in my hand, pointing outwards.

*Run!* Every bone shouts it. *You should have run sooner.*

We stand together and watch. Watch as the dark shape comes towards us out of the snow. He appears slowly out of the mass of dirty grey. And he doesn't shiver, even though he's only wearing a T-shirt . . . and he's smiling, that's what's really frightening, that Kef's smiling at us as though he's finally found just exactly what he's always wanted.

I've never realised how white he is before. Skimmed-milk-white. Bone-white.

He doesn't look at me, not really, just a glance, and at first that gives me hope – but he looks at Neesh as though . . . as though he wants to peel all her skin back just to take a look and see what's underneath.

'Hi Paki,' he says.

She doesn't look at him. She looks down. Down at the snow as it lands on the pavement. Blink. Blink, blink.

I think of her emptying her lashes on to my cheek, of her soft scared smile, and without thinking I move towards her.

'Mistake!' Kef says. He doesn't shout. He talks very slowly, like everything's in his control, but only just. He gives me the feeling that if we move a centimetre, no, a millimetre away from exactly where he thinks we should be, his control will snap completely. I see the knife . . . he's pulling it out of his pocket, slowly, carefully . . . and I move again, towards Neesh.

'One more step,' he almost sings, and that's what's really frightening, the fact that he's talking in a voice that doesn't really sound like his. 'One more step and I'll rip your feckin' head off and shit in it.'

I stop moving.

Stop dead.

'Got anything to say now?' he asks, stepping closer to Neesh, and I have to fight myself to stand by her side, not to step back, not to run. I want to. I can feel all the terror inside me running down my leg.

Piss-scared.

This is it.

He holds the knife up to Neesh's chin, forcing her face up. The snow lands on it, but she looks past him, up into the air above him. I notice her lips are pressed together hard, as though she's willing herself not to speak. Everything in this moment is absolutely clear and sharp against the falling snow.

'Know what my dad says?' Kef asks. Neesh doesn't move a muscle, doesn't even blink. She turns her eyes to his hand on the knife, as though just by looking at it she could keep it steady. The tip of the blade makes a sharp dent as it presses against her skin, and for a moment I wonder if she's actually breathing. 'He says we should castrate the lot of you, that'd stop you breedin'.' He presses harder.

*But she's a girl, you freakin' dork,* I'm thinking, *you can't castrate a girl,* but I don't say a word. Not a word.

'So what do you know?' he asks Neesh, but she still doesn't answer, just blinks, like she's trying to get the world back into focus and where she wants it to be.

'Think you're very clever, dontcha, bitch?' he says. 'Sneaky rats, sewer scum, the lot of ya, eh?' I think maybe she shrugs, just the slightest, faintest movement, but he catches it all the same. 'Ah, ah!' he says, 'now what did I say about moving?' and he presses harder, and this time the blood does come up, a sharp drip of it, startling and red against her golden skin.

'Thought you'd find me out, dincha?' he says, 'calling up my nan! Very clever,' he says, and I don't know what he's talking about. It's obvious he's mad, but I'm not about to say so. The snow's gathering on Neesh's upturned cheeks, but she doesn't move a muscle. 'Bet you don't feel so clever now, do you? What have I done, then? – go on, tell me, what've I done?'

She looks at him, asking permission to speak, he nods.

'I don't know,' she whispers.

'That's right,' he says. 'So you just take your coat off nice and slow and we'll see what's underneath it, shall we?'

Neesh doesn't move. Her eyes flicker and I realise she's shaking, but not just with fear. She's trying to hold something back, and she can't . . . and then it's like a dam bursting and all the water pouring out and everything happens at once.

Neesh's mouth opens and a voice comes out of her. Not her own lovely, gentle voice, but a high, wavery, indignant old lady's voice.

'*Kef, you know exactly what you done!*' it says.

And for a split second it's Kef who looks terrified. When I move it's pure instinct, like a catch at first slip, over before I even know I've done it. My arm just comes up and knocks his away from her. The knife slips sideways across her jaw as she turns to look at me, her eyes wide, and her hand clapped over her mouth. Kef's knife arm rises up in the air and I can see it heading for my hand, the one that's holding her chin where it's been cut, heading straight for us like a guillotine about to slice us apart . . .

And then I hear somebody scream my name.

'Sammy!'

And it all happens so quickly I can't get it straight in my head. Kef turns around at the sound of the voice, the knife still in his hand.

Neesh screams in her granny-voice.

*'Kef, NO!'*

And then there's this strange inhalation of breath in my ear, right next to me, and when I turn towards it, Gita's there – but she looks different. Her eyes are too wide, too open, and she's trying to back away from something. And then I see the knife that's sticking out of her chest with Kef's hand still hanging on to it.

'No!' I yell, and I try to grab the knife, to keep it in her body so all the blood doesn't spill out, but I'm too late. Kef pulls the knife back out of her body, out of my hand. Gita stares at me. Her hands fly to the hole in her chest and she blinks.

'Whoa,' she says, 'whoa!', two tiny exhalations of breath that go with the look of total surprise on her face, and then she falls into my arms and knocks us both onto the snow-covered concrete, and there's blood everywhere, turning the pure white into red.

*'Kef, no, no, no, no!'* wails Neesh in her weird voice.

But Kef's already gone.

*What's Gita doing here?* That's what I'm thinking. *Why's*

*she lying in the snow with a bright red splash spreading all the way across her white tee?*

'I saw him . . .' she whispers, '. . . follow you . . . tried to warn . . .'

'Shh, don't talk, Gita!'

I'm trying to hold her away from the cold, feeling for a pulse in her neck.

Neesh stands in the snow, shivering and staring at Gita. And then she puts her old coat over her.

'Hurry, hurry!' she says, 'she's all breaking up,' and she looks up at the empty air all around Gita's body, and strokes it, as though she could coax it back into her body.

'Stop it!' I yell, because it looks so weird.

Neesh looks at me, her eyes wide dark mirrors of my own, as though we both know already. Even as I reach for my phone I'm worrying that Gita isn't here any more, that I'm kneeling next to an empty body. I punch the buttons. I hold my hand over her heart as the colour fades from her lips, and her blood is so hot and wet and red as it pumps itself out all over my hand.

Neesh kneels down. She pushes my hand away and holds her palm out flat, floating above the wound. It looks as though the air is shimmering beneath her hand. Her eyes are closed and she's concentrating so hard it's like there's nothing else in the world except her and Gita.

'Gita!' I call. I put my lips to her ear and whisper her name, as though I could call her back. 'Gita.' I think her eyes flicker.

I don't know how long we wait. How long I watch Neesh holding her hands over the stab wound as though she could will it back together, but when I hear the sirens and see the lights flash I grab her, and we run.

And that's how quickly the world can change. One minute you're part of it, the next you're not. One minute Gita was someone to ignore, the next I couldn't stop longing for her to be alive.

Till now, my world had had things like sanity and clarity and the normality of everyday life in it. But when Kef put the knife into Gita, all that ended.

# Part Two

# Kefin

Kef runs. Jesus! Who the fuck was that?

*Gita, Gita, Gita,* says a voice inside, *it was Gita.*

No! He didn't mean it, it was the knife, the knife that went in. Feckin' hell, he thinks, he's still got it, the knife. The knife's stuck to his hand; he can't get rid of it. He tries, but it stays wrapped up in his fist somehow.

Shit! he thinks.

Stop-it drop-it chuck-it fuck-it –

THE KNIFE.

Again Kef tries to chuck it, but it's stuck, stuck to him, stuck to his skin, and he can't seem to get free.

'I wEnt in liKe a fuCkin' Man U peNalty,' says the knife, whispering to him. 'STraiGht in. RonAldo scores!'

'OMIGOD. Oh my life!' mutters Kef, trying to twist away from the knife in his hand, but it won't let go.

'So much blood, so much blood, and Geet's only tiny,' he whispers.

He crouches in front of the flats, but already he can hear sirens, see blue lights flashing.

Can't go home. Blue lights everywhere. Shit, shit, shit! He sees the hump in front of the fireplace. He smiles. That'll give the feds a bloody shock, when they barge in and Dad finally jumps up and sees who's in his house!

*'What've you done?'*

*What've I done?* Kef answers his nan. More like, what's *she* done? Paki bitch! I can't go home! I'll cut her feckin' coat off for her, all the buttons one by one, and then we'll see who's in there, won't we . . .

'*Behave, Kef!*' He hears his nan's voice and he's scared. What if she's angry? What if she doesn't love him any more?

It wasn't me, Nan, wasn't me.

'*Kef, NO!*' he hears his nan shout after him as he begins to run down the road.

'Not me!' he whispers as he runs. 'It was Knife, it was Knife, Nan, see?' And he holds the knife up before his eyes, and it seems an amazing thing to him in that moment, a thing entirely separate from himself. A frightening, powerful and amazing thing. Something to be appeased.

'It wasn't me, Nan,' he whimpers. 'Knife killed her.'

He runs on and on until he stumbles into an old city graveyard where the snow has found a place to stop and settle. It lies in a warm white blanket across the lumps of earth that mark the old forgotten graves. It lines the tops of stones. Nan must've found it for him, that's what Kef thinks.

He stops running, shakes his head at the glittering fairytale snow, soft and unbroken until his own footsteps disturb it, making dark marks on the pathway. The last light flakes of snow fall silently out of the darkening sky. Kef stares. The silence in the graveyard feels fixed and absolute. Safe. He wanders through the overgrown pathways, forgetting to shiver, full of a sudden wonder at the clean, clear whiteness of it all, and numb with cold and shock, stroking the knife in his pocket again and again, without thinking, without noticing.

He comes upon the dark waters of the canal that mark the boundary of the graveyard, and for a brief moment his hand stops. He thinks of throwing the knife far out into the dark waters, but the thought barely reaches his conscious mind; it's his knife.

His.

All he's got. All Dad's ever given him. He turns away.

He sees the shed. He pushes back the brambles and opens the door. Cobwebs break, the dried-up bodies of dead flies fall across his face. The shed is dark, and he stands still, waiting for his eyes to focus. There are no lights to help him here, no safe orange street-glow. Darkness has fallen. Slowly his eyes adjust to the lack of light; he sees a pile, a hump in the darkness. How did it get here, has it followed him? He holds on tight to his knife. It's his now, his, and what's Dad anyway, without it? He waits for a sign of life, of movement – but nothing comes.

Nothing at all.

Outside, the first stars begin to pierce the night sky. Kef moves. The shed floor creaks and groans under his weight, loud in the silence. He pushes at the dark, humped shadow and feels it roll beneath his hand.

A carpet?

Something scutters across his palm and . . . SHIT! Kef rears up, hits his head on a shelf and feels something land on his foot. A blinding light fills the darkness.

He blinks.

A torch has landed on his foot. He picks it up. Rolls of old carpet are stacked against the shed wall. He cuts the tape and string with his knife, unrolls the top one. A small brown mouse squeaks, runs at his hand. Kef slashes at it. Cornered, the creature leaps at his fingers, bites – and Kef screams in pain, flinging it away from him. It cowers on a shelf, watching him, eyes gleaming. Kef stares at the mouse as he unrolls the carpet. He's shivering now, the numbness fading, fear and words invading him.

*'Useless little fucker,'* yells his dad, *'should've sent you after your mam.'*

Inside the carpet is a nest of wriggling, naked, near-blind mice, mewling. Slowly Kef reaches for them with the blade of his knife. One by one he lifts them on to the edge of his blade and tosses them out into the snow.

He unrolls another carpet, wraps himself in it. After a while he begins to feel his numbed skin tingling and burning, coming back to life until he's shivering uncontrollably, helplessly, and he begins to remember, to whisper . . .

'She came at me, Nan, I couldn't help it, she just came at me, and the knife . . . Knife protected me . . . Knife went in like . . . NO! NO!'

But the picture keeps on coming up like vomit, inside him. Words forming.

REd stain. WhiTe snOw. REd-WhiTe. REd-WhIte MAn U. My fuCkin' coLours!

Then Nan's voice: *'Kef, no!'*

*But it's too late, Nan,* thinks Kef, the knife's done it, gone in, is sticking out of her body. He can still feel it, the way it went in, so soft, so easy, not like in a fish – and that sound she made as it came out in his hands, like breath . . .

'Oh Kef . . . Kef . . . Kef . . . what you done?'

'No!' he cries out to his nan. 'I didn't . . . not me . . . wasn't meant to . . . go in . . . go in . . . like . . . NO! It was Knife, Nan, Knife and Miss Paki-piss . . . pretending to be you, that's what made me do it!' The sound of his wail spins out into the empty graveyard and returns unanswered.

'ShUt it!' says a voice inside. 'Just shUt it, you sniVelling little git!'

And Kef does. He stops immediately, and the voice goes on. 'WE'll soRt old Paki-piss out, neVer you mind!' And slowly the pictures inside him change. He watches as Knife imagines cutting the buttons off Neesh's old coat, imagines cutting off her hair . . .

He forgets to shiver, he feels warm now, now that he's watching Knife. Knife knows what to do. Knife'll help him.

'See, Nan,' he whispers, 'it wasn't me.'

But his nan doesn't answer.

# Grandpa: Kashmir

I move on to the boat. I have to be there. I'm always there anyway, in my mind. Anxious. Waiting. Sure she'll come. Convinced she won't.

I'm asleep on the roof when it finally happens. Late afternoon, lying in the long shadows, a book fallen open beside me. A book I keep on pretending to read, when all I can really see on each page is her. The memory of her face, the feel of her body ... I fall asleep.

Something wakes me.

A tapping beneath me. Insistent. Repetitive. Breaking through my dreams and the heat. At first I think it's a moth trapped in a light, but then I remember it's daytime. I stumble down the ladder and into the kitchen, reaching for the water. Someone grabs my wrist ...

'Jake.'

I don't make a sound, I can't. I think I'm still dreaming. She's leaning against the wall, one hand around my wrist, the other on her lips.

'They know,' she says, and again it's a moment before I realise that she's speaking Urdu.

I still don't speak. The transition from dream to reality's too sudden. Too harsh. At first I don't even notice she's frightened. And then she says my name again. Softly, urgently.

'Jake.'

And we stand there, hand in hand. I whisper her name,

wondering if she'll disappear as soon as I speak and I'll wake up on the roof of the boat, hot and thirsty. Alone.

'Farida.'

She blinks slowly.

'You're back,' I whisper. And she nods. I notice then how frightened she is. She lets go of my hand.

'Jake,' she says again.

'Yes?'

'They know.'

And she falls forward into my arms and she's cold and wet against the heat of my skin, and I realise she swam here.

Thank God my uncle doesn't have a house-boy on the boat.

No one will know she's here. No one has seen her.

'It's OK,' I say. 'You can stay here, you're safe now.'

I whisper to her, 'You're safe.'

# Sammy

We run all the way across the city in the falling snow, to my house. I wait for someone to stop us, to shout out. Neesh's chin is still dripping and the blood on my hands is streaked all over my shirt.

I stick to my original plan, to get Neesh back to my grandpa's place. There's a boat there, it's hidden on a small lake deep in the woods – and best of all it's empty for the next few months. Nobody will know she's there except for me – and she'll be safe.

Even now, looking back, I still wonder if it was really me who made the decision to go to the lake, or was it some- thing inside me, some feeling passed on to me from Grandpa? As powerful as the gene that gave me his nose, as strong as the need to re-do something, and this time to get it right? I don't know. But I do know that if Grandpa and Mum had told me the truth, the whole story right from the beginning to the end, about what really happened out in India, I would never have taken Neesh there.

We sit in Mum's car with the heater on full blast, wait- ing for the windows to clear.

I can still see myself, starting the car and taking off to a place where I thought no one would ever find us. White Barn, a safe place, that's what I thought then. Safe from Kef, and safe from Neesh's friends and relations. Safe enough for her to be alone there. I always knew that would have to happen, even before Kef; that I would have to carry on as though everything was normal. If we disappeared together then it would be obvious what had happened, wouldn't it? Now it was even more important that nobody guessed we were together.

We stare through the windscreen at the world moving past.

'I think we must be in shock!' I say, but Neesh doesn't answer, she just takes in a big breath like she can't get enough air, like she suddenly realises how lucky we are just to be able to keep on breathing.

'Whoa! Whoa!' I hear myself say, and I shudder because that's what Gita said, and I think that maybe she felt like I do right now. Like I want the world to stop, to rewind. Want to understand where and how and why we got here, and what the hell has just happened. But time isn't playing. Time keeps right on moving and we've got to keep on trying to stick with it, or even one step ahead of it, if we can.

It's grey-dark by the time we get to the woods. The car tyres stick and grind on the snowy mud paths and I pull in. We'll have to walk from here. The snow's stopped falling and Neesh is silent, like all the words have been pushed right back down inside her. I'm freezing. Neesh has got my coat and I don't want to think about her old one lying over Gita. There's an old blanket in the boot so I grab that, wrap it round me, but the cold just goes right on beating at my bones. Get to the lake, get to the lake, that's what I'm thinking. If I can only get us there we'll be safe.

# Neesh

I follow Sammy into the woods. I'm scared I'll lose sight of
him as we stumble through the snow. He's all I've got now,
my only link with the world outside. If I lost him now I'd
have no one and nothing.

I keep seeing all the life leaving Gita, all her colours joining together, turning white on the air and streaming out of
her before beginning to fade away. I keep seeing it over and
over, Kef turning the knife on Sammy, Gita getting in the
way, and the look of sudden surprise on her face, like it
wasn't even her body it was happening to. The strange
silence of it – it was so quiet that I thought I could hear
the blood pumping out of her body with each beat of her
heart. We left her there. We ran before I'd finished saving
her, not all the life was back in her yet.

We come to a fence. It's sudden and surprising in the
middle of a wood, and Sammy's tapping numbers on a little box, near a gate, and the gate swings open. Sammy pulls
me through and closes it.

'We're here,' he says.

We both lean against the fence, eyes closed, breathing
hard. I can smell pine trees on the air, and when I open my
eyes they can't believe themselves. I blink.

Blink. Blink, blink.

But the picture doesn't dissolve. It doesn't turn into a
teacher waving his hands in front of my face, or the ceiling
of my bedroom, or the street through the window. It stays

exactly the same.

The lake is huge, but not so big that I can't see the end of it. It's the shape of a figure of eight, and right now the water is iced over and still, laced with shreds of snow. The high banks of grass that surround it are planted with pines and poplars and birches, their budding branches still and pale against the dusky sky. Out on the water, in the centre of the lake, two small islands drift like shadows, hidden and secret.

How has it all got here? Is it real, or am I imagining it? It's just like the lake I've always seen in my head, but smaller, it doesn't stretch all the way to the horizon. I realise I'm still waiting for it to disappear, but it doesn't, it stays there, right in front of my eyes. And at the sight of it something snaps inside me, like a barrier tipping over and the crowd rushing through. I begin to hear a strange chanting like praying inside me, and the air isn't just cold and crisp any more, but hot and limp as well, and beyond the dusk it's somehow already dark . . .

*I hear an owl hoot and see stars wheeling above my head, deep and huge and yellow, and I can hear a voice chanting whispered words, strange, unknown yet familiar words, words of comfort, words that sound something like a prayer . . .*

And then Sammy breaks away and runs down to the edge of the lake and picks up a stone. He hurls it across the ice, where it makes a strange singing noise as he screams out:

'Fuck!'

The noise echoes out in wide circles and disappears up into the trees; his colours glow an angry red–black, fire and ash mingle above his head.

Blink. Blink, blink.

Blink. Blink, blink.

I pull Sammy's coat closer around me and follow him. He looks out over the frozen lake, another stone raised in his hand. He must be freezing: his hoodie's covered in wet snow under the blanket around his shoulders.

'Fuckin' Kef!' And he hurls another stone across the ice.

*Don't!* I want to scream at him. *Don't make so much noise.*

'Shh!' I say. And for some reason that makes him laugh. I don't know why, but he just sits on the ground and laughs in such a crazy hopeless way that it frightens me.

'Shit, shit, shit, shit, shit,' he says. '*You* telling *me* to be quiet. Good one, Neesh!'

'Sss . . . !' I try to say his name and he stops as suddenly as he started.

He looks around at the frozen lake and the snow-laden trees and he shivers. 'Maybe this wasn't such a good idea,' he says, and his hands hang empty by his sides.

'Ss . . .' I want to say his name. I want to hold his hand and feel it warm beneath my fingers. I want to tell him it's all right, but suddenly the words are stuck again, won't come.

'Sing?' he shouts at me. 'Sing? Why would I want to fuckin' sing, Neesh? Oh God!' he shouts. 'What if she dies? No!' The word echoes around the lake. 'No!'

His anger makes my eyes blink fast. Scares me. I see a

body falling. I shake my head; I didn't want him to sing, I wanted to say his name, that's all. I want to hear his voice because I want to block out the sound in my head that's wiping everything else out. I look at the lake, and the chant inside me gets louder, and I hear myself think, *Where is it? I mean, if this is the lake, where's the boat?* I know it must be here somewhere – and straight away the chant grows even stronger, drawing me forwards.

'Where are you going?' shouts Sammy, but I'm not listening.

I follow the sandy track around the lake past an old, ruined boathouse. Then the path runs out and I have to push my way through the rhododendron bushes. Sammy follows me with a strange, worried look on his face.

I'm getting closer, I know I am. I'm like a wave being pulled by the moon. The bushes press closer together around the lake, but I squeeze right through them till I'm covered in loosened snow and right by the edge of the lake. There's an old jetty, made of rotting planks, swaying ropes and struts that stretch out over the frozen water. I stare at it, afraid to look up, afraid the houseboat will really be there, afraid it won't.

'How did you know how to find it?' asks Sammy.

I don't say anything. I look up, and sure enough it's there. A Kashmiri houseboat, floating on the water in the fading light, almost as though it has always known I would arrive. Behind the boat floats a shikara, a punt, but there are no flowers heaped over its bows like in the pictures I see. It's a lovely faded dusty blue. Its insides are empty.

'I . . . I . . .' I try to answer, but the words are still stuck. The words are stuck but the pictures inside me jump and crackle and catch like a video trying to find the right channel. The images come clear for just a second before fading into reality again . . .

. . . *a pool of light on water, the thump of a stone. Flowers falling, spinning, dancing, and then the sharp catch of a breath . . . the feel of skin . . .*

I look at Sammy. He's staring at me. We look at the boat and at each other and slowly our hands reach out for each other, but just as they touch a spark jumps straight from his fingers to mine, driving us apart.

'Static!' he laughs.

*Yeah, right, Sammy,* I think, *like the earth's made of polyester.* Our breath makes icy clouds and the air feels like it's waiting to see what we'll do next. I step on to the black ice of the jetty.

'No!' Sammy's voice rings out like his stone thrown over the ice, strange and disturbing. For just a flash I see a body again, falling, imagine the cold water closing over my own head like a blessing, and I stop and turn. He reaches for my hand. 'No, Neesh!' he says again, but quietly this time, more like himself.

*Why?* I mouth at him.

'I don't know,' he says slowly. 'I don't want you to be on the boat . . . I mean, it's cold and I don't know if the generator's working, and . . .' He shakes his head.

I turn away from him and walk over the swaying jetty. I can't do anything else. I feel like I'm meant to be here somehow. I feel something I've never felt before. I feel like I belong. I keep walking and a weight falls over me, over my body and through my skin. I'm not me, I'm walking in someone else's footsteps. The real me wants to run, to run towards whatever it is that's waiting for me on the boat; but the chanting inside me drags its feet, can barely lift its face, walks like a soldier after a lost battle, barely alive and already knowing he has no home to go to.

I step on to the boat and the words of the prayer finally come clear . . .

*Allah the great, the merciful, the compassionate and wise* . . .

The words weave themselves together as though they are holding bones tight, stopping skin from bursting at its seams . . .

I shiver.

Something bad happened here.

When I feel Sammy's hand on my shoulder, I jump, frightened until I hear his voice.

'It's here,' says Sammy, and he points out the door of the boat. I grasp the handle, but my hands don't seem to have enough strength to open it, not until Sammy is beside me and curling his fingers over mine. Together we twist the wooden handle, it feels smooth and worn and it fits the palm of my hand perfectly. We twist it and a bolt of heat sears through me as the door handle gives swiftly beneath our fingers and we fall over the threshold, straight into each other's arms. The walls of the boat pulsate, like hot, dusty, sun-ridden skin. The smell of long-dead flowers fills the air. I hold out my hands to steady myself and find they're full of Sammy. I hold on to him tight . . .

And then we're kissing: clinging, fierce and sudden. Holding on to each other's lips and faces and hair, pushing and pulling at the clothes that are between us. Clothes that I want to dissolve, just like the world feels like it's dissolving and spinning away from us as the boat rocks suddenly and sharply beneath our feet, tipping us to the floor.

It's wordless, violent, frightening, wonderful and shocking.

And then the door bangs behind us, a flurry of cold flakes and wind flings itself at us, and we draw apart, stunned. We stare at each other, at his coat slipping off my shoulders, at his blanket lying like a puddle on the floor. We don't speak, we can't, we just stumble through the door and back out into the dusk.

He climbs up to the roof and unlocks a huge box, searches for a torch. 'Neesh?' he asks, and just for a second I wonder who he means, and then I remember that it's me he means, I'm Neesh.

*What?* I mouth at him. We're shaking, afraid to touch each other, longing to touch each other. We stand on the roof of the boat surrounded by silence. We watch as the darkness falls and stars begin to punch tiny little holes of light and hope into the night. We stand apart just beyond each other's reach, staring into the night, as though we

could see something. Anything, other than each other —
and the sensation that it wasn't just us kissing and touching
and ripping the clothes off each other . . . it was . . . something else . . . or maybe some*one* else . . .

# Sammy

I've got stuff to do. I've got to unlock the box on the roof,
I've got to get the generator going, grab a torch before it's
so dark that we can't even see. *Stuff to do,* that's what I whisper to the feeling still echoing through my body. The touch
of her hair, the smell of it, like strawberries; her lips, so
much fuller than I thought, and her . . .

I find the keys under the old plant pot, unlock the box,
switch on the generator, hear it hum, and then I turn to
her. She's just a shadow in the darkness. 'Neesh,' I say, and
it seems like it takes her a second to realise that it's actually
her I mean — and that's exactly what I want to say to her.
That wasn't me. *It wasn't me,* I want to shout, but I know it
was. It was exactly what I wanted to do. But I wouldn't
have chosen right then, the timing, that wasn't me.

I flick on the torch, test it out. On, off, on, off.

'Neesh?'

'What?'

'I'm sorry, I mean the timing, it was hardly . . . I . . .'

'Pass-i-ons moo-ve,' she whispers, and it's a relief to hear
her voice; for a moment I thought she'd lost it again. She
looks out across the sky.

'I think we're in shock, Neesh,' I whisper back, but she doesn't answer. 'I've heard of it,' I say. 'I mean, it happens, like in wars and stuff, when you're near death you . . . you want to, well . . . make life. It's just an instinct, a thing we can't control!'

She doesn't say anything, and I wonder who I'm trying to convince anyway.

I shine the torch into the darkness where its light wavers, picks out the trees and the railings of the boat and falls on the water, turning it dark beyond the small circle of light.

I hear Neesh gasp and hold on to me, she clings to my arm making the arc of light sweep and swoop up into the sky where it loses all its power.


# Neesh

The light on the water terrifies me. Pictures jump and stop and start behind my eyes like broken glass trying to mend itself . . .

*. . . stones landing . . . light on the water . . . dark sky . . . far-away stars . . . broken words of a prayer . . .*

And then the generator whirrs and the boat lights come on, soft and naphtha-yellow, and Sammy's guiding me down the ladder and I cling to the feel of his hand on my arm, holding me tight as we squeeze into the kitchen, where he flicks on the gas and lights all the rings on the stove and tries to get us warm.

I stand up and look in the small cupboard. I want to

cook. I want to be back in my kitchen at home, mixing and stirring and making something for everyone to eat, but I can't go back. It feels like an ache all the way from my guts up to my chest. I can't go home. I have no home because I've made my choice. I'm not allowed to love Sammy *and* Mum and Jammi, even if the truth is that I do. I can see them in the kitchen, without me. I wonder what they'll eat; I wonder if somehow they'll miss me?

There's hardly anything in the boat's kitchen cupboard, no real food, just a few small bottles and some cans.

'We need brandy,' says Sammy, and so I hand him some.

## Sammy

She's looking into the cupboard as though she wishes she could just step into it and disappear. I boil the water. I make the tea and tip a capful of brandy into it. I look at my watch and wonder how only a few hours can have passed since we left the park.

I hand the mug to Neesh and she takes it, holds it up to her lips and coughs, then looks up at me through the steam, questioning. 'Oh, shit!' I say. 'You haven't ever had alcohol, have you?' She shakes her head. 'I'll make you another one, or you could have it medicinally, I mean, that's probably allowed, isn't it?'

She nods, and her eyes are so huge and wide and lonely in her face that I wonder how we can go on, and what we think we're doing. Everything feels different now that we're really here and on our own.

'Are you sure you can't go home?' I ask her. 'I mean, not even to *my* home? Or you can stay up at the house here. I can explain to Mum, she'll be cool . . .' But even as I'm saying it I know it's not true, Mum wouldn't be cool with it at all. Anything else, any*one* else, maybe. But not me and Neesh.

'I haven't got a home, Sammy,' I hear her say, 'and if you tell your mum or anyone else where I am, I'm a dead girl!' And her voice is dead too, numb and dead sounding.

'What?' I say. 'I mean, I know you can't now, but never?' And as soon as the question's out I realise that a bit of me wishes that she could say yes, wishes that I didn't feel so totally like I'm her only hope. It doesn't seem like much to rely on to me.

'No,' she shakes her head. 'I'm . . . I'm not . . . worth anything.'

'But Neesh, we haven't . . . I mean, you and me . . . we haven't done anything! I mean . . . '

She stares at me, and slowly sips the tea and brandy. 'I know what you mean,' she says, 'but you're wrong. We *have* done something, we've broken the rules, broken izzat, taken their honour. Where I come from, once you've done that, you can't mend it.' Her words sound hard and cruel.

'Are you serious?' I ask. 'I mean, I know your mum's a bit nuts, but . . .'

'It's not really Mum, it's Jammi, Jammi and . . . others.'

'But why? I mean if . . . um . . . er . . . I haven't touched you . . .'

'Sammy!' she says suddenly, shifting her eyes to mine. 'Just don't tell anyone I'm here, will you?'

'I won't!' I say.

And I move towards her to hug her, to hold her against me where she can't see the doubt in my eyes, but something stops us touching. We're frightened. Frightened of what we'll set loose if we touch again. We both draw back at the same time.

'Neesh, I . . . I have to get back, otherwise everyone'll be asking where we *both* are. Listen, let me drive us up to the house. It'll be warmer, and it's better than in here.'

She shakes her head. 'I think I need to stay here, on the boat, Sammy. Even though I'm scared. I feel like . . .' She stops and she looks like I feel when I'm searching for a tune I can't quite remember, a lost tune. 'I feel like I'm meant to be here,' she says.

'Are you sure? I'll bring some proper food and stuff tomorrow. I wish I could stay,' I say, but the awful truth is I *want* to go. The boat feels tight and claustrophobic, like I can't breathe. She doesn't answer. 'Neesh, I'll be back as soon as I can.'

'Sammy,' she asks suddenly, 'do you know what happened?'

'What do you mean?'

'Here, on this boat, something happened, didn't it? Something bad.'

'No,' I say, 'I think it's just Grandpa's "Homage to India" – at least, that's what he calls it.'

'That smell, what is it?' she asks.

'Not me!' I say, and laugh, but she doesn't laugh, just breathes in. I do the same, and our eyes catch and it's in the air again. The smell of flowers, sweet-sour-red-hot flowers, their petals wide open in the heat. Our eyes lock on to each other and I'm about to step towards her, closer, but she manages to close her eyes, slowly, effort-fully, breaking the connection between us – just like she did the first time we met. The smell of flowers fades.

'It's the generator turning on the heat,' I explain. 'It brings out the old smells hanging around in the wood,' and she nods, but not like she believes me.

'I'll be OK,' she whispers, and I'm six again, locked out and on the other side of wherever she is.

'Why don't I just stay?' I say.

But we both know why. We both know everything in my life's got to look as normal and everyday as possible, because if anyone wants to look for me, this is the first place they'd come – and then they'd find her.

'See you,' she says.

'See you early tomorrow,' I say back. 'No one can find you here, Neesh. You're safe now.'

I walk back to the car. At the top of the sloping wood I turn and look back to where the boat's just a tiny glow on a dark sea. A glimmer that's got Neesh all alone in it.

# Neesh

I watch Sammy leave from behind the sitting-room window. I push my face up against the cold glass and use my hands to cut out the light from the room. I watch his waving torchlight disappear through the gate and then reappear higher up in the woods. I watch it weave between the trees. I watch until it's a tiny dot, as far away as a star. I watch it until I'm only imagining that I can still see it, when I know that I can't, not really. He's gone and I'm alone on the boat.

Slowly, I turn around to face the sitting room, to face the feeling that, somehow, this boat I've never seen before, or even heard of, has been waiting for me. Waiting to tell me something. I stare at the deep window seats, the dusty silk curtains and wooden dining table. I keep thinking of the dark night trapped in the black hole of the window behind me. I imagine people looking in when I can't see out.

The whole boat's humming, and whatever Sammy says, it's *not* just the generator. I think it's the memories trapped in the old wood, torturing and twisting it until I wonder how the boat manages to stay afloat under the weight of it.

I walk quickly back to the kitchen, where it feels safest. The kitchen is right at the back of the boat and runs the whole width of it. A small window looks out over the lake, but the shutters are closed, so it's still warm and cosy from the stove.

I reach for my bag and fish around for the small plastic

box inside it, but when I actually see the razor blades, I can't do it. I remember all the blood pumping out of Gita's heart and I stop. I clean the cut on my jaw; it's only a scratch really, but it makes me shudder, makes me think of Kef's face as he held the blade against my skin. I look at the kitchen door. I'm tired, but I want to know where everything is, all the entrances and exits. The kitchen door leads to a narrow passageway that runs down the middle of the boat, there are two bedrooms off it, one to the left and one to the right. The one to the right is locked. The one to the left has an amazing bed in it, a huge carved four-poster that creaks with dust. A woven threadbare carpet covers most of the floor. The humming sound in here *is* only from the generator, and I think that maybe I'll be OK; I can grab some covers and sleep in the kitchen, or even in this bedroom.

And now there's only the door to the sitting room left. I don't want to open it. This is the room I'm scared of. The room where we fell into each other's arms. I can still feel Sammy's skin under my fingertips, soft and smooth, feel the stretch of his muscles, tight across his stomach. I open the door to the sitting room quickly, like I could fool myself I'm not really doing it. Whatever's in there is so strong it makes the lights flicker. On. Off. On. Off. As though they have to fight to stay alight. The room takes up the whole width of the boat but the space inside it feels pained, constricted. There are two huge windows, one looking out over the lake, the other facing the land, and I think, for just a split second, that if I look outside I won't see woods and darkness, I'll see a wide, endless expanse of water with a backdrop of mountains against a pale blue sky.

And a man, poling a boat full of flowers.

My head starts to spin. I close my eyes. Blink. Blink, blink, and when I open them the room is exactly the same, except for two things: over by the door opposite me, the door we came through, lies a shining heap of flowers. They spill through the doorway like a golden river as the sun glances off them, in orange and red and yellow and gold. The huge French windows are shut. I know they are, and yet somehow they're also wide open, and beyond them there's a faint red rim on the horizon, holding its line of light against the dark sky. Standing in front of the window is a shadow, a silhouette of a girl, waiting. As I watch she turns and looks at me, her eyes are huge, dark holes, and as I look into them I'm filled with a terrible fear that Sammy will never come back.

I close the door, quickly, because I've seen something else. Something worse. The girl looks just like me.

I take a deep breath. I think of Dad. *Dad,* I say in my mind, *seeing ghosts is just like dislocating your knee, it hurts, but somewhere inside you, you know that if you can just stand the pain and the shock, then soon you'll be brave enough to pull your knee straight and click the world back into place.*

*Ucha,* says Dad, as though it was the most normal thing in the world.

And so I open the door again, slowly. But there's nothing there, nothing except the untouched, dust-laden furniture.

I close the door. *You should rest now, uppi,* says Dad's voice in my ear. And so I go back to the bedroom. I empty the old chest at the end of the bed and pile the dusty duvet and blankets high. I turn all the lights out. I lie in the dark with all the covers I can find over me.

I try to sleep but I can't, my mind keeps on seeing Gita and Sammy falling onto the snow, feeling the scratch of Kef's knife against my jaw. There's no sound at all now except the low hum of the generator. I imagine the boat, the lake, the woods and the silence all around me. I've never been anywhere this quiet – *except for the village*, a voice inside me whispers. *Yeah, but I don't remember that.* I listen for the hum of traffic, some shouting, a slamming door or a car revving, anything that feels familiar. But there's only the movement of the boat beneath me, sometimes steady, sometimes rocking.

I must have fallen asleep somehow because I'm falling through my dreams, falling until, with a heart-stopping lurch, my hands grasp at nothing but air, and then there's that sudden feeling of safety. Of hands beneath me – and I'm wide awake and sitting up, heart beating hard in the darkness. I remember Sammy catching me as I fell; I see it like it's happening over and over and over again, a film stuck in a loop, endless and forever. I feel my fingers around his wrists, the bones beneath his muscle, the spark and fizz of skin against skin. I feel dislocated again, stuck in the wrong place, panic-stricken. I've got to do something to make it stop or we'll go on forever, falling over and catching each other, falling over and catching each other.

I push my feet out into the freezing air and stand up. I walk straight to the small ladder and begin to climb up on to the roof of the boat. I feel the night air on my face. But even as I step out I feel the air shift against my body and become as warm as an Indian day; and there they are, a boy and a girl, standing on the roof of the boat, caught in a bubble of broad daylight . . .

*The boy coughs and the girl turns and falls, turns and falls, turns and falls, and the boy's hands reach out to her and catch her, reach out to her and catch her, and slowly they both sink to the ground. And then it all starts again, over and over . . .*

In my head I'm chanting something . . . I think of *Star Wars* with Princess Leia stuck in a fading flickering picture doing the same thing over and over. For ever. Unless somebody helps her. And as I watch, the chant turns into a prayer again, a desperate plea – but as soon as I step forward to help, the air empties itself and they're gone.

I look up. The girl is alone now. She balances on the low railings of the roof. She balances perfectly like a slim column of air against a dawn sky. Her back is straight and determined. Slowly she lifts her arms and drops her veil from her head. I gasp: her beautiful hair has gone, it's all been cut off, cut badly so that it sticks out from her head in clumps and bumps. She doesn't move, just stares straight ahead of her, and when I follow her gaze, I see that . . .

*. . . far in the distance, on a shining lake, there's a boat. Only you can't really see that it's a boat because it's so buried in flowers, so heavy with them that the whole boat's sinking, leaving only a flowery boat-shape like an echo of itself floating low in the water. There's a man standing at one end with a pole, a stick man with stick-thin arms, punting all the flowers slowly through the water.*

*And he's so far away that it looks like they're hardly moving.*

*Behind and above them the mountains make themselves out of the sky.*

*Below them the same mountains hang motionless in the clear water, reflected, suspended upside down. The whole world is pale. Pale-blue sky and snow-capped mountains.*

*The water takes on the colours of everything around it.*

*Only the man and the boat are bright, because the flowers are red and gold and orange.*

*And the man is brown.*

*They look like they're stuck on, like collage. And they cut the sky and lake in two.*

*Marking the difference between where the sky starts and the earth ends . . .*

I blink. Blink, blink, blink. For a moment I think I actually stop breathing. I'm seeing it, the picture I've always seen . . . seeing it through her eyes. Why? Will it move now? I wait, breath held, to see what will happen next. I wait for the girl to turn and for the picture to finally unfold, to turn into a story. But she doesn't turn. She doesn't look back at all. She just steps off the boat, like she's stepping off a pavement into traffic – and then she falls like a knife towards the water.

'No!' My scream sounds loud in the night, my head feels the cold gasping pain of the freezing water. I think I hear the echo of a scream from the edges of the lake calling back at me. *'No!'*

And then I'm alone, standing in the freezing cold on the roof of a boat, with the stars small and white in the distance. I feel like a sheet that's been shaken out and held wide open to the breeze. I run to the side of the boat and look over but the ice is still all in one piece, whole and unbroken.

Like nothing at all has happened.


# Kefin

The hard white morning light breaks slowly through the small grimy windows of the shed. Kef stirs in his sleep, shifts his thin body in the stiff cold carpet, fighting away the daylight, the waking up that's to come, the knowing. He wants to stay asleep and warm but the daylight goes on creeping across the floor towards him, until it steps up and lands on his flickering eyelids.

He's dreaming. In his dream someone is reaching for him, stretching out the tips of their waving fingers towards him and calling his name.

*'Ke-fin!'* his nan's voice calls. *'C'mon Kef! You can do it!'* But there are acres of space between him and the floating

fingers, acres of frightening floor, and he clings on to whatever it is he's holding. He can't let go.

'*C'mon!*' Nan's voice floods right through him with its promise of warmth and he takes a step towards it. He lets go. He takes a stumbling, falling, wobbling step . . .

'*Well done!*' says the voice, and he looks at his feet in wonder, and when he looks up, her hands are gone and he's falling, falling through an endless, bottomless, black-filled pit, and somewhere above him another voice is screaming, screaming his name:

'*KEF!*' it screams. '*KEFIN!*'

His heart leaps. He's a rabbit, trapped and scrabbling through the dark earth towards escape, but there's only more earth piled up above him. He just goes on falling, falling awake.

*Mum!* The word doesn't make it past his lips as he opens his eyes to the light. It disappears deep into the recesses of his mind, along with the dream.

Buried.

'Neesh.'

That's the first conscious word he mutters. And her image fills his mind as he reaches for his knife, just to check it's there, and strokes it. Neesh has got all the voices inside her, is what he thinks. Neesh knows everything, and what if she tells Nan? What if she tells Dad? Is Nan on her side now? Does Nan know what he did? Wasn't him anyway, it was Knife. Knife did it.

He turns his head to the west, past the faint orange glow

of the town to the darkness of the wooded hills beyond it. He thinks of Neesh. He gets Knife out of his pocket.

'You saved me,' he whispers to it. 'Perhaps that's why Dad gave you to me, perhaps that's why?' Kef thinks that maybe Dad knew that one day he'd have to kill him. So he gave him the knife, he *let* Kef kill him, because it's Kef's turn now.

'Yeah,' he whispers to himself. Suddenly, he feels good, good and strong. How many people can say they killed someone?

'SoMe tWo!' says Knife suddenly, and Kef looks up, startled, not knowing where the voice came from, or what it means.

'Not soMe oNe, soMe tWo. We kiLled GiTa, don't forget GiTa! BUt I s'poSe she's a PaKi, ent sHe. Does thAt coUnt thouGh, I meAn if you oNly kiLl a PaKi?' asks Knife.

'It was *Gita!*' whispers Kef, and shakes his head.

He hears Dad's voice. *'Once you let one in, they're at it like rabbits, like rats!'*

And he'd killed one, hadn't he? And so now they were all after him.

'YEAH,' he hears Knife say, 'but bloOdy heLl, she aSked for iT, diDn't she, shouLdn't a got in oUr way, shoUld she?'

Kef looks at Knife. Knife took everything out of Gita when she tried to stop him, all the life, all the blood.

'Oh!' he gasps, whispers, twisting his fingers in anxiety. 'Should chuck it-chuck it-chuck it.' He looks at his hands clutching the knife tight.

He runs his finger over the blade and he hears Knife's voice. 'ThEy see tHe blood, the poLice? ThEy can fiNd it, can't thEy?'

'Oh, oh, oh,' Kef whispers, his body writhing, legs twisting, torso bent. 'Clothes! Fuck-shit-bugger – it's on me, blood everywhere, on my clothes.'

'AlL oVer you,' says Knife, with a satisfied sigh, and he sounds like Dad, but it can't be Dad, can it, because he's dead, isn't he?

'Got to, got to,' Kef gasps, 'chuck-it-ditch-it-dump-it-sling-it-leg-it.'

And he looks at the knife. He closes it, opens it. Its blade gleams, its wooden handle is worn almost to the shape of his palm.

Fuck Dad.

'Drop-it-chuck-it-lob-it-kick-it-fuck-it-sling-it.   Drop it!' Kef whispers to himself, hoping the knife can't hear.

*Drop-it-in-the-canal.*

He stumbles out of the shed and looks down into the water of the canal. Slowly he holds the knife over the dark water, lightly, between his two fingers, whispering words to himself, chanting: 'Drop-it-chuck-it-fuck-it!'

Finally he manages to let the knife go, but almost without him knowing it, his other hand shoots out and catches it just before it hits the water. Voices rage and compete inside him.

*Drop-it-sling-it-ling-it-chuck-it.*

My knife.

Mine.

Saved me.

Not Dad's. Not any more.

He drops it, catches it, drops it, catches it. Each time it gets closer to the water.

Until finally he lets it go, sits back and watches as the knife plunges below the inky surface of the water. Watches as the water begins to close over it, ripples spreading and dying across the flattening surface.

NO!

Kef drives his fist into the water and brings the knife up again. It's dripping. He takes a deep breath; it's his knife, his. He won't let anyone take it from him, ever, whatever.

Kef unfolds the blade and holds it up, testing the air with it.

'I'll kill the lot of 'em,' he whispers to it, but it's Neesh's face he sees in the blade as it gleams in the cold hard light.

'ARe yOu a kiLler?' Knife asks. 'ARe yOu haRd enough?' Knife whispers to him. 'EH, WiMp?'

Kef doesn't answer, not in words, words aren't hard enough. He makes the first cut. He knows what Knife needs and he cuts swiftly and easily along the inside of his arm, all the way from his wrist to his elbow.

'Yeah,' he says, 'I'm hard enough.'

'YoU aNd mE Kef, yoU aNd mE,' says Knife, just the way Dad used to when he wanted Kef to go fishing.

# Sammy

Mum's face is as frozen and hard as the ice on the roads. It's taken me ages to get back, driving so slowly in the snow. And all the way I've been wishing I'd never left Neesh. I keep on seeing her face and feeling this terror that when I get back to the boat she'll be gone. 'But it's the safest place on earth,' I whisper to myself. A hidden boat on a hidden lake. What could be safer?

'Where the hell have you been?' Mum shouts, as soon as I'm through the door. 'And what could possibly justify you taking the car out in weather like this?'

'I was—'

'David rang to ask where you were, so don't even try to tell me you were with the band!'

'I wasn't going to—'

'For chrissakes, Sam, haven't you heard what's happened? It's all over the local news! Some kid's freaked out and stabbed a girl, and when the police get to his flat there's a dead body in there and God knows what else, and you pick today to go walkabout!'

'What?' For some reason it surprises me that anybody else knows about what happened to Gita, but Mum doesn't notice, just goes right on talking.

'I thought you were dead. I thought you were lying on the roadside somewhere waiting to be found! How can you justify that?'

'I can't,' I say. 'I'm not trying to!' But she's so angry she can't hear me.

'And every time the phone went, I just thought . . .' She can't even say it.

'I'm sorry, really Mum, I—' But she's not listening.

'And who do you think *did* ring?' she shouts. 'Neesh's mum. That woman needs a bloody bomb putting under her, and her son's even worse!'

'What did they want?' I ask, heart thumping.

'I don't know,' she shouts. 'I told them I couldn't speak to them, I was waiting for a call!'

'But, Mum . . .'

'I was,' she yells again. 'I was waiting for a call to tell me you were dead!'

*I nearly was*, I want to scream back at her, *and if I was, do you somehow think you could shout me back to life?* And then I think of Gita's mum and dad and I start to shake.

'You're shaking.' She finally notices. 'Your clothes are wet, where've you been?'

'I . . . I . . .'

'Never mind, oh Sammio!' she says, and she wraps her arms around me and hugs me like she's only really just realised I'm here, and she's about to fight off imaginary lions for me. But that's Mum – changeable, like the weather.

'Let's make you some of Grandpa's tea!' And she does, and I try not to think of Neesh, all alone on the boat as I pump Mum for info.

'It's awful!' she says. 'Apparently this boy, Kefin – weird name – went crazy and stabbed some poor girl in the

187

street, and when the police went to his flat, they found a man's body!'

'How do they know it was Kefin?' I ask, but she just shrugs.

'They're not saying much, just not to approach him and that he's dangerous and that he needs help.' She shudders. 'Honestly,' she says, 'someone actually put a coat over her, rang the police and then walked away. Imagine, stopping to do that but not staying! Some people!'

I take a deep breath.

'Is she dead?' I ask. 'The girl?'

'No!' says Mum. 'Doctors say it's a total miracle, they've no idea how she survived, but she's hanging on, somehow!'

Thank you, God.

Mum looks at me. 'Do you know her?'

I nod. And Mum stares at me.


'Omigod!' she says. 'I forgot to ask — do you know where Neesh is?'

'Why?'

'Well, Jammi rang after his mum, and for some reason he thought she might be with you, but then there's some rumour that this boy, Kefin, was after her too, and they're worried sick!' She looks at me. 'I said I'd ask you as soon as you got home . . . but I was so relieved, so angry . . . I . . . *do* you know where she is, Sammy?'

I shake my head but I don't actually say anything, so that's not quite lying, is it?

'Sammy, where *have* you been?'

'Walkin'?' I suggest, and she doesn't even correct me.

'Walking? Why did you take the car if you were walking?'

'Just, you know . . .' I'm too exhausted to make anything up.

'No,' she says slowly, suspiciously, 'no, I don't know, tell me.'

I sigh. I am completely knackered, but she's still staring at me, so I do what I always do *in extremis* – I tell a partial truth.

'I just . . . I just felt like going to Grandpa's for a bit, see what it looks like in the snow and pick up some extra amps!' I'm careful to say Grandpa's, not the lake, or the garden.

'Oh!' she says, still suspicious, but I'm warming up now.

'And I thought if I stayed for a bit, the weather might pick up!'

'Mmm, did you get the amps?' she asks.

'Couldn't find them, it was freezin' in that garage.'

'FreezinG!' she says, and then I know it's OK.

'So you haven't seen Neesh?'

I shake again.

'They sounded pretty desperate to find her, Sammy. Jammi said something about a trip back home and how she'd miss the flight if they didn't find her. I wonder if that's why she's gone missing?'

'Uh?'

'Well, you know, she's at that age, isn't she, when they marry them off.'

'Mum! She's only sixteen!'

'Well, *I* know that, it's not as if it's something *I'd* do, but it was always her father who wanted her educated, her mother's never been . . .' and she trails off. 'Good God, I hope not!' she says.

'Hope not what?' And I can feel my heart beating wildly.

'Hope she's not run off with a boy, got involved, and . . .'

'Why? Why shouldn't she?' I ask, and I am utterly amazed at the sound of my voice, at its normality, at the sheer bloody casual indifference of it; even as I'm terrified I'm congratulating myself.

'Well, I don't know, but times haven't changed that much, Sammy, not in her world. I mean, why do you think I've always tried to keep you two apart?'

'What?!'

'Like I said, ask your grandpa. I only *think* I know – he really does!'

I say nothing. What can I say? But I'm worried – are they after her to save her, or to harm her? Perhaps they really are scared for her. I mean, everyone knows that Kef's always hated their family. He *is* after her, and for all they know he's already got her.

I shiver.

'Jesus, child! Get into the shower, and make it hot!'

I do, I turn the temperature all the way to the top, but

somehow I'm still shivering. I lie in bed and try to get it all straight in my head, and now I'm here, at home in bed, things feel clearer. We need to stop behaving as though *we're* the criminals, we need to tell someone.

What we really need is Grandpa, I think, he'd be able to make it all make sense, but he's not here. He's a million miles away.

# Grandpa: Kashmir

I think I thought it could last forever, the two of us together on the boat. I was fooled by the stillness and the beauty of the place. The way the whole world seemed to float above the lake as if it were glass, a mirror, only reflecting an image of me and my desires. But of course the lake had its depths, depths I could never have imagined, hidden monsters of the deep that she tried to tell me existed . . .

'They'll find me,' she whispered.

'Why?' I ask. 'Why should they want to?'

And then she says it.

'I'm a daa'in.'

'A what?' She glances at me, half smiles.

'Daa'in,' she says, slowly and clearly, but her mouth twists at the word like it causes her pain. That's the bad word for it. It means *witch*. I like to call it sahira, a good witch.

I say the word, roll it around my tongue. Sa-hi-ra. I have a crazy thought that maybe one day it's what we'll call our child.

Slowly she explains. Everybody has energy and some people, sahira, daa'ini like her, can see it. She can lay her hands on people, cure them. She smiles and picks up the dried remains of a marigold. 'See this,' she says, 'it cures soreness and cleanses wounds.'

'Bloody hell!' I say, because of course she must be amazing if Mum was going to let her anywhere near her!

'And, Jake, they have to punish me, don't they? I mean, if I run away with you then anyone might think they can . . .' she tails off, the flower falls from her hand.

'Jake, I'm scared.'

She only ever said it once, but her whole body shivered and I remembered England in winter, grey and damp and cold in your bones. She shivered like that, like my touch defeated the sun in her, turning it into something grey.

'Don't be,' I said, and I held her in my arms, unable to believe that I still could. With a part of me I was always expecting her to dissolve, to disappear or go up in smoke. I couldn't – still can't, really – believe that she loved me. But she did.

'We have to ask for my uncle's help,' I say.

'We can't,' she answers, and she looks at me, and then away again. She stands by the side of the window, hidden but watching. Watching and waiting.

The heat increases. The air is so heavy with unfallen rain that it's hard to breathe.

Dog days, days when it's hard to move or think of anything beyond the next nimbu pani. Outside the boatmen still pole their wares – flowers and carpets and jewellery – around the lake, calling for buyers, but the air soaks up their voices. Somewhere in the woods above the lake the group of boys out from England are still camping. We watch them swim in the early morning from behind the windows. The heat under canvas must be unbearable. The only sound that can pierce the heavy air is the early morning call to mosque.

I go home. I tell everyone how hot it is on the lake, unbearable, not the faintest breeze.

I don't say how the water is never hot but always cool, or how the weeds curl around your limbs as you swim. How delicious it is at night to slip together, perfectly synchronised so that we only make one slight splash, into the dark water. To swim beneath the moon.

I think it can go on for ever. For as long as it takes her to see that we must tell someone.

I was wrong. Soon it would end. Very soon.

'Please,' I say, 'please let me tell my uncle at least, he'll help us!'

But she just shakes her head and watches through the window, as though she's paralysed.

As though she knew exactly what was coming.

# Sammy

As soon as the sun's up, so am I. I nick the car again and, in my head, I promise I'll be back by dark so Mum doesn't worry. I tell her I'm going to the hospital to see if I can find out about Gita.

As I drive I'm full of the fear that when I get there the boat will be floating empty on the water, the way it's always been. That I won't be able to find Neesh, won't be able to make anyone believe that she was ever in danger or was even with me. I'm afraid they'll find her.

I don't want us to hide away for ever, only I don't know how to convince her that it's safe not to. I'm not even sure it *is* safe. For the first time I wonder if we should make a run for it, but then I think that's madness, because what if her family did catch up with us, and hurt her or make her disappear? How would I get anyone to believe that she was ever really with me?

'Neesh!' I climb on the boat and shout her name. The lake echoes. The sound is eerie on the icy air but there's no answer. Is she in the woods? I listen. Nothing.

She's not in the sitting room or the bedroom. She's in the kitchen, sitting scrunched up under a duvet.

'What happened?' I ask, but she doesn't answer; she just shakes her head and holds out her hands. Mute, elective mute, that's what they call it, but there's nothing mute about her for me. True, she has no words sometimes, but her face is cold and pale and small and desperate. It speaks volumes. Her eyes are dark, and her hands talk for her, playing invisible music in the air . . . she's terrified. I hold her hands still.

'What is it, Neesh, what's happened?'

She still doesn't answer, just blinks like she's making sure I'm real.

Blink. Blink, blink.

I light all the rings on the stove, and then I get under the duvet beside her and hold her ice-cold hands between my own.

'It's OK, it's OK,' I whisper. 'Guess what? Gita's not dead! And the police know Kef's involved. They're looking for him.' No answer, so I reach for the iPod in my rucksack and flick through the options, decide on some Bach and link us up to the earplugs. Then I lean back against the cupboards with her head on my shoulder, the duvet wrapped around us both, and wait. After a while her hands aren't like ice any more.

'I saw it through her eyes,' she says. I nod. I think of Grandpa, and how he'd know, just like I do, that she hasn't finished yet and that it doesn't matter that she's not making any sense, that sometimes you just have to wait.

'She fell,' she whispers. I shiver, hold her tighter. I feel Gita in my arms, feel us falling into the soft snow before hitting hard concrete. Neesh shakes her head as though she hasn't got it right. 'She just stepped off,' she says, 'like she *wanted* to die.'

'Gita didn't want to die, Neesh!' I whisper back, and she

stops and looks at me. She takes the ear plug out and pushes herself away from my chest.

'I don't mean Gita,' she says.

'What?'

'I mean a girl I saw on the boat last night.'

'And that's what scared you?'

She nods.

'But there can't be any girl, there isn't anyone else here, Neesh. This place is right off the map. I mean, you couldn't have.'

She looks at me for a long time before she answers. She looks above my head and into my eyes, and then she holds my hands tight and says, 'Sammy, it wasn't someone *real,* it was a . . . I don't know, like a ghost or a memory . . .'

'Right,' I say, but I'm worried. For the first time I wonder if she's not just a bit off-beat, but really crazy. I mean, how could I tell? She takes her hands away and moves apart a bit, like she knows what I'm thinking.

'Perhaps it was, like, a dream?' I suggest.

She stares at me.

'She was a ghost!' she says, as though I'm the crazy one. 'But the weird thing is, the really horrible thing, is that I didn't just see *her.* I saw what *she* was seeing before she fell, and it was . . . it was . . .' She sighs and blinks. Blink, blink, as though she's still straining to see something.

'What?'

She takes a deep breath, like she's going right under and doesn't know how long it'll be before she comes up again.

'It was something I've seen before, a picture, one I've always seen. The one I write about, the one that's mine. So how could it be in *her* head? And Sammy, the girl – she looked like me!'

She's almost gabbling, I think. Wow! I've never heard Neesh gabble! We look at each other for a bit, while I think.

'First it's not in *her* head, is it, Neesh, not if *you* saw it! I mean, maybe what happened yesterday is scaring you into imagining things? And the second thing is,' I take my own deep breath, 'I think we need help; we need to tell someone about us. I've thought it through, Neesh, and if we don't tell, you don't exist, do you? And if you don't exist and your family find you, they can do anything they want, can't they, because no one'll know!'

She gives me a look like I'm just not hearing her right, and then carries right on.

'Why, though, Sammy? Why have I always seen that picture? Why did she jump? What happened to her? Something happened on this boat, Sammy,' she whispers, 'something bad.'

Hasn't she heard me at all? I shake my head. I feel as though I've got to keep us both afloat, up above Neesh's fear and craziness.

'Neesh,' I try again, 'weird things happen when you're stressed, waking dreams, seeing things. I mean, it's not that surprising, is it? You've seen someone stabbed. You've left home! We don't know what to do . . . but we can't stay here for ever . . . we've got to tell someone . . .'

Neesh stands up, walks into the sitting room and looks out of the window. She stands close to the wall so that she can see, but not be seen.

She frowns and blinks.

'I keep seeing her falling,' she says and she rubs at the glass of the window, stares intently over at the bank of the lake.

'So do I,' I say, and I shiver. 'I feel Gita landing in my arms and us falling.'

'No, I don't *mean* that,' whispers Neesh. 'I keep seeing the other girl falling, stepping off the railings, but like I'm seeing it from the other side of the lake and she's falling, over and over, and I keep seeing *me* fall, and you catch me, and then . . .'

'See what I mean, Neesh? You're just trying to make connections, your mind can't make sense of it. It was Gita who fell. I caught her. End of story. Isn't that bad enough?'

She turns away from the window and stares at me, and I get the weird feeling that she's looking right through me and out to the other side.

'It's weird,' she says, 'but I feel like the girl I saw . . . I feel like she's trying to tell me something.'

'Yeah,' I say, 'like maybe it would be a good idea to tell someone we're here? I mean, think, Neesh! What would we do if Jammi and his army turned up right now, or if Kef happened to drop by? Can't you see our only option is to find help? There must be some place out there that helps people like us, or like you, to get away?'

She stares at me. My heart's beating fast. Surely she can see that what I'm saying makes sense?

'No!' she says suddenly, sharply. 'We can't tell *anybody* where I am, *can't you see?* If they know I'm *anything* to do with you they'll find me, and then . . .' She wraps her arms around herself.

'Exactly, that's why you shouldn't be here . . .!'

She shudders and turns to look out of the huge windows, and for a second it looks as though she's seeing a different world; her eyes are far away, looking right through the trees, at something I can't see.

'I don't know,' she whispers. 'I know you're making sense, but I just . . .'

# Neesh

I don't know how to answer him, I don't know how to say that there's more than one world, more than just his world that only turns one way and has words for everything.

I can't stop seeing the girl, falling like a leaf from a tree down into the water, slowly, inevitably, as though it was always bound to happen, and the voice in the background screaming, 'No!'

What happened to her, why did she step off the boat? What happened to make her want to die? I hear my mum's voice: *Do you want to feel so bad you want to die?* I push it away, I have to. I have to put my old life behind me. I can never go back. And it's there again, the ache in my guts and chest at that word, *home*, and the weird feeling that somehow I'm already home, right here, on the boat.

I look out of the window. I feel a shadow of something, or *someone*, land over me, and out on the lake I see a faint haze of colour, like an echo of a boat full of flowers, and beyond it on the bank a sudden flock of crows land, caw and fly away. I step back quickly so I can't be seen. When I turn around Sammy's staring at me, and I don't know how long he's been standing there, waiting for me to answer a question I've already forgotten.

'Was this always your grandpa's boat?' I ask.

Sammy sighs.

'No, Grandpa's uncle rented it every year while he was posted in Kashmir. I mean, he had a government house in Srinagar, but the boat was for weekends and for Grandpa and his mum to use really. Everyone rented them.'

'So why bring it back here?' I ask him, but he just looks angry now.

'Neesh!' he says, like I'm suddenly a moron. 'Don't you think it's a bit weird worrying about how a boat got here, when somewhere out there is a *real Kef* with a *real knife* who thinks you know something about what he *really did*, and I don't mean just stabbing Gita! And then there's your brother's barmy army who could be out there hunting us down to marry you off, or whatever it is they do. Do you even get what a serious psycho Kef is? – I mean, wait till you hear what else he's done . . .'

'I already know what Kef's done,' I say. I make sure I say the words slowly, clearly. I make sure they come out so that they can't be misheard, or misunderstood. For the first time ever I'm grateful to my old speech therapist.

Sammy falls silent. He takes a deep breath. 'You can't know, Neesh,' he almost whispers, 'you've been on the boat all night!'

And his colours are scared, so worried sick that they shiver in a liver-brown. I can see them wavering, wondering if I'm crazy.

'How can you know?' he asks, and I take a deep breath and tell him.

'Because I can see inside people sometimes.' And the words surprise me, they're so simple to say.


## Sammy

I'm gobsmacked. For a moment I can't do or say anything, because there's something about the way she says it that's so clear and simple that I actually ask:

'What did he do, then?'

And she begins to tell me.

'Kef already killed someone before Gita,' she says. 'I think it was his dad, but I can't see clearly because the body's hidden under a duvet. They had a row; I'm not sure, but I think it was an accident.'

I'm stunned.

'How, Neesh . . . how *can* you know all that?' I ask. It

doesn't make any sense for her to know. She *can't* know. I look around the room as though I might see an answer. A radio or a TV might appear, but there aren't any, never have been. 'How?' I ask again, and she tells me.

She tells me in words that don't halt and stop and stall and stutter any more. She tells me she sees colours in the air that show her how people feel, and as she speaks she checks the air above me constantly, and now I know why it's always unnerved me. She tells me that she knows when people are ill, and why. Being able to make people better is the good bit; but she doesn't like the voices she hears, the troubled voices that need to speak. That's how Kef's nan started, just a voice, a voice she thought was in her head, a voice that became a picture, a picture that became a person who haunted her bedroom.

'You see Kef's nan?!' I ask, trying to take it in.

She nods. She actually laughs. Somewhere inside me I get that this might be a shock for me, but for her it's a relief to tell someone.

'When I was a kid I thought everybody had an old lady who lived in the walls! She's always been there, but since Kef's dad died she's been desperate to get to Kef. It wasn't me who knew what he'd done really, it was her, his nan – and then when he tried to attack me, the picture of his fight with his dad was so strong inside him it just all spilled out! I mean I try not to do it . . .' She stops. 'You can't hear me any more, can you?'

I shake my head. She's right, I can't take it in:

information overload.

'Sammy,' she says, 'I'm not just making things up. I've always been this way, always, I've just never been able to . . . to . . .'

'Tell anyone?' I finish for her, and she nods her head.

'It's just the way I am,' she says, so quietly I can barely hear her. 'It's in my family; my great-aunt was like it too. She healed others, but she ended up killing herself.' She holds her hands in her lap, curled up together like they're comforting each other.

Mum's words echo in my mind − *It's in her family* − is this what she meant, this madness? Is that why she doesn't want me and Neesh to be together?

'You don't believe me, do you?' she says. 'But, Sammy, I just know there's something about this boat. I mean when we fell through that door, and we . . . we . . . touched, didn't you feel it then, like it wasn't really us, like it was something or someone else taking us over . . .?'

It throws me, her changing the subject like that. I feel my skin blush and I don't have an answer for her, only an intense memory of the feel of her skin, smooth beneath my fingers, and a longing in my bones that's bigger than me, but somewhere in the back of my mind is an answer, that yes, it *did* feel like being taken over − but then again, isn't that what it's *meant* to feel like when you fall for someone, isn't that what feelings *are*? Only, maybe, if you actually, really let them take you over completely, then . . . then . . . well, maybe that's when you go crazy?

I try to take each thought slowly, carefully, let each one take shape and make sense and keep away the fear that's rising in me. I think it goes like this: minds are just like muscles really, aren't they? I mean, they can snap or ping or break completely, only minds are much cleverer than muscles. Minds can play nasty tricks, especially when they don't want to have to face up to a problem. They can make us see things that aren't there, imagine things. And when we're scared, well, sometimes we can only make sense of things by making up our own story, just the way we want it.

I suppose the problem is, it all *feels* real — I mean, I really, really, really believed that my dad left us because I lost a cricket match that Sunday. Mad, maybe, but still better than believing the truth, which was that he just didn't care enough to stay. But how do I get Neesh to see that's what might be happening?

'Let's get out of this room!' I say, because she's scared herself senseless and maybe in the air she'll be able to clear her head. I make some hot chocolate and we sit on the lockup on the roof, each wrapped in a blanket and staring at the trees and the melting snow and ice.

We talk to each other like we're strangers.

'Sammy,' she says, suddenly, 'does your grandpa like this boat?'

'Well, he loves having it here, but he never really uses it. I suppose it's only me that's ever really used it.'

'So why keep it here?'

'That's his business,' I say, shortly.

'Sammy,' she says so softly that I have to lean close to hear her, 'do you know, when you talk about your grandpa, your colours are a blue I've never seen before, it's so . . . so . . . sad. Why?'

I think of Grandpa's eyes darkening in the sunlight, of the way he sometimes glances out across the garden towards the boat and the lake, and the way I know, just *know*, that the questions have to stop; and that's exactly what I want now. I want Neesh's questions to stop. I can already feel the fear fizzing in my guts, the fear I always feel when Grandpa's eyes shut down and I know there's no more to be said; no more that *can* be said.

'Just leave it, Neesh!' I snap at her. I don't mean to, but that's the way it comes out.

And she just explodes.

If I could see people's colours like she says she can, then her colours would be an absolute fizz of fireworks. I had no idea she could be like this, the words just fly out of her mouth in a long string, one right after the other, so fast I can't hold on to all the meanings.

'Leave it, yeah?' she says. 'And then what? It'll get better, will it?' she hisses at me. 'Like teachers thinking it was best not to ask my mum why I was always late for school? Answer: because my brother was busy making me cook food for him to sell at his posh school. Or like no one bothering to find out why I never had a coat that would fit me? Answer: once Dad had gone, no one ever noticed I was cold. They left it. Or maybe you mean like just not noticing that everyone avoids me, and trying to help me think about why, or if it could be any different. Tell you what, Sammy, let's just leave it.

'You want us to ask the grown-ups for help? Well, where were they when the whole school knew Kef was searching for me? Why do half of them walk right past when they've just heard him call me a fucking Paki? Answer: they're as scared as we are, so they leave it. Do you mean like that, Sammy, do you mean that kind of leaving it?'

'But those are things that happened, Neesh,' I manage to say after a bit, 'they're awful and terrible, but that doesn't mean—'

'The things and colours I see are real *too*, Sammy, I've always seen them. How do you think I always knew where you were hiding when we were kids? Your colours were fizzing right through the curtains, through cupboards. Sammy, you glowed! How do you think I can tell how you're feeling right now, like you're scared I'm crazy but you don't know what to think, you're excited and freaked and angry and . . . well, anyway?' She stops.

'I am, but Neesh . . . I . . .'

'Sammy, I've tried leaving it, really. . .'

And then she tells me this; that sometimes it all drives her so crazy that she cuts herself to make it stop.

She holds out her hand. We're both shaking. I reach for it. I realise I've only ever held it curled up like a small ball in the palm of my hand. I can feel my heart beating as I slowly uncurl it.

Her palm is pink and raised, lacerated, cut and healed. Her lifeline is nothing but a long scar, still bleeding. I have to close my eyes when I see it, as though that could block it out. I have to remind myself to breathe. I want to be sick. I want to make it better. So that's why her hand is always curled at her side.

'Don't you think they ever noticed that in the medical room?' she says. 'But maybe they just thought it was some weird custom, and left it? Sammy?'

I hold her hand, her curled-up hand, in mine. I can't think. *Jesus. Jesus. Jesus*, my mind goes, *all I ever did was fancy you*.

'Sammy? Sammy?' she says. I open my eyes, and she goes on.

'I don't want to leave it any more. I can't. I can't pretend nothing's happening. That I don't see things or know things or get treated like shit.'

*Why not?* I actually hear myself think back at her, but thankfully the words don't make it to my mouth.

'I want to stay on this boat and work out why I can see the girl and what she wants to tell me. I want us to be together. I want to know what the hell is happening to me and why, why, why!'

I open my eyes. I can't take it all in, but for once I don't have to say anything at all, because she's doing all the talking.

'The girl, she's trying to tell us something, something about what happened to her, and I'm going to listen,

Sammy, because I've got this horrible feeling that if I don't it could happen to me too . . . and . . . I feel like I know who she is, but I can't remember, like a word on the tip of my tongue . . .'

'Just stop talking for a bit!' I say.

And she does. I let go of her hand.

'First off, where are the razors, or whatever it is you do that with?'

She looks up at me, surprised, and says, 'In my bag, why?'

I don't answer, I just go to get her Tesco's bag and find the small plastic box.

'They were my dad's,' she whispers, and her mouth twists in a small sharp way that actually causes me physical pain to see, so I take out the blades, re-fold the wax paper as though they were still in there, put it all back in the box and hand it back over to her. I wrap the blades up to take away with me.

'Thanks,' she whispers. 'I wasn't going to, I mean, after Gita I couldn't . . .'

'Well, now you can't,' I say.

'Sammy,' she stops for a moment, 'don't you think it's like we're *meant* to be here? I mean, starting from when I slipped and you caught me . . . that spark . . . and when you asked me to marry you . . . I mean, was that you, or was it like something else overpowering you, like a feeling you couldn't stop . . . like us on the boat?'

And when she says that I know exactly what she means, but I can't remember when it happened or where, and then

I remember her falling into my arms, remember the right-ness of it, the way she fitted and . . . I shake it away. It can't be true that something else is controlling us.

'But Neesh, I've always wanted to catch you, from the first moment I saw you,' is all I say. 'I wanted to kiss you when we got here, and you wanted . . . wanted to kiss me . . . didn't you?' I ask, because maybe this is just the weird-est way in the world of blowing me out?

'Yes!' she says. 'Yes, I did! I'm just saying that maybe we're connecting with something that happened on this boat. I don't know what, but I know it was wonderful, as well as frightening, and I think it gets inside us somehow, and that it . . . it feels dangerous!'

'But that's what feelings are!' I hear myself shout. 'They *are* inside you, and they *are* dangerous and sometimes you just wish you didn't have them, but then you'd be dead . . . wouldn't you?'

'Well, *you* might be,' she shouts right back, 'but what if your *feelings* aren't? What if someone else's feelings are still right here on this boat, making pictures, like I think they are? And what if they're connecting with us and trying to tell us something?'

'Jesus, Neesh, and what if you're just imagining it all? What if? Isn't that possible too?'

She doesn't answer, she just turns and walks away from me, and after a few steps she just stops dead and falls back, her arms flinging out, flailing.

She does it so quickly I react without thinking. My arms

reach out to catch her, her shoulders land in my palms, and she wraps her fingers around my wrists and a spark jumps across our skin, like the lightning between the fingers on the Sistine chapel. I can feel the weight of her in my hands, bird-light, and my heart muscle feels suddenly squeezed too tight and now I know. I know exactly what she means. Because it's like it's not just that I caught her. It's like I'm somehow *meant* to catch her, like somewhere, somehow there's a place in the universe where all I ever do is catch her – and just for this one moment the real world and this other place are completely aligned and it . . . it feels so right.

'See?' she asks. 'You'll always catch me!' But then her eyes become thoughtful, doubtful, and she glances towards the low railings of the boat.

I don't like this feeling. I don't like the way it connects with the fear. The way it makes me think of words like *chaos* and *danger*, and what if I'd dropped her?

'For fuck's sake, Neesh! We need help. We can't deal with this alone! We need to TELL someone!' I say, and what I really mean is this, that she's scaring me.

'And you think *I'm* the one who sees things, Sammy. Look around you, the world doesn't like anything that doesn't fit – and in case you hadn't noticed, that means me! We can't *ever* be together, not without cutting our families out of our lives completely, and that means yours too, don't you get that?' she says. With a voice like that she doesn't need razor blades to cut skin. She shakes her head at me.

'No, I don't believe that, Neesh, and what I want to know is, what's so wrong with normal? Normal's always been good enough for me!' I shout back. Because that's exactly what I want. I want to walk down the street and hold her hand. I want to sit on a bar stool next to her, and watch her drink whatever she likes. Coke and water included. I want us to eat hot chips straight from the bag right on the street, where everyone can see us . . .

'Like your mates, like that kind of normal?' she asks.

And then all the fear ignites into furious, ugly words that we throw at each other like stones; neither of us mean them, but once they're said it's too late.

'Your problem, Neesh!'

'Oh!' she gasps. '*Is* it? It's not as though your mates were inviting me down the Anchor every night!'

'Why should they? You don't drink!'

'What's water?'

'Great! Come down the pub for a water!'

'I don't need to get drunk to have fun!'

'No,' I shout back, 'you friggin' well see things anyway!'

Sudden silence.

'Neesh! I . . .'

'Don't tell anyone, don't go *near* my family, or tell your mum!' she says. 'Just *promise* me you won't do anything stupid!'

'Jesus!' I say.

'Peace be upon him too!' she hisses.

'Why are we arguing?' I ask suddenly, but she doesn't

answer, she just gets up and walks off the boat.

We stand by the lake. 'Sammy,' she says, 'maybe we're arguing because . . .'

I sigh. 'Right, because the boat made us?'

She shrugs. 'Maybe.'

And then there's nothing left to do or say, so we walk to the car to collect the things I brought. The new leaves on the trees hang damp and dejected. We unload the car, put stuff in cupboards.

'I've gotta go,' I say. 'If Mum finds out I'm driving the car again we won't have any future anyway, and I'm meant to be in school by two!'

She doesn't answer, but as I leave the boat she calls me.

'Sammy!' I turn and look at her, watch as she struggles to find the right words. 'Watch yourself, be careful . . .'

And the boat seems to shudder beneath us, but that's what happens when you allow the feelings to take over, isn't it? Everything's an omen, everything has a meaning that only you can see. I mean, that's the fear. The paranoia. And once you go down that route, you're buggered.

'Sammy,' she says very slowly and clearly again, 'just don't tell *anyone*.'

I walk through the wood. Jesus, I'm thinking. What if I'd dropped her? What a crazy bloody stunt. My hands tremble, can still feel the blades of her shoulders as they hit my palms. The relief as I caught her, the rightness of her weight in my hands. Why does she have to make it all so difficult?

To me it's simple: if we don't tell *someone* about us we'll never have the chance to be together without having to hide, and I don't want that. And what if her mum goes to the police to say she's missing, what if they connect Neesh disappearing with Kef disappearing, or – worse – what if they find out it's Neesh's coat covering Gita?

I get in the car and start it up; as soon as I'm on the road my mobile bleeps. It's David.

AT SKATE PARK COMING? I risk Mum's hysterics and drive straight there. I could do with the company. And besides, I need to know what everyone's saying. Has anyone connected Neesh and Kef?

There's still snow left up in the park and someone's got vodka. They're filling what's left in the bottle with the snow and some juice, taking turns to swig it. It's great, makes sense of the words 'ice and fire'. Makes it easier to listen to all the chat about Gita and Kef.

'I would've bet Gita's Mulberry it was Neesh who wanted to kill her!' Leah says, and my heart leaps.

'Neesh would never—' I stop myself.

'Ah, bless!' she says 'Still keeping an eye out for the mentally challenged?'

'Fuck off!' I think I manage to make it sound friendly enough.

'Perhaps Kef thought Geet *was* Neesh?' Dunc says.

'Yeah right,' laughs Dan, 'they all look alike to Kef, don't they!'

Everyone laughs, it's a relief.

'They won't let us in to see her,' says Holly, 'she's too ill.'
Some girls start to cry.

'Hey!' says Sean. 'Anyone see Mr Mayhew on TV?' (Mr Mayhew's the school Head.)

'The whole school's just devastated,' mimics Dunc, 'absolutely! She was SUCH a lively girl, Gita, a wonderful student!' Then Dan taps him on the shoulder and whispers something. 'OH,' he says, 'she's NOT dead! In that case I'll see her in the annexe at four p.m. as usual!'

'Suddenly she's Saint Gita!' laughs Holly.

'Yeah, but she could've died, still might!' I say slowly. 'I mean, she's really badly hurt.' And they all turn to stare at me.

'Do you think it really was Kef?' asks Dunc again. 'Where were you,' he says suddenly, swinging an imaginary mike under my face, 'at four p.m. on Monday, and where have you been this morning, Mr Colthurst-Jones?'

'Get lost!' I say.

'No, though!' says Mo. 'Where *were* you, cos you didn't turn up to practice after school yesterday, did you?'

'Yeah, and you rang my mum – thanks, lads!'

'Whoaaa!' they all say. 'But where were you, and who were you with? Someone or something's getting to you, Sammy-boy!'

I shake my head and try to smile, take another swig to hide the confusion: burn, cold, cold, cold, burn.

'Gita probably did it to herself!' someone says. 'Anything for attention!'

'What?' I hear myself shout. 'That's a totally sick thing to say!' *Whoa, calm, calm, calm down*, I whisper to myself. *They didn't see it happen, they don't know, stay cool. Chill.*

'You all right?' asks David, suddenly.

'Not great!' I say. I get up, I realise I can't do this, not any more. I keep seeing how it really was. I see Kef taking the knife out of her body and all the blood coming out. Feel Gita fall into my arms and knock us both to the ground. I've got to go.

'See ya!' I say. And they all stare at me. Or do they? I'm not sure. I'm not sure of anything any more.

I nick David's bike; no way am I driving after all that vodka and ice. I see Gita again, the knife sticking out of her. I'm a witness. The words just appear in my head. *I'm a witness.* And I am. A witness who isn't saying anything. How did that happen? And why?

I see Neesh fall backwards, feel myself catch her, her fingers wrap themselves tight around my wrist – I feel that leap of longing between us. 'Love's a spark, lad, a real thing,' says Grandpa in my ear. My mind's spinning, and when I look up I'm outside her house.

The door's shut. The house looks just the way it always has. They're in there, her mum and Jammi. They might be in the house but really they're standing right between me and Neesh, stopping us telling the truth. Stopping us being witnesses. And they'll always be there unless we face them, won't they? And before I know it the bike's lying in the snow and I'm walking up the pathway.

*'Sammy, watch yourself!'*

*Christ*, I'm thinking, *we've known each other practically all our lives; of course we can sort this!* I'll offer them whatever they want. We'll leave the city, we'll give them money, a dowry, niquat, marriage, whatever; we'll sort it! But we can't hide any more. Because if we do we'll always be waiting, won't we? Waiting for the one moment when we turn a corner and see them. Wherever we go, however far we run, they'll always be just one pace behind us, dictating what we do next. And I can't live with that. We have to face them sooner or later! That's what I think, standing there, swaying slightly from the vodka. And then I open the gate and walk up to the door. I mean, how difficult can it be?

As soon as the door opens I realise this wasn't such a good idea. Jammi doesn't give me a chance to say anything.

'Where is she?' he says. 'Wherever you go, I'm telling you, we'll find you. No one shames us, no one!'

We stare at each other and there's nothing there. I mean, nothing. It's like we never knew each other and never could. It makes me cold just looking at him. My tongue feels thick and numb; the words come off it shaking and slow. 'Somewhere you'll never find her!' I say. And I turn to go, my feet unsteady beneath me, already wondering what I've done.

'Not any more she's not, mate, she's dead meat!' Jammi shouts after me, and when I turn back to look his eyes are dead too, dead and cold. 'She is if we find her!'

I don't answer. I haven't told him anything, I think, but then again, I didn't need to, did I? Because now he knows we're together, doesn't he? Does he know about Grandpa's house? I think his mum might. Fuck, fuck, I'm thinking, this is the twenty-first century, isn't it? But it's not, is it? Neesh has already told me it's not. Mum's told me it's not. I just didn't want to listen. I spin the wheels of the bike as fast as I can, as though they could spin me away from all the pictures inside me. Pictures of Neesh. Neesh falling into my arms. Neesh standing up under the insults raining down from Gita and her mates. Neesh talking, each slow word full of meaning. But most of all I see her standing by the window of the boat, looking out across the lake waiting . . . waiting for me. And suddenly I'm worried it won't be me who'll get there first.

What've I said? Can Jammi work out where she is? But even if he does he'll spend hours in and around the house, won't he? He doesn't know about the lake, and even then he'll have to find the boat – won't he?

*Just don't tell anybody!* Her last words to me.

The words make themselves into a tune and play themselves over and over in my head, crucifying me.

'But it's not us doing anything wrong!' I shout out loud, and Neesh's answer comes straight back at me.

'Oh yes it is, we've broken the rules, we've broken their honour, their *izzat*, and where I come from, once you've done that you can't mend it.'

I see Jammi's face again. He looked like Neesh didn't

exist for him any more, and so perhaps now all he has to do is make that come true. Make her really not exist. How did I end up here, that's what I want to know, in a place where just falling in love is as dangerous an insult as holding up a knife?

'Sammy!' I have to stop the bike hard, because he comes out of nowhere and he's standing right in front of me. It's Kef. He looks like he spent the night in a dustbin. He's shaking and holding on to something in his pocket. The knife.

'I didn't do it!' he says. His words come out all jerky, like a puppet with his strings tangled. He clings to the knife in his pocket. I start to wheel the bike slowly backwards.

'We saw you,' I hear myself say, as I wheel the bike around him – and then I get on and cycle as hard as I friggin' well can back towards the car, hoping it's still parked by the skate park.

I think about Neesh. No wonder she's half crazy with that fuckwit for a brother.

I didn't understand what she was telling me, though, I still don't. How can you just cut your sister out of your life like that, as though she doesn't exist any more, as though she can't feel pain any more, just because she doesn't agree with you? *It's not normal,* I want to scream out loud.

But maybe I'm finally learning there's no such thing as normal, maybe there are just people all trying to live whatever way they think is right. So what do I do now? Do I try the police again, tell them what we saw? Tell Mum?

Ring someone before I head for the boat? I don't know what to do. I lean against the car. I pick up a fistful of snow and bury my head in it . . . but it doesn't make anything any clearer.

# Kefin

Kef wishes Knife would stop. Knife talks all the time now, always whispering in Kef's head, whispering slow words that make meanings in Kef's mind.

'LeT's go back,' whispers Knife, 'let's go bAck and see wHere I went in!' And Knife's so hungry. Sometimes, thinks Kef as Knife draws a line of blood against his shin, it would be nice if someone else could feed Knife. He wonders why someone else can't, why it always has to be him. Then he remembers. Knife is his.

Knife's whispers bring pictures of things he doesn't want to see any more. Like Gita in her white tee. He sees his hand pulling the knife out of her and all the red, red blood that came out on the white tee.

The picture hurts his eyeballs and twists his body and he doesn't know how to make it stop.

'No-no-no-no,' he whispers, 'I don't want to go back, they're looking for me. She'll find me.' And in his mind's eye Neesh's eyes seem bright, too-bright like they can see right inside him.

'She knows,' he whispers, and he sees the hump of a duvet by a fireplace.

'Well tHen!' says Knife. 'Let's go fiNd her!' and Knife laughs, a soft laugh like a sword slipping slowly out of its scabbard.

'REady or nOt wE're coMing!' Knife shouts, and suddenly Kef is filled with an indescribable sense of wellbeing. He feels good and strong and invincible. He doesn't really notice the fear or hunger any more.

He's got Knife.

'Ready or not we're coming,' he repeats, and the words sound good.

But where is she? Where's Neesh?

Back in Nan's house, that's where.

'That was ours by rights,' said Dad, 'bloody Pakis in your nan's house! If your mam hadn't already gone they would've been enough to make her run off!'

And Dad laughs. Kef turns around, scared. Is he here? No, he can't be. Kef realises with a sharp jolt of relief that it's not Dad laughing, it's Knife.

Knife sounds like Dad.

It's all her fault, though, that Neesh. Mum and Nan would still be here if all the Pakis hadn't taken over.

'BlooDy hEll,' whispers Knife, 'it's onLy an islaNd we're liVin' on, thEy'll have us all puShed off the eDges if we're not careful!'

'Yeah,' Kef whispers back to his knife.

'WEll,' Knife whispers again, 'at lEast we goT rid of oNe of 'em!'

And Kef closes his eyes, trying to twist away from the

vision behind them, from the sound Gita made, the sound of her breath coming out, and the look on Sammy's face, of disbelief, of horror.

Sammy doesn't like him any more.

'SaMmy neVer liKed you,' whispers Knife, 'he wAs just bEing kiNd you siLly fuCker!'

'I didn't, I didn't kill Dad – it was an accident,' Kef whispers.

'CoulDn't kill 'im, moRe like!' scorns Knife. 'Not wiThout me.'

Kef nods, that's right, it wasn't him anyway, it was Knife, and Knife licks his lips. 'Let's fiNd Neesh, oNe doWn, two to go, ReAdy or Not wE're coMing,' says Knife.

Kef repeats the words again and they make him laugh out loud. It's OK, he thinks, everything's OK, he just has to hang on to Knife, let Knife do the talkin'.

And when he's killed Neesh, Nan can come back, because the house will be empty again, won't it? And maybe then Mum'll come back too, and then they can all be together again. But what about Dad, he thinks . . . and he begins to shake.

'I'll deAl with It!' he hears Knife say firmly. Knife's strong, he thinks. Knife's a real man.

That's when Kef realises he's been walking, walking all this time, getting closer and closer to Neesh's house. Now he's very close. His heart beats hard with excitement. He feels alive. So does Knife; Knife's shaking in his hands.

Kef's heart rate leaps and he strokes the knife in his

pocket, soothing its excitement. He wants his mum, wants her badly, suddenly, deeply, like a flash of lightning across a dark sky: there for a second and then gone. He has a brief sense that if only she was here with him, she could save him from something; but what?

He's confused. Why did she go away? He hears Dad's voice.

'Think she'll come back for *you*, you snotty little wanker?'

'Will,' he says, 'she will!' But his heart's already dropping inside him. What if she doesn't? What if she never comes back? And she didn't. Why not? Was it him?

'Jesus, you were such a miserable git, always whinge-ing . . .'

'ShUt it!' warns Knife, but Kef can't.

*'You've your dad in you!'*

But Knife cuts short the sound of Nan's voice: 'BetTer than havin' 'iM in ya liFe!'

And it's weird, thinks Kef as he looks at the knife, cos Knife reminds him of someone, if only he could . . . remember.

But he can't. Knife's rage is confusing him. Knife's rage feels red, like red stains dancing in his head. Kef holds on to the knife hard, and he can't think properly, can't manage all the feelings racing through his head.

'C'Mon!' yells Knife, and Kef wonders why everyone crosses the road to get past him.

'Nigger in your own country!' says Dad.

'LeT's gEt her,' says Knife, 'or are you tOo yeller?'

'Aren't!' Kef shouts.

'GO oN THeN!'

'Will.'

'OH YeAH?'

'Yeah.'

'LiKe whEn?'

Kef wants Knife to be quiet. Something's stirring in his mind. What if Gita isn't dead, what if he isn't a killer? He tries to hang on to it. Slowly he begins to close the blade to fold it away. It could be all right, couldn't it? And then he sees Sammy. Sees him come out of the gate of his nan's house and get on to his bike, fast, and start to cycle away.

'Sammy!' he shouts, and Sammy screeches to a halt, stares at him for a second, before whispering one word.

'Fuck.'

'I didn't do it!' Kef says quickly.

'We saw you.'

'Didn't, wasn't me.'

But Sammy just stares at Kef, keeps him in his sights as he moves away slowly. 'Right, Kef,' he says and he gets on the bike and cycles away, fast.

'It wAsn't Me!' Kef shouts after him.

He wonders why Sammy looks scared. Sammy's never scared.

'SEe?' whispers Knife. 'No oNe on yoUr side. They saw you, KEf, they know, and you know wHat that means?'

'No,' says Kef.

'We haVe to gEt rId of them!'

'No!' whispers Kef.

'No woRries, mAte,' says Knife, 'yOu just sit baCk, and waTch the maSter at work. I'll sort it!'

Kef follows Knife up to the door of Neesh's house and rings the bell. If it wasn't for her he wouldn't be so cold and starving and lonely, would he? And she saw him, she saw him do it and so did Sammy; he's got to find them. But what then? Kef doesn't want to think about it, but Knife isn't scared, Knife bangs on the door, loud!

'I just can't get you out of my head!' sings Kylie.

'Shit!' says Kef.

Her fat brother answers. Kef looks at him; now he's here, he doesn't know what to do or say.

'PaKi!' says Knife.

'You got a problem with that, guriya?' says fat bro, and Knife wonders whether he should kill fat brother. Kef can hear Knife thinking it. *Nah*, thinks Knife, *too far through all that fat to the blood.*

'WhEre Is she?' Knife says.

'I dunno.'

'She's hEre, I waNt her!'

'You find her, you can have her, mate!' says her brother.

'SCORE HIM,' says Knife, to Kef. 'Make him TELL!'

So Kef does, lightly, just a scratch, same as Neesh's – a line across his jaw.

'TRADEMARK, MATE, THAT'S MY MARK, SEE IT, REMEMBER ME!' Knife's words come out of his mouth, and Kef hears Knife laugh.

Kef smiles, he feels good and strong. 'That's just the beginning, mate,' he says. 'See this knife, it's hungry. You or her, don't matter to us, you lot all look the same to us lot anyways! So where is she?'

'She's safe, that's all Sammy told me! Honest!' Knife notes fat bro's sweating; sweat's good, it smells of fear, but not as good as blood.

'Not anY more sHe's not,' says Knife.

Fat bro's sweat mixes with his blood and rolls down his neck. Knife watches and waits.

'Try Sammy's grandpa's place, posh place up in Bagley Woods. That's where me and the crew are headed, after we decide what to do with her when we find her.'

'You make me sick, you lot, hunting down your own sister,' says Kef, but Knife doesn't agree.

'I'LL be sure and seNd 'er yoUr lOvE, MaTe,' says Knife, pulling away from Jammi's neck.

Jammi stares at them both all the way to the gate, and then he shouts, 'Don't bother, mate, just send back the pieces!' and he slams the door.

Kef's laughing. Kef laughs at the sound of the knife's voice. *Knife's so clever, funny, not like me*, he thinks.

*Send her your love.*

Good one. I'd never've thought of that one, thinks Kef.

He heads off. He doesn't have a plan, he doesn't need one. He's got Knife.

Knife'll sort it.

# Neesh

Sammy's gone.

A grey mist hangs low over the lake. The last remnants of snow drips off the trees. I stand by the window. I stand well back, where no one can see me watching, waiting – but for what? The boat creaks as the ice melts and frees it. The jetty sways, and it comes again, that feeling of time dislocating, folding over and meeting at its edges. Danger. I can feel it in my guts, in my hair and in the air all around me, waiting to happen. The indecipherable words of a prayer start up again inside me and a hot, pumping fear fills my body so that I can barely breathe.

I climb the ladder to the roof and she's there again, *a shape in the mist standing on the railings wrapped in white like a shroud, like a slim column of air, her back to me* . . . and at the sight of her I'm paralysed, unable to move a muscle, but something inside me reaches out to her in recognition like a thought already had – and she turns towards me and looks right through me to the edges of the lake beyond. Even as I turn to follow her gaze I can feel the colours forming out of the heavy damp air; they are black and grey, and slowly they become figures, figures who surround something . . . someone . . . her . . .

*The chains above the heads of the women swing and clank against each other angrily, linking them together. One of the women spits and then holds her hands out, muttering a counter-curse.*

'Witch!' she says.

It's as though the word has given the women a sign. They stand back. The girl lifts her shorn head on her exposed neck and begins to walk away, she hasn't got very far when the first stone hits. She turns like a deer at bay and stares at them. As each stone lands she shouts a name, the name of the woman who has thrown it. The sound of the chains writhing and intertwining is deafening. The stones come faster, thicker, driving the girl backwards, towards the woods, and she turns to run . . .

My eyes close against the picture. Blink. Blink, blink. I don't want to see it. Fear screeches through my body like tyres on a tight corner, burning, smoking.

The girl on the railings stares at me, and through the dark almond-shaped holes of her eyes . . .

I see the story of her time on the boat over and over. I see her fall into the boy's arms, I see a river of flowers, I see her tunnel through them, dive into them, open her arms out wide and fall backwards into them, I see her shadow staring through the windows of the boat. I see her being stoned, and then there's a gap, or a space where the story's scratched so badly that the pictures jump and hiss and fragment, and the sound of the prayer is like a terrible re-mix, no one word is clear, and then the whole thing goes back to the beginning and starts again, until I see her right where she is now, standing on the railings, staring at me . . .

Something's wrong. There's a space, a gap in her story that's not filled in. She's trapped, trapped in the same place, telling the same story, over and over again, trapped in the boat, trapped by a world that doesn't know what happened to her – or doesn't care.

Like me.

I'm trapped too, not just on the boat but in my life, in the minds of all the people around me who think they know what I should do, or how I should be. Her eyes hold mine, trace the thoughts as they run through my mind. I try to shiver, but I can't move. Am I right? The question rises in my mind and I think she nods, the slightest incline, a darkening of the pupils, a faint glow in the air above her, and then her eyes release me and I can move again, but before I can get to her . . . *she steps out into the air and drops like a stone . . .*

And now it's me balancing on the railings, me about to fall; for a split second I feel the railings beneath me, see the lake, not as it is now, but stretching ahead of me, all the way to the horizon, where there's a man, poling a boat full of flowers. I wobble, I step back quickly, feel the wooden deck safe and solid beneath my feet.

I wonder if Sammy's right. I wonder if I'm what they call mad. I stagger back inside the boat. I touch the carved wooden walls; feel the semicircles meeting at the edges of each panel, making circles beneath my fingers. I stand up. I cling to the sides of the boat. I touch them and I wonder what makes things solid and real, and then I see him through the windows, like an answer to my question. Sammy. He's running, running through the woods towards the boat, towards me, calling out my name, shouting it so loud that the birds rise up from the trees and the water and the damp air echoes.

'Neesh!'

'Sammy!'

'Oh, thank God you're still here, you're OK!' he whispers in my ear and I hold on to him, solid and real and here and now. I let my head fall on to his chest, feel my arms wrap themselves around his body. We hold each other, pressed up as close as forever. There is no smell of flowers, no echoes of other people's lives for us to step into. For now there's just him and me.

Sammy and Neesh.

# Grandpa: Kashmir

I'm telling you a story. The story of my life. Do you believe in stories? Do you know that they cry sometimes just to be told? And so here we are, at this moment, this now.

This part of the story that no one has ever spoken, including me, even though we all think we know what's on the other side. We can sense that over this fence the world as we know it drops away. This is the time when your feet fail to land safe and sure and solid on the other side, you put them down on the ground, only to find . . . there's nothing there.

And you just keep on falling.

As she did. Stepping off the boat and crashing right through the surface of the water that looked like glass. Shattering my world into a billion fragments.

Why?

That's the story that's crying to be told.

# Neesh

'I'm sorry,' he says after a while. 'Neesh, I don't know what to say, I'm so, so sorry!'

And I can *see* he is, his despair floats above his head in a rich inky black, punched yellow with sorrow.

'It's OK . . . I'll make it OK,' he says, and I know he wishes he could. I wish he could too, but it's not in his power. He can't change the world.

'What happened?' I ask.

'I went to your house,' he says.

*So they know,* I think. I feel the fear blossom inside me, swell like a poppadum hitting oil. I know I have to make a decision. Shall I stay here, or shall I run? I hear my mum's words: *Do you want to feel so bad that you want to die?*

Q: What now? What do we do now?

A: I don't know.

'How much do they know?' I ask.

Sammy looks grey.

'Nothing! But I went there, Neesh. They saw me, they know we're together.'

'Are they going to know where to look for me?'

'I don't think so, I . . . I don't know, Neesh.' His words sound so unsure and sad that suddenly I miss the Sammy who thought there was a place where everything could be OK. A different world. His world.

'They'll find me,' I say, 'and when they do . . . what then?'

He shudders. 'Neesh, I don't know. It felt, it felt like you didn't exist. It felt like Jammi had to wipe you off the face of the earth now you . . . you've left them.'

'I tried to tell you,' I whisper. Sammy puts his head in his hands and doesn't come up for a while. The air around him is so blue, a deep, grey, impenetrable sad and sorrowful blue that can't be helped, and so I don't say anything.

'Neesh,' he says after a while, 'what are they going to do? I mean, when, if . . .'

'I don't know,' I say quickly, but inside I feel the hiss and crack of the girl's story jumping.

We sit there, trying to think, but we can't, not really. There are no real colours left above Sammy now, nothing except a numb pale haze of shock, and I know I'm feeling the same.

'It's whatever happened here on this boat. That's what will happen to me!' I hear myself say slowly, not even sure where the words are coming from.

'You mean, like, you'll step off the roof of the boat . . . and then . . .'

We stare at each other. 'I don't know. I don't think it's that, I think it's . . .' and again Mum's words come – *Do you want to feel so bad you want to die?* – along with the broken words of a prayer. And I say, 'It's whatever happened before that. That's the bit of the story that's missing. What *made* her want to jump.'

'So what do you see, Neesh? I mean when you, when you . . . uh . . . see things?' he asks. I look at him but the air above his head is clear and clean, waiting for an answer, waiting to listen, not just to tell me I'm crazy, and so I begin to tell him.

'Well, first I saw the man poling a boat full of flowers on a lake. That's the picture I've always seen, and then when . . . when I was locked up at home and heard your song, I saw a girl and a boy standing in flowers. Loads of them, like a whole river of flowers. Red and gold and orange and—'

'Marigolds . . .' whispers Sammy suddenly, 'were they marigolds?'

'Yeah, the same as the ones in the boat the man's punting.'

It feels weird to be talking about the things I see, to be making them into words, to think that they might be a picture, now, in Sammy's mind too.

'And that first night on the boat I saw her falling, Sammy, just like I did when you caught me, only I saw it happening over and over and over again, like it would never stop.'

Sammy mutters something, and a faint rose-like colour slowly dawns above his head, like the beginnings of an idea.

'And now when I see her she's standing on the railings with all her hair cut off, or by the window, and she's so—' but he doesn't let me finish.

'Flowers . . .' he repeats, 'he bought her a whole boat full of flowers.'

And he gets that look on his face, like he's trying to catch a memory of the wind.

# Sammy

I can feel an idea beginning to form as she speaks. One of those ideas that you realise has been staring you in the face all along, only it's been up so close that you were looking straight through it. I hear my own voice in my head, young and high and excited:

'You bought the flowers for *Granny*!'

And I see Grandpa's face. I see it fall and darken as he looks out over the lake, towards the boat. Grandpa's words and pictures flash through my mind as Neesh speaks: 'a boat full of flowers'; '*niquat*, like a promise, Sammy'; 'Love's a real thing, lad, like a spark'. And my own question: 'Have you ever bought anyone a boat full of flowers?'

And his answer: 'Yes.'

It all starts coming together in my mind, slowly. The flowers he bought weren't for Granny, but they were for someone else, someone he loved, someone he met on *this boat*, the one we're standing on right now, and that's why he brought it here.

'India, where I met the light of my life and had my soul extinguished!' Grandpa words, words that sound so normal but have never made any sense.

Until now.

I look over at Neesh, staring out of the window of the boat. For a moment it's almost like the lines of her are blurring and blending in the misty air beyond the window.

'What happens, Neesh, what happened to the girl you saw?' I ask.

'I told you,' she says, and shudders, 'she steps off the railings, she just steps off them like she was stepping off a pavement, like her life was nothing – and then she drops towards the water like a knife, like a stone.'

'But why?' I hear myself ask.

'I don't know. I don't know, Sammy, but I think she *wants* me to know why . . . and that she's been waiting, waiting for so long . . .'

'Neesh?'

She looks away from the window, from whatever it is she can see that I can't, and she frowns slightly at the colours above my head.

'Perhaps she's been waiting for *you*, Neesh?' I say, and she walks towards me almost as though she already knows what I'm about to say.

'Wh—' she begins, but I put my finger to her lips.

'Is she about so high?' I ask, holding my palm on her head. 'And is she about this wide?' I say, circling her waist, and I see the idea grow in her eyes as she nods her head to each question.

And her long eyelashes trap her unfallen tears so that her eyes shine.

'Are her eyelashes so long that they trap tears?' I ask, and now I know I'm right. The girl Grandpa fell in love with out in India was Neesh's great-aunt, the one just like her.

Neesh blinks. Blink. Blink, blink. Freeing her tears.

'I think you're seeing your mother's aunt,' I say. 'What do you think?'

# Neesh

I nod, I can't speak, it makes too much sense.

'It's them!' says Sammy. 'It has to be, your great-aunt and my grandpa! That's why he brought the boat back here, it's where they fell in love!'

I take a deep breath. I can feel her in the air all around us. My great-aunt Farida, a healer, or a witch if you want to call it that − like me. A girl who thought she could choose, a girl who did something as terrifying as falling in love without anyone's say-so. She slept with a boy who wasn't chosen for her. She broke free of all the chains that held the women together, that swing in the air above them, and that's why they stoned her and . . . and what else?

'Why did she kill herself, Sammy?'

'Maybe she came back up?' he says.

'No, Mum always said she killed herself.'

He's silent.

'Is that what'll happen to me?' I hear my voice ask, as though he could answer.

'No, Neesh, she's trying to help us, to warn us!' he says.

'To stay apart!' I say back.

'Neesh!' says Sammy, and I can feel his voice trying to call me back to normal. 'I know it's difficult. I know you're scared, but the world is a different place these days, I mean there are people who have no problem at all with us being together – most people, I'd say – but back then they never had a chance!'

*Is that what'll happen to me too?* I'm thinking. I mean, if I look like her and I heal like her, do I have to die like her?

'It's OK, it's OK, it's OK, Neesh, it can't happen again!' Sammy's voice goes on, sane and calm and reasonable . . .

'It hasn't changed,' I say. Because I already *know* it will all happen again. I know it for certain, like knowing you're about to be sick and there's nothing you can do except wait in horror and feel your gorge rising. They're coming for me. I can't be allowed to get away, or set a bad example; neither could my aunt. The chains have to be kept linked above us all.

'But *why* would she want to die, Neesh, what happened to her?' and now his own voice sounds full of fear, of panic. 'If we know what we're up against, we can be ready for it!'

'They were together on this boat,' I hear myself say, and I don't want to turn to face the windows where I saw her shadow standing, but I do, and as I look out of it I see her standing with her hand held up to the feel of the air on her naked neck, and I turn away, fast.

'What?' asks Sammy.

'My great-aunt Farida, she was here. When they found out about them, they . . . cut her hair off . . . and she was stoned . . . I . . .'

'It's OK, it's OK, Neesh, that's not gonna happen! Don't think about it!'

'But I have to, don't I, because that's where her story stops and the picture's all broken up. We have to know what happened to her.'

# Sammy

Neesh stops and looks out again, over the lake, far away, and when I follow her gaze the lake seems bigger, wider somehow, as though the surface of it stretched all the way to the horizon.

She shivers, and her eyes darken as she watches the picture unfolding again behind her eyes, and I recognise her expression. I've seen it in Grandpa's eyes, that same darkening, and I can feel the same sinking in my stomach, the fear that's always there between us whenever I ask too many questions about the boat, or about India.

'Neesh?'

'Yeah?'

'Let's go!'

'What?' She stares at me, not getting it.

'Let's leave,' I say again, and as soon as I hear the words it makes perfect sense to me, and they're all tumbling out over each other, hardly able to wait to be said. 'Let's go, let's get away from where you live, from where I live, from this boat where they lived! Let's go, let's take off. Not your world, not my world, let's find our world!'

She stares at me as if she's thinking it through, trying to work out what to do.

'But I have to go home.'

'What?' I can't believe what I'm hearing. 'You said you can't, you said . . .'

'I know!' she says. 'But I . . . if we're really going then I need some stuff.'

'Why, Neesh? We can buy stuff.'

'Not that kind of stuff. I want some of my dad's music, and the blanket he bought me!'

'But you said it was too dangerous. We don't know what they'd do to you!'

'But they won't do anything if they're not there, will they?' she says. 'If we go to my house now we can make it before my mum gets back from the market – she always goes on Friday, five till seven, for the bargains. And Jammi's got football from five!'

'OK, but we ring the house as soon as we're round the corner, just to make sure it's empty. And tomorrow, we go away, right?'

She looks round the boat. 'Tomorrow,' she says, 'we'll leave tomorrow, early.' But she doesn't really sound like she believes it.

We run across the jetty and down through the woods to where the last of the mist is lifting as a weak sun breaks through. The trees' leaves unfold, and I remember that it's May, and everything's singing with life, like it thinks it has a future.

# Neesh

The house is empty, and it feels different, smaller. When I put my key in the lock, I almost don't think it will fit.

'Just get whatever it is you need, Neesh, and then we'll go. I'll be lookout!' I can feel our hearts pumping, beating together, and wonder how much time, how many hours we've really got left together.

Sammy stays on guard downstairs and I head for the bedroom. I open the door, and for a second I can't take it in. It's not my room. I mean, nothing in it is mine. Everything's changed. Jammi's computer's in here and all his speakers. There are piles of his stuff – games, wires, two great big speakers – and the walls have been painted, and before I know it the tears aren't just pricking the backs of my eyes, they're stabbing them. It looks like I was never here. I haven't just gone, I've been wiped clean.

'*Hello, dear,*' says a voice, and I turn. Kef's nan! And you know what? I'm pleased, so pleased to see someone who expects me to be here that the tears begin to make tracks down my cheeks.

'*It's a hard thing, change, isn't it?*' she whispers, but I can only nod.

'What did you want to tell Kef? Because I'm leaving now,' I say very slowly, very carefully, 'and I can't ever come back.'

'*Kef,*' she says and her face lights up at the sound of his name, and it shocks me, still shocks me that anyone could ever love him that much.

'*Tell Kef,*' she says, very clearly, '*that his mum wouldn't ever leave him . . . not from choice, and that I was wrong not to tell him what happened to her, and I regret it, but I thought it was for the best that he should have his father with him, even after what he'd done . . . and tell him from me . . . you can't kill someone, however hard you try, not once they've got inside you. You'll help him now, won't you, dearie?*'

And she's already fading away, turning, disappearing into the walls.

'NO!' My hand disappears inside her arm as I try to grab it and she shudders; the air around her burns a deep, deep blue. 'What do you mean?' I shout.

'*Warm!*' she says, with a great big smile on her face. '*Now, that's what I call a treat!*'

And she smiles at me.

'What did his dad do?'

'*He killed her! His father killed his mother and he did for me too, the rotten bastard. When I cottoned on to what he'd done he pushed me down the stairs, he did! Still, should never've turned my back, should I? Always was too trusting!*'

And then she gives me a sharp look. '*Why else d'you think Kef would kill his dad? He taunted him with it, his dad, good as told him he'd pushed me down those stairs! But you make sure Kef knows this, young lady: his mother would never've left him. He still doesn't know that bastard killed her . . . but two wrongs don't make a right . . . that boy . . .*' She looks so sad and lost for a moment, the old woman, and her hands twist. '*He seen things no child should see, and . . .*' Then she looks at me, right at me.

'*Thanks, love!*' she says, and then she's gone.

Completely.

I run my fingers over the air where she burned, fierce and white, for just the trace of a second before disappearing, and there's still the faintest hint of warmth in the air where she stood, but even as I feel it, it's gone.

I sit down.

Kef's mum didn't leave him. Kef's dad killed her. It *is* Kef's dad who's dead, who's the lump on the floor. And then the door bangs. It bangs once, loudly, and I hear Sammy shout out: 'Hey, Neesh!' and his voice has a tinge of terror in it.

Mum's back, I can hear her. 'And what are you robbing from me, my daughter isn't enough, you are coming back for me!' She's standing at the bottom of the stairs, hitting him with her rolled-up umbrella, then she sees me.

'Why are you standing doing nothing?' she shouts. 'Is it that there is nothing to do? Is that it, and most of it in the kitchen?' She looks Sammy straight up and down, and then she cracks him one with the umbrella, quite slowly, on the arm.

'Didn't your grandpa do enough to our family, must you join in too?' she yells at him, and then she turns to me. 'Always I told your father to leave it alone, but no, he must bring you to England, well, here we are! History running itself!' She stares at Sammy. 'Have you also taken my daughter's jewels?' she shouts.

We stare at each other, and then we get what she means,

and we can't help it, we start laughing. All the hopeless, helpless tension just rises up out of us in laughter.

'No!' Sammy manages to say. 'No, I haven't, Mrs Hussein!'

'Is it a laughing matter, a girl's jewels? Who are you thinking you are?' she says, staring up at me. 'Madonna herself, running with this man, that man − as though jewels were nothing! Your uncles found you a nice man, and now will he have you?'

I look at Mum. 'I didn't choose him, did I, Mum, so it doesn't really matter how nice he is, does it?' I say very slowly and clearly, and she draws back in horror, as though I've struck her. And then she grabs her mobile and begins pressing numbers.

She's ringing for backup.

## Sammy

Neesh takes slow, stunned steps down the stairs and wraps her hand around mine, tight. We're not laughing now, we're facing her mum who's standing in the way of the front door, speaking into her phone: 'Yes, yes, I have her here . . . and the boy!'

'No!' she says to Neesh. 'There will be no more throwing away on boys.'

I try to get past and she pushes my shoulder back, hard. That's OK, it's a hard shoulder. I keep it where it is. She puts the phone in her pocket.

'We're leaving,' I say, but she ignores me completely.

'They will be here shortly,' she says to Neesh, and then she finally looks at me. 'You should leave, you have no place here at all!' and she lifts her umbrella again.

'Don't!' Neesh's voice comes out of nowhere. 'Don't touch him!' And her mum turns to stare at her, unable to believe what she's really hearing, and that's the moment we need; we push past her and run.

'No!' her mother screams after us down the street, and I grab hold of Neesh's hand, frightened she'll turn back. She looks back over her shoulder at her mother, but she doesn't stop running.

'Jesus, your mum's crazy!' I say as the car screeches away from the kerb. But Neesh doesn't answer, and when I look at her I see she's crying silent tears. I realise I've never seen her really cry before. Not ever.

'She's not crazy,' she says after a while, when she can speak.

'No? Seems it to me!'

'What would you do, Sammy, if you knew your aunt had been treated so badly that she killed herself, and then you had a daughter who everyone said was exactly the same?'

'What do you mean?'

'I think,' she says, 'I think Mum believes she's trying to save me!' And she sounds startled and lost. I rub my arm where the umbrella made an angry dent in my bone.

'She's mad, Neesh, do you think she'll ever . . .'

'What?'

'Well, will she ever . . . well . . . like me?'

'No,' she says, flatly.

'After this, maybe, I mean, when . . .' but I don't get any further because I know I'm kidding myself, still imagining happy endings, still thinking I can change the whole world and make it see things my way. I feel hopeless and stupid.

'Where shall we head – tomorrow, I mean?' I ask. She shakes her head.

'I can't see anything after this, Sammy,' she says slowly. 'I'm not sure I want to.'

'Neesh, don't ever, you won't ever . . .?'

'What?'

'Do anything stupid, like your great-aunt did.'

'I think that's what my mum's scared of,' she says, as though she's only just worked it out. And then she does laugh, a bitter, angry laugh, and what she says next isn't especially reassuring.

'What if it's right?' she says. 'What if, one day, you realise that the "stupid thing" is the only thing left to be done? What if you'd rather die than be stoned, or locked up, or worse?'

And I don't have any answer to that, only a feeling like ants crawling through my guts, and the fear that lies behind everything I do.


# Kefin

'The woods,' that's what Jammi said, 'the woods.' The words bounce. The woods. The woods. And the picture comes without warning. Sharpens into sudden focus in Kef's mind. A wood. A lake. A place he's never meant to go. A place where Dad went fishing.

'WhAt for?' asks Knife, 'FiShing for wHat?'

'Fish!' says Kef quickly, but the thing he sees rising out of the water doesn't look like a fish, it looks like . . . Knife jabs him hard. Ow! The thought fades.

'If yOU Go doWn to the WOods today,' Knife sings. That's what Dad used to sing. He'd look at Kef as he sang it and Kef would look away.

'YoU're in for a bIg surPrise!' sings Knife. Kef looks away. He doesn't remember. He doesn't remember anything, but his feet do. Kef's feet are on the move. They know the way to the woods. The lake.

'If you go down to the woods today . . .' Kef hums as his feet move.

## Sammy

We get out of the car and walk through the woods. The air's warm and damp, flattening everything. The boat floats on the water, the way it always has, and I still don't want Neesh to be on it.

'Stay in the house, Neesh,' I say. 'Please! You don't have to stay on the boat. There's no way Grandpa would mind.'

But she just goes on staring at it as her hand slowly slips from mine. 'It's only a night. And it's weird, Sammy, but I kind of want to be near my aunt. It's not her I'm scared of, is it? – it's what happened to her.'

'You mean, the stoning?' I ask. It's hard to say the words, hard to believe it could really happen. Not here, I think, not in England in the twenty-first century. It's what happens in the Bible! 'They wouldn't do that to you, Neesh, not here – they'd have a job finding the stones!' I say, but she doesn't smile, and neither do I.

We sit down on the bank near the jetty, looking at the boat.

'But there are people who would stone me if they could,' she says slowly. 'I think I've always known it, Sammy, that if I made a wrong move I could end up here.'

'What, with me?' I try to laugh, but it still doesn't work, not for either of us.

'There's something my great-aunt needs to tell me; there's a gap, a piece of her story that's missing. Like something else happened between the time she was stoned and the time she killed herself. When I see the boat, the man and the flowers ... I ... I ...'

I wait.

'I know it's the last thing she saw before she died – and that I've spent all my life trying to make the picture move, to see what happens next, and ...'

'Yeah?'

'I couldn't, not till I was with you.'

'And?'

'And now I can't stop it moving, only I can't work out which bit goes where ...'

'Like seeing a film out of sequence?' I ask. She looks at me, and the smile she gives me is startling and sweet.

'What?' I ask.

'I didn't know . . .' she says.

'Didn't know what?'

'That people could, well, think together,' she says. 'You wouldn't know what I mean, but I've never had anyone to do that with before,' and then she laughs, 'except Kef's nan!'

I don't answer, still don't smile, just hold her hand tight and try to imagine what she means.

'I think my great-aunt Farida left me that memory,' she says, 'so I could fill in the gap in her story, find out what made her want to die.'

I smile, try not to feel too frightened. Try to understand.

'You mean, like the memory's in your genes, like the colour of your hair?'

'Maybe,' she says, 'and maybe if we can work it out we can stop it happening again.' There's a long pause.

'You mean stop it happening to you,' I say. She doesn't answer.

'Neesh, I know you want to stay here. I know you want to find out and so do I, but is it safe? Suppose Jammi works out you're here? And what about Kef?'

'I keep forgetting about Kef,' she says, and she sighs. 'What do you think it was like for them, falling in love back then, in Kashmir?'

I look at her and hear myself say, 'I don't know. Well, I

suppose we do, kind of, don't we?'

And then we do smile. 'You mean, that's what happened when we fell through that door into the sitting room?' And she grins. 'The past catching up with us? Not crazy, then?' she asks.

'No,' I say, and I hold out my hand. She takes it, and we stand up and walk over the jetty together to the front door of the boat. The door where Neesh sees flowers spilling in a golden heap. I try to imagine what she sees. To imagine marigolds piled up high between us, like a river of gold.

'Ready?' I whisper.

'Ready,' I think I hear her say, but we're not, not really. Because how can you ever be ready for that feeling when it comes? Unbidden, uncontrollable, unstoppable desire, rolling all the way through you. We stand in the doorway and we reach out for each other. A current runs through our fingers, our bodies; a connection clicks, and in the charged air between us a spark leaps. The space between us is breached and crossed over, barriers break and we're touching each other. We feel the longing inside us made real under our hands, and this time I can tell the difference between the pull from the air around us, and the longing inside me . . . I touch her face, run my fingers over the cut on her jaw, tangle my fingers in her hair, but we don't kiss.

Something stops us; because when we do we want to be sure, completely sure, that the old story's over and ours can begin. I let go of her fingers and neither of us speaks.

So that's what it's like. The way it always is, whether it's now or then, whether it's us or them, whether it's right or wrong, it always feels the same: to want someone. And sometimes, like now, it's dangerous.

We step apart. We don't want to touch each other and it's not just that it's weird knowing that stuff about your grandpa and your great-aunt, it's knowing that beyond the love and the flowers and all the feeling they had for each other is the price they had to pay.

Neesh is right. I can feel the danger in the air. No doors fly open or windows bang, but I can feel it, and we step back even further from the edges of each other, and everything feels sharp.

And in focus.

So this is the fear I've always felt somewhere deep inside me. The fear that's made me sing and work and play until there's no space left to think. This fear and sadness. Grandpa's sadness. A nameless dread. A fear of having set something terrible in motion, something so terrible that you lose the person you love the most. Neesh's hand hangs suspended between us and I want to take it in mine, but I can't.

The shock of recognition is physical, painful, like your head hitting a lamppost and only afterwards realising you've always known it was there, you've seen it every day. You just hadn't noticed it – until now.

He did this, my grandpa. Whatever happened to Neesh's aunt was because of him.

Neesh's hand drops to her side.

# Grandpa: Kashmir

I told him. In spite of everything she said, I told my uncle. He was furious.

'But we're in love!' I said over and over, and even now, all these years later, it still amazes me. That we were. That it can happen like that sometimes — with a single touch — and that once it has, the whole world has changed and can never go back on itself. Because love is a thing. It's real. A spark and then an understanding, just like knowledge.

But all I could say then was this: 'I love her!'

My uncle worked quickly. He called the servants in and told them not a word — if any had been heard — was ever to be repeated, anywhere.

'She's not something to be ashamed of!' I hissed at him.

'But your actions are; the risk you've taken with her *is* something to be ashamed of.'

'But I love her,' I howled again. And then the bearer came and whispered something in my uncle's ear.

'Too late,' he said.

By now it was dusk, and I was frantic. She was alone on the boat, waiting.

My uncle turned to me. 'You should have told me sooner! You're too late!' I still shudder when I think of his face. Of how the British white, beneath all the sunburnt Indian years, seemed to seep through his skin.

'If you had loved a single bone of her native body,' my uncle says, slowly and clearly, 'you would have had the decency to leave her alone.'

I'm stunned to silence.

'This is not a place where you can keep secrets, and it's not you who'll pay for this, is it?' His face goes even paler, and I notice that he's shaking. 'It's her!'

'What will they do?' I whisper. The sky is already dark as he leaves me.

'Stay here! You've done quite enough damage already!'

He makes sure I can't leave. To my great shame, he locks me in my room and tells the servants to guard me.

'If they find you, you might not be safe.'

And then he leaves the house.

# Sammy

I look at Neesh. I can't speak. Somehow in all the fear and understanding the words have gone. I blink at her. Blink. Blink, blink.

'Sammy?' she asks.

I stare at her. Can't she see that I've got it? I've finally got what everyone's been trying to say to me all along. It's impossible. We can't happen. The price is far too high. I stand up and go out on to the roof and after a while she follows me. We sit on the lock-up. It's hard to believe that I sat here this morning thinking so many things were possible.

In the same world. In a different world.

'You're safe as long as I'm not with you, aren't you?' I finally say. 'That's what it's all been about, hasn't it? Your aunt trying to make us see we *can't* be together, not without you paying some terrible price . . . like you being hurt, or even dying, and me having to live the rest of my life knowing I was part of the reason it happened. Like Grandpa.'

'We've already done it, Sammy. You leaving me now won't make any difference. It's too late.'

I'm stunned. Stunned like you are when you wake up in a dream; you know you're already wide awake, only then the alarm goes off and you realise you've been asleep all the time. This can't be happening.

'But it's dangerous . . . Neesh, isn't that what's happening? – we're being warned. If we're together something will happen.'

'It's *always* been dangerous,' she says, looking at me, at my eyes, at the colours above my head. The way she does it makes me feel naked, exposed. 'Nothing's changed, has it, Sammy? Except now we've decided to run away together.'

She stops and I find I have to look away from her eyes that suddenly feel too bright, that delve too deep inside me. 'Perhaps you don't want to, perhaps that's what's changed?' she asks slowly.

I shake my head, raise my eyes. 'It's not that, Neesh. I'm scared, scared for you. I mean, if what you say is right, then it's you that suffers, isn't it? I mean, Kef might come after me, but Jammi won't, he'll go for you . . . and I can't, I didn't . . .'

'What?'

'I didn't realise, Neesh, how hard it's been for Grandpa all these years, knowing that she died because of him. I can't imagine . . . I don't . . . I mean, I . . .'

'You didn't realise how dangerous it was, mixing with me,' she says, and I nod, because it's nothing but the truth.

I always thought I could make everything all right, make everyone see reason. I didn't see until now what impossible might really mean. It doesn't mean *can't happen*, which is what I always thought; it means not worth the price you might have to pay if it *does* happen. So that's how the world works. You can make a choice; we always have a choice, don't we? But what if it's not us who pays? What is it right to do then? I don't know. I don't know. I feel like I'll never know anything for sure ever again.

'I don't know what's right any more, Neesh,' I hear myself say. 'I mean, I know I want to be with you, I just don't know what to do for the best . . .'

She nods.

'I can see it,' she says.

'How?'

'Your colours have changed.'

'To nasty-bastard colours?' I say, but she doesn't even smile, just shakes her head.

'It's like they shimmer,' she says. 'They're not definite any more!'

I don't know what to say, so I don't say anything.

'Lots of people have colours like it,' she says, like she has to reassure me. 'Good people, people who think, people who don't always know the answers.' And then she smiles, a sad smile.

'What shall we do?' I ask, because I need it to be her decision, her who decides. Even if that makes me a coward, I need to know that no matter what happens she made the decisions. Neesh stares at me for a long while. She closes her eyes, and then she stands near the window and watches as dusk arrives. I don't know what she sees, or why, but I know I trust that weird bit of her that knows things. Things I never thought possible.

I wait. And as I wait the thought of ever leaving her feels less and less possible – and then she speaks.

'Go home, Sammy,' she says.

'And tomorrow?' I ask. Does she still want to leave with me?

'Sammy, I can't go back and I can't go forward, not yet. I need to know what happened to my great-aunt, and for that I need to be here tonight.'

I nod. 'OK, but tomorrow we can both leave together, right?'

She nods. 'But tonight you *need* to go, Sammy. We need stuff if we're really leaving. I don't even know what stuff, but you do. And you need to see your mum, say goodbye.'

I feel a stab in my guts at the thought of leaving Mum, leaving like Dad did. I bury it under the usual stuff, stuff like thinking that we can't leave without the guitar so that I can busk for cash. We need food for a few days, and I should get all my cash out on the way home tonight. I need to load up the tent, the camping gear. How much can we fit in the car?

When I look at Neesh she's almost smiling.

'Wh—?' I begin.

But before I can finish she says, 'There's this particular shade of green and it nearly always means lists . . .'

'I don't want to go,' I say.

She holds up her palm to stop me talking. I place my own against it, and we stand there, palm to palm, not moving, not speaking, not wanting time to continue, but it does, doesn't it?

It always does.

It's Neesh who lets her hand drop first. I watch as my legs take me to the door, the deck, across the gangplank . . . and she stands by the windows and watches me leave. When I turn back at the gate she's still there, staring into the growing darkness for my shape. When I stop at the top of the hill, in the last place you can see the boat, she's still there, and I think I see her lift her hand, and the brief flash of her palm as she waves.

And I wonder. Are we ever really in control, or are we just stepping in footprints that are already there and waiting for us?

# Grandpa: Kashmir

Sitting here, looking out over the lake every evening watching the sun leave the sky, I wish so many things.

But most of all I wish this.

I wish that I had never left her there on the boat.

Waiting.

Waiting for me to come back.

# Sammy

I get in the car and sit there as though I've been hit. I look at my watch like it could explain something to me, but it just says it's Friday. I don't know how long I sit there, but when I next look at my watch it's nine p.m. and it's still Friday and I think, they'll all be down the Anchor, the whole crowd. I start the car, I worry about Jammi, but even if he works out where she is he'll probably spend ages trying to get into the house. With any luck the alarm'll go off and he'll end up in a police cell. He won't be able to find the boat in the dark, no way. So I reckon Neesh is still safe, at least for one more night.

Kef only appears in my mind briefly, a flash in the dark. I mean, there's no way he can know where she is. And in the morning, I hold the thought to myself, in the morning we'll be gone. I press my foot down . . . faster.

When I get home I lean against the car door and take a deep breath before going in. I look at the sky. It's that deep, deep blue-black it can only ever be in spring. A bird sings and the stars are spaced out across the heavens. I hear Neesh's voice asking me, 'Do the stars move?'

*No. They don't*, I think, *they're stuck, stuck just like people.* People like Sean and Leah and Dunc and all that lot. They can't move, not like the earth. Not like us. And I'm glad we're leaving, even if I'm still standing here outside, too scared to go indoors because I don't know how to leave Mum without saying goodbye. I lock the car and go in.

She's reading, her legs curled beneath her and her glasses slipping down her nose.

'Sammy! Hi!' she says. 'Not down the Anchor?'

'Nah,' I say, 'not in the mood.'

'Not surprised,' she says. 'How's Gita?'

'Oh! Er . . . hanging on, but we're not allowed to see her or anything.'

She looks at me.

'You look awful!' she says.

'Thanks, Mum!'

'Glass of wine? Beer?'

'Sounds good.'

And we smile.

And it's a normal night, until she remembers it tomorrow.


# Neesh

The light seems to disappear from the sky in the time it takes Sammy to get from the boat to the brow of the hill. I wave at him. I know he'll try to come back, what I don't know is if he'll actually make it. I already know life doesn't always turn out the way you want it.

I turn back to the boat. The door's half open, the light spilling on to the veranda, breaking through the darkness like a river of flowers.

'What happened?' I whisper to myself, to my aunt Farida, and I try not to notice that I'm in exactly the same place as she was all those years ago, standing on a boat, waiting. Waiting for Sammy to come back, waiting for the girl, my great-aunt, to tell me her story. Waiting for whatever it is that's coming next.

Slowly I walk through the spilled light, through the sitting room and up the ladder on to the roof of the boat, and she's there, standing on the railings, perfectly balanced between the past and the future, between life and death, between me and *my* future.

She's not looking out over the lake but back behind me, over her shoulder. I turn in the direction of her gaze to see what she's looking at. The dislocation between worlds is brutal this time, wrenching . . .

*Fear. Feet thumping. Heart pumping as she heads for the woods. She's stopped. Runs into something, hits it hard and stops. Stands back.*

*She keeps her eyes down, tries to lift her dupatta over her shorn head, as though it could cover her up, as though it could save her. But it's too late.*

*Her arms are caught from behind. She doesn't fight, she's too scared.*

*She can't be saved.*

*She has broken the code, and now she has to be broken herself. That's what she thinks at first, and then she looks up and sees their faces . . .*

I tear my gaze away. Straighten up, remind myself of where I really am.

I look up at the stars that seem so cold and far away. I

remember something Sammy once told me, that the stars we see aren't really shining now; that it takes so long for their light to reach us that some stars are as old as the prophet himself (peace be upon him) shining in a sky full of memories.

I keep my eyes away from the shape on the railings. I'm frightened but I don't want to cut my palm or hold my breath, or do any of the things I've always done to stop the fear inside me, because I know now what I'm really frightened of; I'm frightened of all the life that's inside me now, of the hope and the desire to live – of the longing. I don't know what to do with it all, but my body does.

It does something I haven't done for a long time. Something I thought I'd forgotten how to do. It turns to face east, towards dawn and all hope of a tomorrow.

I kneel with my head to the floor and the words come slowly at first, in a trickle ... *Allah most great, most merciful, most compassionate and most kind* ... before they begin to flow like a deep remembered river all the way through me. The words move past my lips and out into the night sky. Return to the world, to each living thing they've grown from. And I don't know if Mohammed (peace be upon him) is up there, or if he can really hear me. All I know is that this is my plea, my prayer in the dark of night for everything that lives, including me and Sammy. I ask for us to be allowed to think, to be allowed to feel and to be allowed to live and make our choices, even if they're bad ones.

The night is breezeless and the soft lamplight falls on the dark water. My prayer is finished and I'm ready now to look up into the dark eyes of my aunt as she balances on the railings. She waits as she has always waited, for Sammy's grandpa, for me, for her story to be told and for justice to follow. I watch over her . . .

*They don't take her far. Far enough away to be amongst the trees. She can still see the light that falls from the soft lamp of the boat, like a pool on the dark water. Steady and bright. She turns her head to it as she feels her back hit the grit of the sandy earth. The light's a link and she clings to the sight of it across the black water, in another world, a world before this.*

*She stares at the light. She looks up at the stars that stare back at her, cold, unmoved. She doesn't look, but she can still feel them, one after the other, quick and brutal.*

*She remembers flowers falling through the air, landing all around her.*

She is dead meat.

*She hears the words whispered in her ear, insults issued like engines to power them.*

*She watches the stars slowly crossing the sky, feels the earth beneath her back and the heaviness of the bodies one after the other beating against her, inside her.*

*She answers the whispered insults with a prayer. She whispers the words to herself, and they make a rope, a rope she holds on to, the words holding her ceaselessly as the stars go on shining above her and the earth slides beneath her back until it can no longer hold her up as the world slowly loses its meaning.*

Dead meat.

*They disappear as though they'd never been. She doesn't move. She doesn't know what's mud and what's her, where her body ends and this new shell-sharp world begins. Perhaps they think she's dead, but she isn't. Slowly she crawls back to the boat, retracing the stones and rocks that lie in a trail. She picks up the largest, holds them.*

*She dresses in white and slowly walks on to the roof of the boat. The rocks are in her pockets. The world is pale and blue and cold as breath.*

*She sees a man, a man poling a boat full of flowers across the lake, caught between the land and the sky. Between the perfect reflection of the mountains in the water and the mountains themselves, reaching up to the clouds.*

*She remembers, from somewhere deep and lost inside her, the touch of a boy's wrists beneath her fingers and the feel of his hands beneath her, breaking her fall. She wonders about the mountains below the water. She wonders if maybe there's a whole universe under there, perfect and inverted, where maybe they'll meet. Where his hands still wait, held out, and ready and waiting to catch her.*

*And then she steps up on to the rails . . . the man still punts his flowers through the water. As she knows he will tomorrow, and tomorrow and forever, in a world that will go on without her . . . and so she steps out into the air and she thinks she hears him cry out, the boy, but by then it's too late. By then she's already falling.*

*'No!' The boy's scream echoes over the lake, shatters the still-ness of the morning.*

*She hits the water and the glass-like surface of it shatters, the*

*whole world fractures, her legs catch in the strangling weed and it's
too late to turn back . . .*

I turn away. I close my eyes. I realise I'm standing on the
roof of the boat holding my arms out as though they could
catch her. At least I think that's what I'm doing, only my
arms are wrapped right around myself and I'm rocking, and
rocking.

'He did come!' I say to her. 'He did come back!'

Sammy's grandpa nearly got there, and she heard him,
but she was already falling. It was too late. I hear Mum's
words, '*Don't ever throw yourself away, like her.*'

I look up. She's back on the railings looking out over the
lake, seeing what I have always seen. A lake, a man and a
boat full of flowers, stuck on like collage – and I wonder
what it might be like to be stuck for all eternity in one
moment, the moment you wish had never happened. The
moment you realised it was too late to turn back. And then
my great-aunt turns and looks straight at me.

'It's OK,' I whisper to her – well, to myself really – 'I'm
not going to hurt myself any more.' And it's true, I'm not.
I'm not going to slit my wrists, or hold my breath till I faint
or kill myself, and I'm not going to hang my head in shame
– because I don't want to die. I used to. I used to think it
was always something I could do to get away, the one final
place where no one could follow me. But now I want to
live, even though being alive is often mostly shit. Life's
frightening and it hurts and it doesn't matter whether you
wear a dupatta or a beanie, nothing can protect you from

life itself.

Q: Is that what it's all really about? Do Mum and Jammi think that if I stay at home and wear the right things and marry who they choose that I'll never be hurt? Or do they just enjoy the power? I don't know any more.

A: There aren't any answers.

Once more I hear Mum's words: '*If you behave as though you have choices, it gives everyone choices.*'

*Yeah*, I think, *including the choice not to behave like an arse-hole*. I don't know what will happen next, but I do know this: if Jammi or Kef want me they'll have to find me, and if they find me and they don't like what they see they'll have to make their choices. And if I'm still alive afterwards, like she was, they'll have to kill me.

Because I'm not doing it for them.

I'll make them live with their choices. I'll let the world see what they've done.

And when I look up my aunt is right on the rails look-ing at me, and I'm not sure but I think she's smiling, and I hear myself think, *Tell him, tell Sammy's grandpa she heard him: she knew he came back.*

'I will,' I whisper . . .

. . . *and she takes her step, a small step off the railings, and she drops like a stone* . . .

And even though I know it will happen, am expecting it, my heart still drops with her.

And this time, she doesn't come back.

The railings are empty.

# Kefin

By the time Kef gets there it's nearly dark. He begins climbing to the top of a low hill. He's a commando on a mission, but what mission? He turns.

In a split second Knife answers him: 'To rId the WoRld of the fuCkers! At it liKe RaBbits, arEn't thEy?' says Knife. 'I mEan, the mOre baby buNnies, the moRe for them on tHe social, innit. HOw elSe aRe thEy goNna taKe oVer the woRld, and what I waNna know is, wHat've we gOt to deFend ourSelves wiTh?' Knife looks at Kef. 'FuCk aLl, thAt's wHat.'

'Yeah,' whispers Kef, 'that's what Dad used to say.'

Kef holds the knife up in the faint moonlight so that it can guide him. He follows it up the hill through the ancient oak, ash and beech woods. He likes to look at the blade all glistening and shiny-clean. He likes it, how he can just wipe off the blood and make the blade shine again.

'DoN't worry,' says Knife, 'we'll fiNd them. YOu and me, KEf, going fisHing. FiRst little mIss PaKi can plAy raBbits wiv us, and theN she's deAd meat!'

Kef feels a stab of excitement and fear when Knife says that. He stumbles through the wood following Knife. He has no coat, and even though spring has finally come, the nights are cold. He shuffles leaves aside, he's glad he's with Knife. When he reaches the top of the hill he senses the blade faltering in his hand as it drops to his side.

'Tired?' he whispers anxiously to the gleaming metal,

because Kef is, Kef's exhausted. Sometimes he catches himself wishing Knife would sleep, but he never seems to. Kef sits with his back against a tree trunk. Carefully he folds the gleaming blade back into the groove of its resting place.

'Sleep, now,' he whispers, which is what he'd like to do. He holds the knife close, folded up against his chest, like a child at prayer.

But Knife is hungry, hungry, hungry. He can't sleep, he whispers at Kef's nodding head, at his folding legs. 'Hungry, hungry, hungry.'

Silently, Kef lifts the cuff of his trousers and carves a small circle around his ankle. Knife sighs.

'Rest time, rest now, Knife,' whispers Kef, and his voice sounds soft and comforting as he cradles the knife in his pocket.

It's tiring feeding Knife all the time. He only eats one thing, blood. Kef has to find blood for the knife. He has to find Neesh and Sammy; Knife needs feeding, and maybe when he's fed Knife with Neesh then Knife will sleep. Kef would like that. If Knife would sleep, then he could too.

He closes his eyes. Spiders run silently across the leaves and over his sleeping body. It's hard to tell the difference now, between the forest floor and the leaf-strewn muddy boy. Only the occasional twitch shows he's alive, and that he's dreaming . . .

*He's watching, watching through the leaves and mud. He can see two people. He knows them. He knows them intimately, but it's frustrating because in the dream he can't remember their names.*

*He can see two bodies moulding to each other as they turn in the falling sunlight. He can't tell if they're fighting or hugging. And then he hears Dad's voice.*

'Fuck off, Kef! Go and play in the big pond . . .'

In his sleep he holds the knife closer, curls his hand around it and sighs. Even in his sleep, the place he's in, the woods, the trees and the leaves, all feel familiar. And his dreams are right. This place is where Dad took him and Mum fishing. Is this where Kef saw his mum burst up suddenly from the ground, like a startled pheasant, and start running for the lake? He watched Dad gaining on her.

*Run, Mum, run*, he's thinking.

*Run rabbit, run rabbit*, he thinks, like the nursery rhyme, and then Mum's in the water and . . . in his sleep Kef hears his mum call his name. He hears it loud and clear.

'KEFIN!' and the scream drags his heart straight out of sleep and pumps it into sudden wakefulness, so that he finds himself standing, eyes wide open and Knife in hand – yet blinded by the darkness.

'I'm coming!' he shouts, and his words startle the night creatures so that they rustle for safety. He stabs out wildly at the night, at the fear tightening his veins and spreading through his whole body.

'Who's there?' he calls. 'Who are you?'

But there's no answer, only the wood slowly returning to silence and the sound of his own rapidly beating heart and the blade of Knife, casting a faint light into the darkness. He doesn't remember the dream, or the words he screamed out. He only knows he's got to get to his mum.

But where is she?

Maybe Neesh has got her all locked up inside her, like she's got Nan.

Then he feels Knife in his hand, sees the blade in the moonlight. His heart slows. It's all right, Knife's here, Knife will know what to do. He holds the blade close, and whispers, 'It's all right, Mum, it's all right, I'm coming!'

# Neesh

I turn away from the empty railings. The night is dark, but it isn't really silent, it never is. At dusk the waterfowl calls echo and a heron's wings beat over the boat. Sometimes there's the stink of a fox as it passes, hot and musky, or the flutter of a flock of starlings settling on the reeds, disappearing like smoke or a thought forgotten. It's only in these few first moments of true dark that the world is silent and surprised, realising it's night.

'I'm coming!'

The words split the night apart and I know he's here in the dark woods up above me. I stand behind the windows of the boat and glance at the soft lights still shining on the water, and then I turn as fast as I can and switch them off. The dark descends immediately, swiftly, and I feel my way back around the boat searching for a weapon, any weapon. There's nothing. The knives are old and blunt. In the end I find a blowtorch, the type of thing you make crème brûlée with. I search with my fingers in the pitch-black darkness for the igniter.

'*Kefin!*' A woman's voice echoes through my skull and I see a wet face with water streaming down its sides and her mouth is wide open like a fish on land, gasping for air. '*Kefin!*' the mouth screams, and then suddenly the whole face is forced back under, under the water, and the vision's gone.

'I'm coming!' he calls.

His words sink through my skin, crawl over nerve endings and drive me up from where I'm crouched in the dark by the kitchen cupboard. I'm searching, searching for the best place to hide.

*Who for?* I think. *Who are you coming for?*

But I already know the answer: he's coming for me.

# Grandpa: Kashmir

I waited until it was nearly dawn, and then I climbed out of the window and began to run. The sky is as pale as my breath on the chill air, and when I break through the trees that surround the lake I see her in the distance, on the roof of the boat. A shape. A slim pale column of air that I know is her. I gasp, I take a big, deep, drawing breath of relief that she's still there. I watch as she steps up on to the railings on the roof of the boat; she doesn't look down or backwards, but straight ahead to where a man punts a boat full of flowers through the endless pale reflection of the mountains in the water. My eyes drift from her to the man, and when they return, they see her as ... she takes a step forwards and falls. Her veil flies straight up into the air like a kite-tail longing to break free, tethered to the falling kite.

'No!'

I hear my own scream echo around the lake. See the water close over her and become still and endless, an unbroken reflection of the unmoved mountains.

I hear my feet pound on the sandy earth, run faster, ready to dive into the water.

A hand stops me. Pulls me back.

'No, Jake.' His voice is soft but his hands are like steel. I look up.

This is the moment.

They are already lifting her body out of the lake. The men hold her flat between them. I remember the lightness of her landing in my arms. The water pours off the planes of her face, weighs down her white clothes so that they cling to her body like my hands. The water drips from the cloth in rivers, slowing already to bright drops. Her hair is shorn and her neck bare. Her face is like marble, already sculptured and unreal.

I move to hold her, to save her from the glare of others. But my uncle's arms close around my chest like a band holding my heart in place. I don't know where the women come from. They land like crows and they take her from the men. They begin to walk away, her body hanging loose between them like a carcass.

It's only then that I realise they aren't going to save her.

I pull against my uncle's arms.

'No, Jake,' he says again. His arms are so tight I can barely breathe, but his words are soft and sad, despairing. 'You *must* realise, this *is* another country.'

I struggle then. I struggle and fight to get to her, knowing that there's a chance for the water to empty from her lungs, for the air to revive them, but my uncle is stronger than me. I know then – in that precise moment – that the world is not just a backdrop for us to act our lives out against, but a thing in itself, a force that will always be bigger, greater, stronger and more in control than we are; my mind collapses under the knowledge of it.

It's a surprisingly physical feeling, a young mind breaking. Like a green twig bent over and over and twisted beyond endurance until finally it snaps.

I start to weep, and you might think it was the agony of it, the loss; and yet, more than any of that, it was the sheer frustration, the hopeless, useless, pointless bloody stupidity, and the waste of it all.

We didn't speak of it, that wasn't the way then. But there were whispers. That was the way too. What else is there when the truth can't be spoken?

I sit on my bed. I see her. I see her over and over, her sleeves rolled up and her golden arms spread out as wide as her smile as she lets herself fall backwards into a river of flowers, not knowing if they will hold her up, will catch her.

I hold on to that picture. I've held on to it for years. When I inherited White Barn I built a monument to each moment I had with her. I dug a lake, planted trees, shipped a boat halfway across the world and kept it near me.

But now I'm back here. Here, where it really all happened. I can feel her rising up in me with every glimpse of the lake, with each dawn, and with every sunset her presence unfolds.

Is it haunting?

Is it memory?

Is there a difference?

I don't know. I only know this, that there is no justice to be had in a story that remains untold.

And now I'm back where I can feel her presence, I know this too: that there can never be only the moments that we choose to remember, however beautiful, because there is also this: there is the truth.

# Sammy

The day hasn't quite broken when I sit bolt upright in bed and realise I'm awake, with my heart beating so fast I think it might break right through my chest. I don't stop to think, I just get up and run. I'm still dressed, with the car keys in my pocket. I've already packed everything. I drive fast along the empty roads, making every single speed camera flash behind me. When I get to the woods I run straight for the lake. I've never seen it like this before; it's so silent. A high mist is rising off the water, obscuring the trees, so that the whole place looks like it's been etched on crumpled tissue paper, like it barely exists. For just a moment I think I see Neesh floating on the water – no, above it, as though she was being carried, with the water running off the clothes that cling to her body, but it's just my freaked-out mind and the mist making pictures.

'Neesh!' I shout, but there's no answer. 'Neesh?'

And then I'm standing just outside the door of the boat. 'It's me, Sammy!' I shout, and something tells me not to open the door straight away, not without being very, very careful. I'm scared, I realise I don't know what I'll find. I twist the handle, imagine my hand over hers, see us both falling through the door and into each other's arms.

The door opens slowly and the part of the room I can see is empty, but I can't open the door the whole way back because there's someone, or something, behind it. For a moment it's stalemate, no one moves. I imagine smashing the door against the wall, but I don't, I still think it might be Neesh behind there.

'Neesh?' I say again. No answer. I reach out for the door and slowly begin to pull it back towards me, so I can look around it.

She's standing just behind the door, and she's holding Grandpa's crème brûlée blowtorch in one hand and an igniter in the other. And for a moment, even though her eyes are open as wide as the whole sky, I don't think she can see me. And then she focuses and she falls forward, her head hitting my chest, her hands still holding on to her weapons.

'I heard him,' she says. 'I heard him in the night, he's here, in the woods.'

'Who?'

'Kef.' She just says the one word, but it's enough for me to understand why she's spent the whole night waiting behind the door, an igniter in one hand and a blowtorch in the other. I don't know how I do it but I smile, and I reach out for her weapons and try to take them off her, but I can't; her fists are set rigid, can't let go. I guide her to the window seat.

'Sammy.' She says my name like somewhere along the way she forgot I was real, like it's all she's had to cling to through a long night. 'I didn't think you'd come, I thought they'd come.'

'Who, Neesh?'

'Just . . . them,' she stutters. 'The boys,' I think I hear her say.

'They wouldn't stand a chance,' I whisper, 'not against you and your blowtorch! They'd be syrup!' I see her face try to smile, but it's forgotten how, it's set rigid in a mask of fear. 'But it's me here now,' I say. 'I came, I'm here, and we're going now, Neesh, we're going to go as fast and as far away as we can. Away from here, so drop the blowtorch and get packed.'

'Too late!' she whispers. 'He's here, and if he's here, Sammy . . .' She can't say it, neither can I . . . where are the others?

'I don't see anyone standing at the gate, and has Jammi got a car? 'Cos I have!' She looks at me then, and something seems to dawn across her face, like hope.

'Here,' I say, 'let me take these.' And she lets go, and then gazes at the blowtorch and igniter in my hands like she doesn't know what they are, or what they're doing here.

'Go?' she asks.

'Yeah, we're going, right now. We're leaving the city.'

She shakes her head. 'You can't. You can't leave all this, it . . . it's . . . yours,' she stutters, 'it's where you . . . you . . .' and she seems to wrench the word out of herself, '. . . belong.'

'Neesh,' I say quietly, 'I've been scared of losing things my whole life, but never of losing places, only people. I can see what Grandpa's life's been like after he lost the girl he loved. I've lived with how angry my mum is that he didn't love her mum best, and so I don't give a flying fuck for any place that hasn't got you in it. Got that?'

She turns her face to me, and the look in her eyes is like a cold sunflower unexpectedly finding the sun, and then she looks away, unable to believe me. I don't bother with words any more, I just pick her up and walk out of the door. I look around at the lake and the trees and the world I've always known and I say goodbye to it, just like she's had to, and it hurts more than I ever thought it could – and now I understand what Neesh has already done for me. Given up her world. So now we're quits.

'We're off,' I whisper, but only a coot answers. I put Neesh down on the jetty but her knees give way. She's exhausted, and I realise we can't make it through the woods like this. I need to get the car up closer. It is possible, but it means driving carefully through the trees and that takes time. It also means leaving her, which is something I don't want to do, not with Kef around, but I know it'll be quicker than us both crashing through the woods together like an open target.

I stop to think.

I'm not so scared of Kef – one on one, and feeling the way I'm feeling and armed with the blowtorch, I think I can manage him – but I am totally freaked by the idea of Jammi and his army, by what they might do to Neesh if they find her and by how easily they could take me out.

'Who's out here, Neesh, do you know?'

She shakes her head. 'Kef, I think.'

'Just Kef?' She shrugs. I make a decision.

'Neesh,' I say, 'I've got to get the car closer. We have to be quick and we have to be quiet, it's the best way. I'll be five minutes at most. Look,' I give her my watch, point out the minutes. She nods, and I give her my iPod too, just for company, and so she knows I mean it, I'll be back. She nods, swallows, blinks. Blink. Blink, blink. I hand her the torch and igniter and she holds them close.

'Second thoughts,' I say, 'don't use the iPod, keep listening.' A shadow of a nod again, and I stand up. 'I'll be back,' I say, 'sooner than you can light that thing.'

## Kefin

Kef wakes up suddenly, frighteningly, unaware that he's been asleep. Something's woken him. He hears it, the sound of a car somewhere beneath him, in the woods. He slowly slips Knife out of his pocket and together they stand up.

He sees a red car on the track below, going slowly enough for him to dodge through the trees on the hill and keep it in sight. He watches as it stops, and he sees Sammy leap out and begin to run.

'BINGO!' whispers Knife. 'Six numBers in a wEekeNd . . . feCkin' lOttery.'

Sammy runs quickly through the trees. Kef and Knife follow him. The boy's hard to keep in sight. He's running fast and they can barely keep up with him. Then he just seems to disappear.

Slowly Kef hunkers down, knees up, feet slipping under the leaves. What if it's a trap?

What if Sammy's waiting for them behind a tree? He reaches for some mud and smears some under his eyes: that's better, he's invisible now. Slowly he circles the place where Sammy disappeared, round and round he goes, until he sees the gate.

Knife smiles.

'We gOt 'em. WaTch out Mr aNd Mrs RaBbit,' he whispers, 'we're coMin' to the buRrow!'

Kef climbs back up the hill, to where they can see what's behind the fence. There's a lake.

*'Go play in the big pond, Kef!'*

The words ring in his ears, in his dad's voice.

There's a houseboat. They can see Sammy standing at the door.

'C'Mon, come oUt to play, little bunny!' Knife says, and Kef feels a cold shiver all the way down his spine. It's freaky when Knife does that.

'I uSed to shOot raBbits,' says Knife.

'I used to fish,' says Kef.

'I don't thiNk so!' says Knife, but his eyes never leave the boat.

They watch as Sammy slowly pushes the door open. Kef shivers. What if Dad jumps out, what if he's in there? But nothing happens except that Sammy slowly brings the door back towards him and looks behind it.

'CoMe on oUt, little bunny,' whispers Knife.

Sammy disappears. Kef and Knife wait until he comes back, with Neesh in his arms, and walks towards the edge of the boat, and suddenly Kef finds he's standing up . . .

'No! No!' he shouts. 'Not near the water!' Knife has leapt to his hand, is with him.

Kef hears his mum's voice. He hears it, hears it loud and clear in his mind, screaming his name.

*KEFIN!*

'FuCk's saKe, shUt it!' whispers Knife. 'We'Ll neVer caTch a raBbit wiTh you maKin' thAt raCket!'

Kef sits down suddenly as though the breath's been knocked right out of him. He tries to breathe but the voice goes on pounding in his head, calling him. Knife jabs him hard in the thigh.

'Fuck!' says Kef, but it stops the voice. He's grateful.

'TiMe to PiCk up BuNny-Boy!' says Knife.

And they get up, the knife and the boy, and head down the hill – hand in hand.

# Sammy

I run to the car; we're close, so close to getting away. I picture the roads we'll take, the A40 all the way west to Wales. The names of the places run through my head: Witney, Cheltenham, Monmouth, Crickhowell, Bwlch, all the way until we begin to head off the map somewhere between Llandovery and Lampeter. We can camp near a lake I know right in the middle of all the green, green woods . . . thank God summer's finally arrived, it'll get warmer . . . me and Neesh . . . in a tent under the stars . . . free . . . away from all the . . . and then I see the car. Did I really leave the door wide open? I'm leaning in and checking the packing, because we'll need room for a camping stove, a—

I don't hear him at all, I just feel it on my neck, and I know straight away exactly what it is and who's holding it – it's a blade. And the weird thing is, the steel doesn't feel cold at all. It feels warm, as warm as skin.

'Don't move!'

I don't.

Kef moves the knife from my neck all the way down my spine, and he's telling me to move slowly, very slowly, all the way up the hill. And I do. I do exactly what he says, but I can't make my mind go slowly. My mind's pumping. My mind knows Neesh is all alone on the boat, waiting for me. I wonder how long she'll wait? *Please, not too long, don't wait too long*, I think as I'm prodded up the hill; I can see her alone and terrified and waiting for the thing she always said would happen, the thing I thought we could escape, and my insides turn liquid with fear and I hear my words to her, *I'll be back,* but I won't, will I? She'll be waiting, but it won't be me who comes through the door this time. Will it?

I try to run, but before my foot's even hit the ground I feel the knife press its tip deeper into my back as though it could read my mind.

'You wOn't be any gooD to MiSs BuNny if you're deAd, now, will yOu?'

I go very, very still. Suddenly I'm not sure it's Kef behind me, his voice doesn't sound right.

'GoOd boY, now you Just sIt here by this tRee and do as you're toLd.'

I sit down. The knife doesn't move – it follows me as I slide all the way down the trunk of the tree.

'Hands behind the tree,' the voice says, and I put them there. Is it Kef talking? I can't work it out, and then I feel my hands being tied, quickly, tightly, irrevocably, and I realise what they took from the car. The rope.

And I go crazy struggling against the ropes, but they've tied me tight to a tree, and I've lost my chance, can't run now, can't do anything.

'TCh, Tch, TCh,' says the voice from behind me. 'You really ought to know better, consorting with the enemy!'

'What?' What does he mean?

And then Kef appears. He looks like a freak. He is a freak. He's got long streaks of mud all over his face and his eyes look unnaturally shiny. He looks like a wild creature, haunted by demons. I try to back away, but I'm tied up. He doesn't seem to even notice that I want to get away from him. He's talking to me like I'm his friend!

'Sorry about this, Sammy,' he whispers, and then he leans in close. 'I have to do it.' He holds the knife up to my face. I back my head up, steady it against the tree. At first I think he's going to cut my throat. I wonder if it will hurt.

I hope it's not Mum who finds me. I hope someone *does* find me. But he doesn't cut my throat. He cuts me from under my ear all the way down to the point of my chin. He does it slowly and cleanly and he looks so totally concentrated, he looks like a child with his tongue out, drawing. He's so into it that for one sick moment, I think he's going to actually lick the knife clean – but he doesn't. He just cleans the knife carefully on the grass, and disappears again.

It doesn't even hurt, I'm so scared. I'm shaking. I can feel the blood dripping down my neck. What's he going to do, what are they going to do?

What are they going to do to Neesh? Through the trees I can see the glitter of the water of the lake. How can I keep them up here with me, away from her?

*Neesh, Neesh, Neesh.* I find I'm calling her name over and over and over inside till it twists and turns in my guts. I repeat it over and over as though she could hear me.

# Neesh

I wait. After a while I stand up. I walk to the windows and look out, wondering where he is. Slowly I begin to realise that he might not be coming. The numbers on the face of his iPod turn over. I watch the time passing – and he still doesn't come. The mist disappears, the leaves of the trees unfurl in the sun. I begin to think that if I don't move soon, someone will come to find me – but not Sammy.

It won't be Sammy.

'Dad?' I whisper.

*Hahnji*, I imagine him reply.

'What am I waiting for?' I ask him. But before he can answer I look out of the windows. I imagine Gita and her gang cutting my hair. I imagine them throwing stones. I think I see shadows hovering on the edge of the lake, waiting for me against the line of the trees. *There's nothing there, Neesh*, Dad whispers, and he's right. There's nothing but the sun shining on the lake and the odd gentle breeze through the newly spread leaves. I reach for my dupatta to cover my head; that's not there either. It's gone.

Where are you, Sammy?

*I'll be back*. I hear his words again and I know he meant each one of them, but I also know this: I know the world is bigger than us and sometimes we can't stop it. Is he in his car? Has it overturned? Is he crawling through the woods, trying to get to me? Is he standing facing Jammi, eyes flicking from face to face, wondering how to get away?

Where are you, Sammy?

And this time the answer comes almost as soon as I ask the question. I hear him chanting my name over and over. I let my body go, let it listen, let it answer Sammy the way it always has. Slowly I feel myself begin to turn like a stick finding water, like a needle pointing north. I begin to spin, to search for him until I stop. I'm facing the long hill up from the boat, and my own name flies down the hill towards me – *Neesh, Neesh, Neesh*. My heels rock on the boat and I struggle to stay standing. I'm rubbing the new scab on my jaw and it suddenly feels raw and new, wide open. And now I know. It's Kef and he's cut him, he's cut Sammy.

I walk into the kitchen. I don't know what to do. The numbers on the iPod turn over and over, making time pass, and I feel like the whole world's waiting, waiting, waiting for me to make a decision. I reach for the old blunt scissors and lift them, begin to hack at my hair.

My great-aunt Farida waited. She waited and look what happened to her. I imagine her running. I feel the sudden halt as she crashes blindly into a body. I feel the breath leave her body as her back hits the forest floor. I close my eyes, squeeze them tight.

Blink. Blink, blink.

But when I open them everything is exactly the same, and waiting for me to make a decision.


## Sammy

The sun's behind me, my phone's fallen out of my pocket and it beeps, low battery. If I can just position it right, I'm thinking, the sun might flash off its screen – that's how desperate I am. I kick at it.

'It's no good without your hands,' says Kef calmly. He lights up and takes a long, slow drag, never taking his eyes off the lake. The boat is bathed in sunshine. Nothing moves on the water. If Neesh is in there she's staying very, very still. From where we are her only option is to slip out of the other kitchen window down the side of the boat, and slide along the bank until she's under cover, but how would she know that?

*Don't come out, please, don't come out,* I think to myself, and then I try to get Kef to look away.

'You don't smoke!' I say. Kef hates smoking. His dad smoked about a hundred a day.

'I do now,' is all he says, eyes unmoving.

'Are you alone?' I ask, because I've still got this weird feeling it wasn't him holding the knife to my neck, that it's not just him and me here somehow.

Kef looks shifty, and I wonder. I mean, he's never really had any mates, so maybe this is how he's got one, by promising me and Neesh as bait. My heart hammers in my chest, the cut on my jaw throbs. What's happening?

I don't know how Kef has found us, but if he can, so can Jammi.

I wonder how long it'll be before he's in the woods.

'Watch out, Kef, you know Jammi's after me, don't you?' I try anything to build up some communication, some hope. He doesn't answer me, just drops his fag and grinds it out in the leaves. I look for any sparks; it makes you nervous being tied up, very nervous. Kef gets his knife out and holds it open, towards me. If he wants to scare me, he's succeeding.

'Meet Knife,' he says.

'Yeah,' I manage, 'we're acquainted.'

'He likes you,' he goes on.

'Yeah,' I say, 'still, it's not that great, the odds, is it? I mean, you and a knife against Jammi and his mates?'

He doesn't answer, just holds the knife closer and bends towards it, almost as though he was listening to it. Christ, he's holding it right up near my eyes.

'Hold it up to the light,' I manage to say – my voice sounds calm, but my heart's banging about in my ribs like a caged wild animal – 'where I can see it properly.'

He does, and the sun glances off the blade, and I call out inside to Neesh.

*Please be looking, please see this. Here. Neesh. Here I am.*

*RUN!* I shout out to her with every bone inside my body. *Don't stay on the boat, NEESH! Please! Don't wait for me!*

Kef's behind me, whispering again. I decide there must be someone with him. Maybe he's deformed, burned or scarred or something, and that's why he won't show his face. I try to get him out into the open, to include him in the conversation, but nothing's working.

'What do you want with Neesh, anyway?' I ask.

'YOu mEan yoU're woRried about Miss BuNny?'

And again I can't work out if it's Kef or not. I feel hands reach around the tree and the knife's back at my throat. I close my eyes. Feel the tip of the blade against the pulse in my neck and realise I don't want to die not here, not alone in the woods with two crazies. It's all I can do not to piss myself.

'We'Re oFf to plAy!' says the scary voice.

'Hey, stay for a bit!' I try.

'NOw, nOw,' he says, 'no keEping little Miss BuNny raBbit all to yourself!'

He giggles, and I know I've never heard Kef sound like this. My mind is leaping around looking for somewhere safe to land – but really it already knows there isn't anywhere, nowhere at all. So it just goes on jumping, always returning to the one thought.

*Run, Neesh, run.*

And the weird Kef-not-Kef voice starts to sing: 'RUn PaKi, rUn PaKi, rUn, rUn, rUn!'

'She's not even from Pakistan!' I yell after them, but the sound of the singing just gets further and further away and then Kef comes into sight. He's walking down the hill, heading straight towards the boat, and now I'm really scared. The blood's freezing in my veins despite the heat, despite the warm, warm sun on my face and all around me in the soft suddenly-summer air.

My blood is frozen.

And so am I.

'Where are you going?' I shout.

But there's no answer, only the sound of him singing: 'Run Paki, run Paki, run, run, run.'

The sound of it sends me crazy. I can see her on the boat and I can imagine Kef, slipping silently over the side with his weird friend, see them standing up together and waiting behind her, waiting for her to turn around and see them, and then . . .

I close my eyes, try to block it out, but the pictures in my head only get worse – I see her turn, suddenly, hopefully, and then I see her face fall and sink into itself with horror . . . not Neesh, not Neesh, not Neesh, not because of me! I scream her name out loud as though that could save her, and cut my wrists against the ropes holding me. Wherever she is, I want her to know I'm coming. Only I'm not, am I?

'NEESH!'

Kef glances back at me and turns away. It looks like he's lost too.

# Neesh

I wait until I think I can actually feel time moving past me, until I begin to imagine that by some miracle it might leave me behind somewhere no one will notice.

'NEESH!'

I hear it. I hear his voice, full of pain and agony and desperation, and I answer. I act before I can think. I grab the blowtorch and igniter and stuff them in Sammy's rucksack. I crawl out of the kitchen window and slide silently down the side of the boat and into the water.

I crawl out on to the bank on my belly, hoping I can't be seen.

When I glance back it looks as though the boat is raining flowers, raining them so hard that they bounce off the wooden deck and back up into the air, where they dissolve into nothing in the daylight.

I turn away. I keep on going.


# Kefin

'*No!*' Kef hears the word as soon as he goes near the lake, and he feels his whole body judder to a stop.

'BUt we're off to plAy with BuNny!' says Knife, blade between his teeth. Kef doesn't answer, all he knows is that he doesn't want to go near the water.

'TouGh sHit!' says Knife. 'I'm huNgry!' And Kef knows it's true. He can feel Knife's hunger in his own stomach; he can feel the need for the drip of blood against the blade. Kef's tired. His brain whirrs and clicks and fails at trying to re-make all his broken connections. He knows something's wrong, but he can't think what.

'Stop – don't want to!' Kef whispers to himself, trying to twist away from his own cut and exhausted body. The brown water of the lake is making pictures in his mind. He sees a face, a mouth in a wide O shape, gasping for breath like a fish.

Water streams across a face.

He closes his eyes, shivers.

'StOp sniVelling, you paThetic little shIte,' says Knife, 'sHe asKed fOr it.'

Kef feels a brief and powerful flare of anger. Knife starts singing. His voice, surprisingly high and clear, rings right through the woods.

'RUn PaKi, rUn PaKi, rUn, rUn, rUn! DoN't let the kniFey get hIs gUn, gun, gUn!'

Kef shivers. Kef's glad Knife is his friend. Knife's scary. Kef runs straight towards the boat even though he's scared of the water. He stays close, right behind Knife, hoping Knife won't turn round, won't notice him.


# Neesh

I'm already buried in mud and undergrowth, halfway up the hill, when I hear the voice. I can hear every word.

'Run Paki, run Paki, run, run, run.'

For a moment it stops me being able to move at all, I'm so scared. I lie in the leaves and mud, breathing, telling myself that I'm still here, still alive. I think if I move, he'll find me, and then, and then . . . what? I breathe in the damp earth. I think of Sammy still out there somewhere, and slowly I begin to move again. Slowly, a slow snaking crawl up the hill, listening to the singing voice all the time.

'Run Paki, run Paki, run, run, run.' Marking it.

Thanks, I think, because now I know where you are and I can make sure I'm heading away from you. The singing is heading towards the boat, and I even manage a small smile. Because I'm not there, not standing by the windows, waiting – like she was.

I move faster. I rise up to a crouch, I circle the hill round and round, searching for Sammy, and then I see a trail of broken branches, trampled leaves of bluebells, a track.

I follow it, trying to stay in cover. I see his hands first, his poor tied-up hands pushing against the tree, twisting against the rope until they're scraped and bleeding.

I'm so relieved I do something stupid then; I call out his name.

'Sammy?'

# Sammy

'Sammy?' I think I hear her voice.

I must be going crazy. I wait, it comes again.

'Sammy?'

'Neesh?'

But she doesn't answer, just appears around the tree. *Thank God*, I think, then immediately think, *shit, shit.* I only saw Kef heading for the boat, where's the mate? Where is he?

'There might be two of them!' I shout, but she just holds her hand to her lips, kneels down and then traces the cut across my chin, and at that moment, she doesn't look scared at all. She looks angry.

'Where is he?' she says.

'I think he's at the boat. Oh God, Neesh, I thought you'd be there, I thought they'd . . .' but I can't say what I thought, it's too terrible. 'Your hair!' I hear myself say, because she's cut her hair off, all of it.

'It was in the way,' is all she says. It makes her look so changed somehow, but good too, kind of.

'Jesus, Neesh, I thought Kef would find you. I thought . . .'

'What?' she says. 'That he'd kill me? Rape me?' and she disappears behind the tree.

# Neesh

I can't untie the ropes on his wrists. He drops his head, as if that way he could block out his thoughts. I get out the blowtorch, light it.

'What are you doing, what is that?' he asks, but by then I've made enough space between the knots to burn the ropes apart, and his bleeding wrists fall to the ground.

'Fucking hell!' he laughs.

We stare at each other and he reaches out for my face. 'Neesh,' but I push his wrist away, gently.

'I couldn't get back, Neesh,' he says. 'I . . .'

I hold his poor damaged hands. 'I know, it's all right, Sammy, I can see how hard you tried.'

'Let's get out of here,' he says, 'quick, before they come back.' He looks around. 'I think he might have someone covering the gate, I'm not sure.'

We crawl away from the clearing on our hands and knees and occasionally we reach out and touch each other, both unable to believe that we're both still really here, and together.

We think it's nearly over. I mean, the odds are on our side now, aren't they? Sammy knows the woods and we've got the blowtorch.

All they've got is an empty boat.

# Kefin

Kef leaps up on to the boat, the knife held high in his hands.

'LiTtle Miss BuNny, coMe oUt to plA-ay-ay!' cries Knife. No one answers. The boat stays silent, silent and empty.

'Ah! WaNna plAy hiDe and sEek? ReAdy or nOt we're coMing!'

'FiNd her!' Knife says to Kef.

Kef searches through the boat, throwing open doors and cupboards, flipping up bedcovers. He can feel Knife getting angrier. Getting hungrier.

'Not Funny, bunNy!' he shouts. 'StuPid Paki, wHere is sHe?'

'Don't know!' whispers Kef. He picks up the long hanks of hair from the kitchen floor, and holds them against his cheek. He has a brief vision of a girl holding her long plait and staring at him as she sucks on the end of it. He wonders who she was. She was pretty.

'CheCk the cupboards, check everYwhere – GaMe over, buNny,' yells Knife, but there's no answer, not a whisper.

Kef shivers and twists away from Knife, he checks everywhere, whispering to himself, 'She's not here, not here.'

And then he stands in the middle of the room, lost.

'NeVer saw tHe poiNt of you meSelf, Kef. Now I know wHy – there Ent one!' shouts Knife, laughing. *That's what Dad used to say*, thinks Kef, again.

Kef stares at the water. He doesn't like it.

'Don't go in there,' he whispers to himself, 'don't go near the water.' And he backs away, but Knife hears everything. *How did he get here?* thinks Kef, briefly.

'DoN't liKe the waTer, do you, snOt-nose?'

Kef stiffens. If Knife can't get Neesh, Knife will get Kef.

'WHat aRe you scaRed of?' Knife asks. 'ReMember somEthing, dO yOu?' Knife prods Kef. A sharp drip of blood appears on his elbow.

'Nothing. I don't remember nothing!' says Kef. He's trembling, trembling all over.

'SAy?' Knife's tip is at his throat.

Kef gulps. He shakes his head, he mustn't . . . he mustn't remember, his whole life depends on it. Knife pushes him forward, down the steps and on to the jetty.

'Go Play iN the poNd?' Knife says.

Kef says nothing, even though the words sound horribly familiar. He never did say anything, did he? Dad told him what he'd do if he did. His mum had left him. That's what Dad told him happened. She left him because he was such a useless fucker – didn't she? Nan was always asking after Mum. Nan didn't believe Mum would ever leave him. She told Dad she didn't believe it. That's why Dad killed her, isn't it? Kef *had* to kill him back, didn't he? Slowly, Kef tries to piece together how he got here, but all the while Knife's pushing him closer and closer to the water.

Dad pretended to be dead, didn't he? But Kef knew, Kef was careful. Kef never turned his back. Never, not till now.

And then Kef gets it. Dad's won, hasn't he? He tricked him in the end, Dad did, because he's right here, right now, isn't he?

Dad *is* Knife.

Kef backs away from the water but Knife holds himself steady, jabbing him in the back. He's right at the lake's edge now.

'Go On!' says Knife, but Kef doesn't move. He can't swim, he's always been afraid of the water, doesn't know why, no one does. He looks up at the sky, he looks anywhere and everywhere, except at the water.

'JuMp,' says Knife. Dad said this would happen, Dad said he would kill him if he ever remembered, and he has.

Remembered what?

Kef doesn't move.

'ARe you goiNg to juMp or do I haVe to I puSh you?' Knife asks.

Pictures start to spin.

He feels a sharp jab in his back. Kef jumps. He feels the cold water close over his head. He feels it run over his face. He sees his mum. He remembers what happened. He sees Mum. Her head is rising from the water. Her face is all wet. He sees Dad's hands holding her down. Kef forces his way up through the cold water. He screams.

He screams with the voice he heard all those years ago, his mum's voice calling for him, longing for him.

'KEFIN!'

Kef hears Mum calling.

He drags himself from the water and begins to run.

'I'm coming!' he screams. His legs feel short and small beneath him. They feel as though he has to take a million steps a minute, and still he'll never get there.

He hears Knife, right behind him.

'CoMe out, CoMe out, wherEver you are!' Knife yells.

'Mum!' yells Kef, and as soon as the word is spoken he knows how he can find her. He sees the tree in the park; he sees Neesh's eyes as she looked into him. Neesh knows everything. She knows what he did, and she knows where his mum is.

Kef's going to find her.


## Sammy

The sound stops us in our tracks, it's bloodcurdling, terrifying.

'KEFIN!'

The sound of his name ricochets in the air around the lake and Neesh's face goes white with shock. I feel her body flinch under my hands as though the sound hurts her, and then she stands up like she's going to answer.

'Neesh! Get down!' I hiss, but she can't hear me. She stands completely still, and even though her eyes are wide open, it's obvious she can't see a thing. She holds her hands stretched out like she's blind and feels the air, touching it, tasting it. It's weird, like watching a snake's tongue, as slowly her whole body begins to sway and spin, until finally she stops. She's facing the lake, pointing straight at it.

'Kef's mum's calling him.'

'What?'

'It's Kef's mum!' she whispers. 'She's here. He can feel her here, and I can feel him feel it. I mean, if you've seen inside someone, Sammy, you can't completely pull out, that's why I don't do it, and why I've always thought he'd find me. I mean . . .' and she lifts her head up, 'once you've done that, you're connected.'

'Get down, now!' I almost yell, and she does. We crawl on fast, because we can hear them coming after us, crashing through the trees and bushes.

'Coming!' yells Kef.

'ReAdy or Not!' says his freaky mate, a split second later.

# Kefin

All Kef knows, or allows himself to know, is that he's running. But no matter how fast he runs, Dad and Knife can keep up with him. He can hear Dad's voice.

'We were fine until the bloody Pakis came!' says Dad, and Kef remembers Neesh's dad's voice, so different to his dad's, so precise and clear and gentle.

'Actu–ally, we are not ev–en from Paki–stan!' he says slowly, gently, sounding each syllable, a smile on his face.

Dad spits at him.

Kef stops running. A sudden silence descends on the woods.

'LisTen!' says Knife. 'We doN't even nEed to fiNd her, do

We?' he says. 'We juSt need to let hEr know wE've got something she wants! We've gOt *Mr* BuNny!'

A slow sadistic smile crosses Kef's face. He'll do anything to get his mum back. He reaches for the knife and runs his fingers lightly over the sharp edge of the blade. And then suddenly, startlingly, the expression on his face changes completely. He opens his mouth and speaks. 'Don't hurt them!' he says to Knife, because he never, ever wants to be like Dad, does he? Not ever.

'WhAt? SamMy your blUd, is he!' laughs Knife. 'GoOd one, thAt, yeAh! EveRyone's bloOd in tHe end!'

They move off up the hill. Kef's face shifts as rapidly as the falling sunlight on the leaves. It shifts from light to shadow, from doubt and horror to the safety of cruel joy. Kef and Knife head up the hill towards Sammy.

Sammy isn't there. Kef smiles with relief for just a split second, before his face contorts into a furious anger.

'WhEre the FuCk is He?' yells Knife.

Kef shrugs.

'You let hIm go, yOu stuPid litTle half-aRsed shIt, diDn't you?

'No! No!' Kef's scared; he doesn't like it when Knife's angry. He wants it to stop. 'Let's pretend he's here!' he says, quickly.

Knife stops, and then he looks up and smiles, and Kef's heart turns over with joy because Knife looks pleased.

'YOu and mE, Kef!' says Knife, and Kef's heart sings. 'We cAn persuade liTtle Miss BuNny out to play with Mr

Bunny. Sit doWn, Kef, you sIt right there. You bE Mr
BunNy. Let's play pretend!'

Kef feels unsure. His head hurts. He's hungry.
Something's wrong, but what? Knife's pleased, isn't he? He
sits down where Sammy was and, in his heart, maybe he's
glad Sammy isn't here. What would Knife have done to
him?

Knife is scary.

Like Dad.


Perhaps Neesh will come. Perhaps Knife can make her.

Kef's in a daze. He sits beneath the wide-arching
branches of the oak tree. He watches Knife's hands as they
move slowly over his body slicing and cutting him. Slicing
and cutting.

He is Kef pretending to be Sammy.

Slowly he stops. He blinks. He stands up.

'Do You like SamMy's pretTy paWs?' he asks. He sits
down. He watches as the tip of the blade draws a long line
following the metacarpals of his hands. He cuts SamMy
neatly, cleanly and with care. He likes him.

Kef stands up.

'WouLd you still loVe him if he dIdn't have a preTty
face?' Knife shouts out into the silence of the woods. Kef
wonders where Neesh is. Will she ever come? SamMy's
weak now. He's bleeding from everywhere. He might not
last much longer. Kef realises he doesn't know how to tell
Knife to stop. He doesn't want to play pretend any more.

He watches as the blade comes closer.

'ThIs is my traDemark, mate,' whispers Knife. He slices Kef's jaw, and Kef feels the cut, is surprised by the pain. Kef knows that he is Knife's now. He's got his mark. He belongs to Knife. He belongs to him just like he belonged to Dad. Like Mum belonged to Dad.

He lies down under the knife. He can feel himself slipping away. It's nice. He sees his mum's face rising up out of the water screaming his name and being pushed down again, but this time he's with her. This time they can both go under together and leave Dad behind – with Knife.

## Sammy

We crawl into a bush.

'Neesh?' I say, but she just looks at me and then she shakes her head.

'I can hear his mum,' she manages to whisper, 'she keeps on asking me to help him, to save him, but I don't know how.'

'Save him? Jesus, Neesh!'

The questions are racing through my head. What will they do when it doesn't work, when Neesh doesn't come out of the woods? Will they come for us? Is Jammi out there listening to this too?

'ThIs is my TrademaRk,' we hear the voice say, and Neesh's fingers suddenly trace the new cut across my jaw, but she whispers Kef's name, not mine.

'Don't!' I flick her fingers away.

# Neesh

Kef's jaw is cut, cut just like mine and Sammy's, but how? His mother is crying and sobbing, repeating Kef's name over and over inside me like rain falling on leaves, like sadness without end, and I'm amazed anyone can love anyone like that, especially Kef . . .

*Kef, Kef, Kef, no, no, my boy, not my beautiful boy . . . save him!*

I touch the cut on Sammy's jaw.

'NEESH!' He flicks me off. 'Don't!'

But it's not me doing it, it's Kef's mum. *Help him!* she wails inside me. Why does she want me to help him? Kef's the one threatening to cut Sammy to pieces.

# Sammy

I edge towards the end of the bush and peer out.

I take the thoughts one at a time; keep my head slow. I think about the fact that I never saw the other guy, not for a second – only thought Kef's voice was odd. Throughout the whole thing I only ever saw Kef, and why would whoever he was with hide, unless I knew him, could identify him. Could it be Jammi? The voice didn't sound like his, but it would be just like him to never be out in the open where you can see him, but always doing the dirty work in the background, so someone else can take the shit.

I fly up above the woods in my head and look down on our position. I picture us all like dots on a map. Them, us and the gate.

'Neesh,' I whisper, 'if Kef's alone we can get to the gate, as long as we know no one else is looking for us!'

She nods, but only just; she's got that look on, the one where she's listening to some faraway voice, the one where it's best to just leave her to get on with it, just like I have to get on with this.

And so I make my decision.

'Neesh, let's go. I think we can make it to the gate.'

She nods, but I can tell it's an effort; she's listening, listening hard to something else that's going on inside her.

Blink. Blink, blink.

She holds my hand and we stand up.


# Neesh

I can't focus properly on what Sammy's saying. The woman inside me is inconsolable, grief-stricken, sobbing Kef's name over and over again inside me. Listening to her is like being stabbed with knives, long, drawn-out cuts that won't heal, can't heal, because she can't get to him. She's so desperate . . .

*Kef . . . Kef . . . Kef . . . no . . . please God . . . no . . . my beautiful, beautiful boy . . . don't make me leave him . . .*

I can see the white haze of concentration all around Sammy, and I squeeze his hand.

*Please. Please, please!* Kef's mum weeps inside me, *save him, save him.*

And I nod at Sammy. I don't really know what he's saying, but I know this: I know I trust him with my life. He takes the rucksack with the blowtorch and igniter in it.

We stand up, hold hands and edge back into the woods.

## Sammy

I'm listening hard. Every note of every bird on every tree in the whole wood is in my ears. Even now I can remember the sound of the leaves beneath my feet going off like gunshots in my head, even as another bit of me knew that we were making the merest rustle.

We head backwards, so that we'll skirt the tree where I was tied up (which is where I reckon Kef is), keeping it as far away as possible. Sound good? Yeah, until you realise you don't have a clue whether that's where they really are, and you know that the cover close by is shit.

I can hear my heartbeat. I can feel the bones in Neesh's fingers.

I look at Neesh. And she's with me, just. We go on, flitting from trunk to trunk, getting closer to the tree I was tied to, closer to the gate just beyond it. The voice is slowing, has been for a while. The tenor of it has changed, it's like Kef's almost forgotten us now and is talking to himself. I'm straining to hear the words, even though we're getting closer.

And then we're as close as we have to be and Neesh trips and a branch cracks.

And we stop.

# Neesh

We stand silent behind the tree, listening, waiting to see if he's noticed.

The closer we get to Kef, the louder his mum cries inside me, louder and louder, drowning out the sound of everything else around me . . .

*Save him*! she's wailing inside me, *please, please, please . . . save him!*

I shout back silently, *Lady, what about us?* but she doesn't pay any attention to me at all.

*Oh, quickly, quickly, quickly . . .*

*But how?* I'm thinking. *I mean, he's the one with the knife.*

# Kefin

'What do you want?' Kef asks the knife, as it hovers over his face, playing lightly over his cheeks. It stops around his eyes, traces his eyebrows with its tip. A thin red line appears, and Knife asks Kef a question.

'I wAnt yOu to tEll me whAt I dId. WhAt did yOu

see, KEf?'

'Nothing, nothing, nothing, nothing,' Kef whimpers.

'SuRe now?' asks Knife, only suddenly it isn't Knife speaking any more. It's Dad.

Kef is stripped bare and bled back to the bone.

Kef is three years old. He is lying on his back, struggling in the leaves and dirt and earth as Dad holds him down.

'Sure?' asks Dad. 'You didn't see what I did? Nothing at all?'

Kef shakes his head, eyes wide and scared.

'Where's Mum, then?' asks Dad's voice.

'Gone,' whispers Kef.

'That's right, son, and don't you forget it.'

Then Knife is back.

'Why diDn't you saVe her, Kef?' Knife whispers, but Kef has no answers. He watches Knife hover over his eyes . . . eyes that saw nothing, said nothing, and Kef knows that Knife is . . . waiting . . . waiting for Kef's permission.

Kef nods.

Knife hovers above Kef's eyes.

Kef's eyes are no longer empty. They are full of pain and memory.

'I didn't save you,' he whispers to his mum. 'I said I didn't see anything. I thought you left me. I didn't help Nan. I killed Dad.'

He nods at the knife. He doesn't want to see anything any more.

A branch cracks, loud and sudden, and Knife hesitates . . .

# Neesh

*'Ke-fin, NO!!'*

The words are like a storm through trees, the wind of her flowing through me, throwing me forward out of my hiding place and into the woods. Beyond life, beyond thinking, my whole body's catapulted into action by her words and the feelings ringing right through me . . . how can I explain it? It's maybe like flying? Or like running, like that moment in amongst all the huffing and puffing and agony where your body just takes off and does what it's best at? That's what it feels like when I answer someone else's desperation.

*Please, Kefin, no! My beautiful boy, stop him, stop him . . .*

I answer, I run towards the tree, towards Kef, but I can't see him, there's nothing there, only a heap of clothes at the bottom of the tree, and . . . what is it? What is that thing at the base of the tree?

OMIGOD! OMIGOD! NO! It's Kef. He's holding up the knife, and he's going to . . . and there's no way I can stop him. I can't get to him in time, unless . . . the knife's hovering above his eyes ready to plunge . . . no!

I let her out.

*'KEFIN! NO!'* His mum's voice rips itself free from somewhere deep inside me.

And I realise that this is what he's wanted all along: the sound of her voice, her memory, her smell. Her being.

And somehow he knew I had it.

# Sammy

Neesh is gone. She's up and running, running out in the open, straight towards the tree, and there's only an empty space beside me. She has no protection, nothing to stop them from killing, raping or torturing her.

'Neesh!' I scream, but she doesn't stop; she's not listening to me, she's answering something else, something inside her. I don't run after her straight away. I empty the rucksack, struggle to light the blowtorch; can't do it, hands shaking too much.

Breathe.

Try again.

Succeed.

And then I'm hearing my own voices in my head.

*Run, Sammy, run, you bastard.*

And I do, and it feels so good not to be running away, to be running forward at last, forward and straight into whatever's waiting for us.

I burst into the clearing with the flame held up high. Where is he? Your turn to feel the fear now, mate . . .

SHIT! HOLY FUCKIN' SHIT!

Kef's holding the knife high above his eyes, staring straight up at the tip of it, there's blood everywhere, all over his hands and face and arms. I look around, spin on my heels, holding the flame. Who did this?

And then Neesh screams. She screams Kef's name. Only it's not in her own voice.

She's standing in the middle of the forest with a lunatic after us, screaming '*KEFIN! NO!*'

In someone else's voice. And it works. Kef stops. His hand holding the knife drops away from his eyes, and he looks straight up into the bright blue-sky. He looks like some crazy long-lost species of man, who's only just begun to comprehend reality. He looks like he's climbed out of the forest floor; he's covered in dirt and blood and debris. His eyes are suddenly confused and full of pain, and he whispers a word.

'Mum?' he asks, and the hope gleams, flashes through his eyes like sudden sunlight.

And in that moment, I get it. He was doing it to himself, the poor crazy fucker.

I watch transfixed as Neesh walks towards him, as she kneels down and holds his head in her hands, and the words flow out of her mouth as she rocks him, rocks his broken body in her lap and whispers the words that as soon as I hear them, I recognise. I recognise them because they come from somewhere deep inside all of us. They're written across our hearts, engraved on our ears and in our bones. They are the basic notes of our race, because amongst all the fear and the hate there's this too, the sound of humankind.

The rhythm that lies behind the words, any words, so long as they have understanding.

*'It's all right,'* Neesh is saying, *'it's OK, there now, sweetheart, shh, shh, my love, good boy, it's all over now . . .'*

And as I watch the knife drops from his hand still covered in blood, his blood, but it looks fine now. The blade is somehow naked and alone; it's just a blade lying in the leaves – powerless without Kef's anger to guide it. But still Neesh moves it out of his grasp, and I pick it up and put it in the rucksack.

Kef's head is lolling, his eyes beginning to close.

'Mum?' he whispers. 'Sorry, sorry, sorry, sorry . . .'

And Neesh, sighs, a huge sigh that seems to have all the voices of all the mothers of lost children in it. I stare at her.

'*It's OK, Kef,*' she says, '*it's OK. You were only a kid.*'

'I didn't save you . . . I didn't remember!' he whispers, and his thin body twists in her arms. 'I thought you'd left me!'

The voice coming out of Neesh twists itself and is full of pain. '*Oh, Kef! My Kefin. I would never ever leave you!*' she says.

I stare at her. I stare at the girl I love because she is amazing, and I know something. I know this: that she can never really, truly and completely be mine, because she's Neesh, she's herself – and that's what's so amazing about her. Even with all the weird words and voices and visions and colours that get into her, she knows just exactly who she is.

And that's what makes her weird.

Being herself like most of us never learn how to.

Because we're too scared, because it makes us different – but it makes her the girl I love.

Always have.

Always will.

# Neesh

Kef's mum's voice runs through me like an underground river, soft and far-away and soothing. I hold out my hands and put his head on my lap.

'Mum?' he whispers, and the pain flows out of him in blue and black and charcoal-purple. All the agony and the terror and the poison his dad poured into him flows out in puke green and acid yellow, until finally he can ask his mother the questions he has inside him, and hear the answers.

And it's my hands holding them. Kef and his mum. I look at them, one still twisted and cut and scarred, one whole and undamaged, and I feel something new inside me. Something like pride.

'Is he dying?' asks Sammy.

But I don't know. I can't do anything about that bit; that's up to Kef, I think.

I look for the knife but it's gone. I wonder how he managed to put all his hate and fear and memories and desire into a thing, instead of a person. And I see that when he did that, it made him a nobody, and that made all of us nobodies, and that's how he could hurt us, hurt himself.

Sammy touches him gently over his eyes, where the red lines of cuts make circles.

'Poor fucker!' he says, and he touches Kef with his lovely long fingers, so whole and undamaged, so soft and gentle and good at catching things. People, music, cricket balls, me.

We smile at each other.

Kef tries to open his eyes. He stares up at the blue, blue sky and then he turns his head slowly, blinking and searching until he finds my eyes. 'I . . . knife . . .'

'It's OK, don't try to speak!'

'Neesh?' He says my name, and suddenly my eyes are full of tears. He's never called me Neesh. He's called me Paki or Wanker or Fucker, but never my name. I nod. 'Sorry,' he says, and then his eyes close and he looks calmer again, almost asleep.

'Let's get him to the car,' says Sammy. 'He needs help.'

And we pick him up and begin to carry him, slowly, over the rough ground.

We never make it back to the car. He's too heavy, and he's groaning like it's only now he's given up the knife that he can feel the pain of what he's done to himself.

# Sammy

We lie him down near the stream that feeds the lake and begin to clean him, and maybe this is wrong but it feels good to finally be safe and together. It feels like lying on clouds. At the back of my mind something's pushing at me, worrying me, but I flick it away, too busy with a sense of relief.

It's like we're suddenly Kef's mum and dad washing away all the bad things and making it better. Neesh is soothing him with her new-found voice. I'm slowly wiping away what he's done, cleaning it up and trying to make it better.

'It's weird,' I say, 'but this feels good!' And she turns to me, her eyes huge and dark and more luminous than ever.

'We're all still alive,' she says in wonder. And I remember that she says the craziest things in the sanest way. I remember that a lot of the time what she says is true.

We smile.

And that's when they come. We should have heard them but we didn't, we were too busy and too relieved. We let ourselves forget the danger; we thought it was all over.

'Don't move!'

Their voices came out of the woods and as soon as I heard them, I knew that the fear inside me had never really left. It had just slipped back to where it's always lived, in the cave of my guts, forever. I reach across Kef's body to touch her, hold her.

'Stay away from her!' they say.


# Neesh

'Don't move!'

I try to let go of Kef but his hand still clings to me. I sit back and see them. I'm small and they're big. There are only two of us, but there are lots of them, that's the way of it. In my weary, tired mind I see the women on the edge of the lake and the boys in the woods, and I close my eyes wishing I couldn't see, but I can.

I look at Sammy.

'Not a muscle!' says the voice and I realise it sounds

scared itself. I turn around and they're standing there, staring back at us. I see what they see. A blood-ridden boy and us leaning over him. I remember picking up the knife and I realise it's got my prints all over it. What happened to it, where did it go?

'Put your hands in the air, both of you, and move away from the boy!'

We look at each other.

Sammy's hands are up but he's talking.

'Thank God you're here. He needs help,' he says, and I wonder why his heart isn't sinking like mine. I wonder why he can't see that they're not here to help us at all, only to judge us, but he can't.

Slowly I stand up, feel them take my hands and cuff them.

'Jesus H Christ!' says one of them, as he looks at Kef.

'I know,' says Sammy, 'but he was ill.'

And he still doesn't get it, can't see the horror in their eyes. Can't see that they think we did it.

'Sammy!' I say, but already I know that it's too late, there's no time. No time to say all the words inside me, like *hold on*, and *never forget*, and *remember me*.

He reaches for my hands.

'What are you doing?' he shouts, but they're already behind him, they grab his hands, and then it begins to dawn on him.

That they think we did it.

And that's what they say afterwards. That it was us cutting Kef, that we did it together over and over, cut him, cleaned him, cut him again, would have cut him to a slow death if we'd had our way. We were punishing him, they said, because he stabbed Gita, because he threatened me.

We stare at each other as they put us in separate cars. We're both thinking the same thing: that we never got to be together in the flowers. We never touched each other until we made the shape of each other's bodies real.

And Kef, Kef who could explain everything? He's dying, in hospital, unable to tell anyone anything.

## Sammy

After the first shock I'm relieved. I mean, I thought it was Jammi behind us, and I'm thanking God it's only the police. And then I can't believe that they're treating us like crims. Throughout the whole journey and even at the police station, and when Mum comes, I keep on talking, trying to explain what happened to everyone. I go on believing that they are actually going to let us go. I still can't really believe it, and I think of Mum's words, 'Just like your grandpa, insisting the world's a better place than it really is.'

I keep thinking weird thoughts, like, *I never tasted her cooking*, and *if she can hear voices, why can't she hear mine right now? Or can she?* That's what I keep thinking. Weird isn't it, what stays in your mind? And I keep thinking this: *whatever you do, whatever happens, Neesh, don't kill yourself. Stay alive.*

*Don't leave me alone. Not this time. Because I will come back.*
*I promise.*


# Neesh

Mum amazes me, she's a whirlwind.

'You cut my daughter's hair!' she screams at the man standing by the door. 'You think she needs lawyer? *You* need lawyer!'

'I cut it,' I say, and she stares at me.

'If you are talking, talk sense!' Her umbrella twitches but she doesn't hit him with it, or me.

I ask for Sammy but they won't let me see him. It's dark here. Not the rooms, but the place where they're keeping me. Some weird remand place. Its soul is grey and sodden, like an old dishcloth that needs boiling, and the other girls are so angry, it makes me tired the way their colours are always clashing and jangling.

'Weirdo, freakoid!'

One throws a cushion at me. I laugh, and soon they're all doing it, throwing everything they can find. They think they're wild and free and rebellious, but really they're just as chained as the women who stoned my aunt.

The lawyers and policeman take statements, lots of them, words going down on pages, but only words that fit with what they already think. At first I tell them easily, with my new-found voice, but then the questions come.

'If you're so innocent, why did you disappear after the

incident in the park?'

'I was scared. *We* were scared!'

'What of?'

'Everybody! Everything! Of Kef. My family.'

They look at each other. One of the women with them says slowly, 'When we're scared, Nushreela, we sometimes do things we wouldn't usually do, don't we?'

I stare at her, say nothing, because slowly I'm beginning to realise that if everybody already thinks that they're right, then there's nothing worth saying, is there? And so I stop talking again.

Sometimes, just faintly, I think I can hear Sammy's voice. I see him standing on the boat in the early morning sunlight, saying, 'I'll be back. I promise.'

I'm here, Sammy. I'm waiting.


# Sammy

It's not looking good for us.

My mates have said I was acting weird at the skate park, and not really around for those few crucial days.

They don't visit.

But Mum does, and in the end I ask her.

'Please, Mum, please visit Neesh; I need to know how she is.'

'Why would I want to do that?' she says coldly. 'Isn't she the reason you're here?'

I stare at her. 'No, no, she isn't,' I say. 'I'm here because of a fuck-up. We didn't do anything. We were helping him!'

'Sammy!' she wails. 'I used to know you.'

'Did you?' I say. 'Then how can you, even for a second, Mum, think I could have done this?'

'I don't for a moment think that you *did* do this, and we'll pay for the best lawyers to prove it. Sammy, I know you think you love her and I know you're loyal; it's a great strength, but sometimes . . . sometimes . . .'

'You have to ditch a dead weight, drop someone you love . . .'

She flinches when I say that word, love, flinches like I've actually hit her.

'There's always a price to be paid, Sammy, when someone breaks the rules – and believe me, it's not you who's going to pay it, whatever you may believe . . .'

'What do you mean? What rules . . .?'

'Society's rules, theirs or ours. You see, my love, it doesn't really matter which. What matters is that you don't live the rest of your life under a cloud! You must tell the truth, you were trying to rescue her from her family!' she says, and her face is hard and cold. 'I've never thought I would say this, but when it comes right down to it, Sammy, you have no choice. If you hadn't met Neesh none of this would've happened, and I hold your grandpa partly responsible . . .'

'What? He's in India! He's not even here!'

'Exactly! He never is here when you need him, is he, but he was around when Neesh's father wanted to move here!

He encouraged you two, and after what happened last time he should have known better!'

'How better?'

'He should have known that history has a way of repeating itself, especially if you go on living in the past! How do you know what'll happen to Neesh even if she does get out of here? Each should stick to their own, that's the conclusion I'm coming to!'

We draw back from each other. We stare at each other like we've both suddenly been slapped in the face, flicked with a cold wet towel. She stands up, and as she walks away I wonder if I've ever known her. Has this always been here, underneath everything – this hatred?

I write to Grandpa.


Mum gets me a new lawyer.

As soon as she comes in there's something different in the air.

'Sammy,' starts the woman. She's youngish, smart, her hair hangs exactly as it should, to just below her ears, her lips are red and seem to pout without her knowing it. She's sharp all over and I don't like her, don't like the I'm-on-your-side look of her, without her even trying to get to know me, or the truth of what's happened to me.

'You had plans for your life,' she goes on, 'presumably, plans that didn't include this.'

I see Neesh. I see her as clearly as if she was right beside me, and she's holding Kef's head in her lap and looking up at me, her face full of pity for the boy who hated her. I remember bowling left arm over the wicket, watching the ball swing out and curve back in. I remember thinking that one day I might wear a cricket shirt with England on it. Now all I want to do is to get out of here – and take Neesh with me.

So yeah, I had plans, I still do, and no, they don't include being here. I nod.

'And then things went wrong, didn't they?'

They certainly did. I nod again.

'And now, Sammy, I have to tell you, they're looking pretty grim. About as grim as they can get, really.'

'How's Kef?'

'Still unconscious. I wouldn't pin your hopes on Kefin, Sammy,' and her voice is gentle, pitying. 'When would you say things began to go wrong for you?' she asks.

'From the moment I was born, I reckon – or, if you're really asking, maybe even before that!'

'Sammy, this is serious.'

I stare at her; does she even know what she's doing? I stare at her without blinking, until she's forced to drop her eyes and look with interest at every other single thing in the room, except me.

'I know what you're going to do,' I say. 'I know you're hoping I'll say that it all began to go wrong when I met Neesh. I know you're hoping that it will slowly dawn upon my dim brain that I've been utterly taken in by her, that this was all her idea and that I've been in her power right from the start. And then, maybe when I'm totally confused and unsure, you'll spring this one on me. You'll say: she's ditched you, you know, she's told us the truth. As if that isn't what you've got already.'

I look at her. She's disgusting; she doesn't give a stuff about me or Neesh, or whether we want to be together. She wants to destroy Neesh to save me, but that's not possible. I don't want memories or monuments, like Grandpa. I don't want a Taj Mahal or a lake and a boat. I want Neesh, the real living girl – and that's all I want.

'What's she ever done to you?' I ask her.

'Sorry?'

'I mean it. What has Neesh ever done to you for you to hate her so much?'

'Don't be ridiculous!' she says. 'I'm not trying to destroy *her*, I'm just trying to help *you*!'

'No,' I say slowly. 'No, what you want is to blame her, and that's easy, isn't it? Because she's not one of us and she hasn't got any lovely money like my family, and so she can spend her whole life being blamed, locked up and hated, and I'll spend my life being free. What you don't get is that I won't be free, will I, because I won't have her!'

I turn away. When I look back all I see in her eyes is anger, anger that she's been sussed. That she's the one who's been got at. That's her job, winning, and deciding who's got the best chance of winning.

Fuck truth.

Fuck justice.

Fuck Neesh.

And fuck me.

Just win.

'It's not gonna happen,' I say. 'We didn't do anything wrong!'

'It's not enough to work with,' is all she says. 'Both of your prints were all over that knife. If you want to continue with those plans you had, Samuel Colthurst-Jones, your best bet is to listen to me.'

'Those plans had her in them!' I shout. 'Not saving my own skin.'

'That might be your only option,' she says. 'Think about it.'

'I do,' I tell her, 'I think about it all the time. Know what? I've been frightened of something like this my whole life-time!'

She turns at the door. 'You might be able to help her more from the outside,' she says, and my heart drops because she's clever, so clever.

I want to be back on the outside.

But the evidence is there in my rucksack, a knife with our prints on it and our faces all scarred in exactly the same places, me, Kef and Neesh, like some bizarre pact.

# Grandpa: Kashmir

We must all bear witness to the lives around us as well as our own lives. I'm waiting here on the lake where I first met her, on a boat that was here then, waiting for a police officer who will tell me what really happened to her.

A man who, I hope, will give words to the whispers of fear that have lived inside me for sixty-five years. Words for the actions that used to be unmentionable and unthinkable, yet happened. And maybe if I'm lucky there will be proof that these things were done. I can feel her with me, near me, alive in me again, and I sometimes imagine that she's here and waiting – beside me.

The policeman's footsteps wake me from my reverie, they're confident, young and powerful. His knock on the wooden door is bold.

'Hello? Cooee?' he shouts in English, and I call him in.

'Id-er-oh!' I shout. 'Come.' And he enters the room, already talking.

'So, you know our language?' he exclaims.

'In words, at least!' I reply, and I smile, but his face remains serious.

'I'm wondering, sir,' he says, 'why you are so interested in the fate of this girl. It was a long time ago.'

I look at him. He is dapper, shoes highly polished, belt buckle gleaming, but his eyes give him away; they are wide almonds fringed with impossibly gentle lashes, their centres dark, questioning, liquid.

'I loved her,' I say, and in the end it makes a simple sentence, like all truth. He stares at me, and with a shock I remember that I'm old. I have been seventeen again these past days, but now I see every one of my years reflected in the pity of his eyes.

'Sir, perhaps you would like to take a seat?'

'Perhaps.' I smile at him; I might need a seat even more later.

'Very well!' he says, and he takes out his notebook, holds it like a slim shield between us as we stand facing each other. We stand to attention like old soldiers ready to hear the truth – and he begins.

'On the last day of the month of August in the year of 1944 the body of Farida Begum Hussein was recovered from Lake Nagin. On autopsy it was discovered that the bruising to the body was suggestive of the practice of stoning . . .'

His voice is strong and steady, holding me up, helping me to listen as he says the words.

'Further evidence suggests that she was multiply dishonoured in the body. She was raped by men unknown and died by drowning . . .'

*I see her body rising from the water, runnels and rivulets gently caressing the shape of her before falling from her face* . . . and then I realise the officer is still talking . . .

'Sir, sir, perhaps a seat now?' He's guiding me to a chair, and shouting for tea.

For a while neither of us speaks. Somewhere within the

pain is a strange sense of relief, of something lifting. We sit in a companionable silence, and maybe, I hear myself think, that's one of the things that's left when the truth is told. Silence.

'Was anyone arrested?' I ask, eventually.

'No.'

'Suspects?'

'As always!'

I take a deep breath.

'And can we re-open the case?'

The police officer rises from his seat; he looks uncomfortable for the first time, awkward.

'I will be very happy to look into the matter, sir, only it may be problematic after all these years, and some things . . .' He tails off.

We stare at each other and his eyes drop to the wooden floor of the boat, away from me.

'Sir?' I say.

'The reports,' he goes on, his gleaming shoe tracing the pattern on the floorboards, unconsciously following it as though it could keep him safe within its boundaries, 'that were made at the time . . . I'm afraid that if they are correct, sir, then the culprits will no longer, be, um, in the country.'

I don't understand. I still don't understand.

'Are they dead?' I ask, but already I know they're not. Already my gorge is rising up inside me at what it senses. Already I can see them, laughing, a group of them, standing on the edge of the lake, camping out in the woods. Boys, like me, on holiday from the war, from England. White boys. When I look up the policeman is still talking.

'It was difficult at the time,' he says, 'for us to proceed, but perhaps . . . perhaps if there is someone suitable and willing to press charges on the dead lady's behalf now?'

'There's me,' I say.

And beside me I think I hear a sigh, a gentle exhalation of a long-held breath. I feel a new space in the world – like someone letting go so that something new can begin.

When the young officer has gone, all that remains of the day is a thin red line of light stretched out across the horizon. As I watch it deepens to an almost impossible red, and flares briefly to gold before disappearing.

And I know she's gone.

Her story told.

And I know it's time for me to go home.

# Kefin

Kef hurts. Kef hurts all over, but he wants to speak. He has something to say. Kef knows that only he can say it. Kef knows that Dad can't say it and Knife can't say it. Sometimes, when the hospital is lit by a soft night-light and Kef comes briefly to consciousness, he hears his mother's voice.

'*I would never, ever leave you,*' she whispers, and Kef knows that he doesn't have to join her under the water because she's inside him now, where he can hold on to her for ever. But it's not her face he sees when he hears her words. It's Neesh's face. It's her eyes looking down on him that make him feel all warm inside. He remembers the feel of her hand in his, the way she laid it aside so gently before they took her away. He wants Neesh to come back.

'I hurt,' he whispers, 'I hurt all over.'

'What can you tell us, Kef?' the policewoman asks him. She isn't gentle like Neesh.

'Neesh,' he whispers, and even the sound of her name on his lips makes him feel better.

'Neesh isn't here, Kef. You're safe from her now. Can you tell us what happened?'

'Safe from Knife.' He shivers.

'We know, we know Neesh had a knife, and Sammy too. It's fine, you're safe from them now.'

'Knife's frightening, like Dad!'

'What happened, Kef?'

329

'Neesh took Knife away. She brought my mum. I want Neesh!'

'What?'

'Neesh,' Kef whispers again. He has a sense now that she is in danger, he wants to save her.

'Neesh saved me from Knife. Knife killed Dad. Knife killed Gita!'

'Gita's not dead, Kef,' says the woman.

Kef sighs and closes his eyes. So he didn't kill Gita.

'How did your dad fall, Kef?'

'I pushed him!' says Kef, because the truth, when it comes at last, is always simple.

Kef settles his head on a pillow. In his head all is quiet now, it's only his body that hurts.

They are always there, the policewoman and the man. Kef begins to like it, the soft presence of them when he wakes up.

Slowly he begins to heal.

Slowly he begins to talk again – in his own voice.

# Neesh

There were no papers at first, but there are now. Papers, and pictures of Mum grinning like Madonna, yep, with the exact same gap in her teeth, only not quite the same smile – and saying things like 'When I was her age all the boys came out to watch me dig the turnips.'

That's true. The next bit, the bit about, 'always we knew

she was special,' is not true; it's how she sees my future. Suddenly me being a witch is good, can make her money. 'Always she can read feelings – cheap price! She can even tell when you are ill, even though she is so skinny.'

Jammi takes the calls from the papers, making sure Mum gets the best offers.

'Lucky, sis,' he says slowly, 'this makes far more than your cooking and witching ever did!'

I don't answer. I hate him.

'You should be flattered,' he says, 'there was a whole crowd of boys out looking for you that day in the woods. Lucky that the police found you first!'

'Fuck off!' The words feel good in my mouth, but sound even better on the air.

He draws his fist back, and then thinks about it. 'Mustn't spoil the goods,' he says, 'but don't push me, sis, they won't be interested in you for ever.'

And I know he's right.


# Sammy

When I get home Grandpa's already standing in the hallway waiting for me.

'I was on my way before I even heard!' he says. 'Goodness gracious, boy, what on earth have you been up to – and on my boat too!'

He's standing in front of me, his blue eyes sparking like the sun off the sea.

'I didn't do—'

'Of *course* you didn't do any of the things they say you did, we know that,' and he glances at Mum, an angry glance, 'but what *were* you doing? That's the question, my boy.'

And just looking at him leaning on his stick, with his wild grey hair sticking up all over the place and his leathery-brown sunburnt skin, makes me want to cry. To just lean against him and cry and ask him, please, to go and get Neesh, who's stuck at home with her God-awful mother giving press interviews while her brother does God knows what. I want him to make it all right, the way he always has – only this time I'm not so sure he can.

'Can I come and stay for a bit, Grandpa?'

He looks at Mum, who nods.

'Whatever you need, Sammy, you know I . . .' says Mum. Her voice fades away. We can't talk in the same way, not yet. I'm still too angry.

'All I want is to be with Neesh,' I say.

'Let's talk,' says Grandpa.

And he takes me home and we sit on the roof of the boat. It's hot.

The woods are full of high ferns and bluebells. The late snow and frost have jumbled everything up, so that the bluebells and the rhododendrons are both lost in flower. They're at their best, the rhododendrons, running wild around the lake like an echo of laughter. Lazing in the sun. It's like having balm rubbed into sore muscles.

Except that Neesh isn't here.

The press can't get near me here, and anyway Grandpa's got someone at every gate. He's made it absolutely clear that anyone who puts a toe on his land without his say-so will end up in court. He hands me a cup of his brew – cinnamon and cardamoms and lots of sugar, black – and I suppose that you have to have been given it since you were a boy to really like it.

I like it.

'Tell me,' he says, and he sits back in the sun, waiting.

And I tell him. I tell him everything, all of it, even the crazy, weird, doesn't-make-the-least-little-bit-of-sense bits of it. And as I do I can feel the sun searching out each sad and lonely bit of me and warming it up. Grandpa listening is like that, like the sun. He doesn't ask questions, just waits, and listens, and lets you stumble and think, and stumble again, and maybe change a few things and then go back a bit, until finally you've found your own way forward. Your way and no one else's. And then he waits some more, just to be sure, and then after a while I find I've finished.

'So you need a way to see her again?' he asks.

I nod.

He looks out over the lake and his eyes are far away like he's looking into the past, or maybe the future. I can't tell which, and right now I'm not even so sure of the difference.

'Sammy,' he says, 'do you know why I dug this lake?'

'Kind of,' I say, 'I mean, Mum says it's like a monument . . . to Neesh's great-aunt.'

He nods.

'So you've worked out some of the story,' he says. 'It's a monument, that's right. To sadness, though, Sammy, that's all monuments can ever be. You can't put love into bricks and mortar.'

'Or into a lake,' I say, 'or a boat, or anywhere really except into people.'

Grandpa nods.

'I've made a mistake, Sammy, I've been living in the past,' he says slowly, 'holding on to the tiny little bit of it that I wished could last for ever.'

'I know,' I say, and I do. I feel like I could live for ever on that feeling we had, me and Neesh, of falling through a door and into each other's arms.

'But, Grandpa,' I say after a while, 'why did she kill herself?'

'I don't know,' he sighs. 'I'll never know, but, Sammy, maybe she just hurt. Maybe she hurt more than she could bear?'

'Like Kef,' I hear my voice say, and he nods.

'Sometimes,' he says, 'I imagine that she's still there, waiting for me, in the mountains under the lake ... and that I'll reach out my arms and ...'

And then he shakes his head, like he's coming up out of the water with mountains on his shoulders.

'Grandpa? What'll they do to Neesh? Can we get her out?'

And he says this. He says: 'Sammio, all we can do is try.'

'Will you? I mean, can you? I mean, I know I'll have to, uh, let her mum know my intentions and everything, but . . .'

'I was just waiting for you to ask,' he says, and he looks up at the sky and at the trees around the lake, and he sighs a deep, deep, sigh. 'Son,' he says, 'it would be my very great pleasure,' as though there's nothing else he wants more in the world. 'It's a chance to put things right, and how many people can say they get the chance to do that?'

And he smiles.

But what about Neesh, that's what I'm thinking; after all that's happened, will she want to come back?

# Neesh

He arrives in a small car, and the photographers hanging around outside barely give him a glance until he comes up to the door and knocks, and then they surround him, shouting questions. I shrink back.

'I've come to see if Neesh would like to stay with me and Sammy for a while,' he says to Mum, as though it's the most normal thing in the world.

Mum stares at him; so do I.

He steps inside and closes the door behind him.

'You are wanting to take my daughter away?' she says. 'For your grandson? She's very precious to me,' and she hugs me to her, too hard, it squashes me, 'and very good cook!'

'Indeed!' says Sammy's grandpa. 'Well, what we can offer is somewhere safe from the hordes,' and he gestures outside at the press pack. 'Anything else is really between Sammy and Neesh, wouldn't you say?'

Mum nods, although it's not what she would say at all, not if she could find her tongue – which she does, eventually.

'You think is chance of marriage?' she asks.

But Sammy's grandpa doesn't hoot, or look horrified, or do any of the things that are making my toes curl so far up my body that they're practically scratching my ears!

He answers her.

'Truth is,' he says, 'you never can really tell with young 'uns, can you?' and Mum nods properly this time, 'not unless you give them the chance, can you?'

'Ah *ucha!*' says Mum, nodding wisely, which means yes in almost any language.

And then Sammy's grandpa does something truly amazing. He starts jabbering away to Mum in Urdu. In Urdu! He talks about *niquat*, bride-price, and other stuff, stuff that gets Mum talking back and nodding away like those little dogs you see in the backs of cars, and in the end, after a long while, he says quietly to me:

'Well, Neesh, we've done our part, the decision's yours now. Yours and Sammy's.'

And they all stare at me, especially Jammi.

I go and pack. Two plastic carrier bags. At the door, Mum presses something small into my hand. It's a small broken painting, on ivory.

'Of my aunt Farida,' she says, 'you know, the one just like you, the witch!'

Sammy's grandpa doesn't talk much on the drive, but he hums just like Sammy does, and I look at him out of the corner of my eyes, and wonder if that's what Sammy will look like one day. I wonder how to tell him what I know.

When we get to the gate to the lake he just stands there for a minute, and then he holds out his hand. I shake it.

'Good luck, Neesh,' he says.

I stare at him. The sun's bright in his blue eyes, and suddenly I feel as though his arms are empty. I reach into my pocket and find the small ivory picture and hold it out to him. He looks at it, holds it, and then he reaches into his own pocket and pulls out his own painting, and puts the two jagged ends together and shows me the miniature: it's a picture of a boy and a girl. A boy and a girl who look a bit like Sammy and me.

'Thank you,' he says.

'Jake?' I say, and he stops and stares at me. 'She heard you,' I say. 'She knew you came.'

'It was too late,' he says sadly, 'but not for you two. For you it's only the beginning!'

'But she heard you,' I say again, 'she knew you came back.'

'Thank you, Neesh,' he says, and then he turns away, still humming.

'Thank *you!*' I shout, but he doesn't turn around, just waves an arm, balances on his stick and hums a morning raga, just the way Sammy does.

I open the wooden gate. Everything around the lake is in bloom. The air is heady with the scent of flowers and the sound of bees. The mayflies dance across the water in the sunlight, flashing blue – and he's standing there.

Sammy.

Standing on the roof of the boat in his tee and cut-offs, waiting for me.

And there's no one but us. No gang of girls, no Kef, no Jammi, just two people waiting for each other. And I begin to walk towards him. I start out slowly, putting one foot in front of the other, watching him closely in the lazy, hazy sunshine just in case he disappears. He doesn't move, doesn't raise a hand – he just watches and waits.

A part of me is waiting too, still waiting for something or someone to stop us, but no one does.

He's still there.

Watching me.

Waiting for me.

And I begin to move faster. I drop my bags and I begin to run. And he moves closer towards the edge of the roof of the boat, and he holds his hand up to his eyes, shading them against the sun.

And he sees it's really me.

# Sammy

I know she's coming. I know if anyone can get her out of that house, Grandpa can. But still, when I see her actually standing there just inside the gate, I can't quite believe it. She stops and looks all around her, up at the trees and the huge jewelled rhododendrons, out over the lake.

And at me.

And I watch. I watch and listen to my heart beat.

And wait.

To see if she'll disappear. But she doesn't. She takes a step towards me, and then another, and I raise my hands to my eyes just to make sure – and then she's running as though the wind was after her, and I call her name, and the whole lake seems to shift and shimmer beneath me.

'NEESH!'

'SAMMY!' she yells back.

And I dive off the boat into the cool, cool, water and head towards her.


# Neesh

The sound of my name rings around the lake as he dives into the water, takes a flying header into the water straight towards me, then he's up and out of the lake and throwing his arms around me, holding me tight. So tight I wonder if we'll ever be able to let go.

And I look up at his lips, lips as surprising as red berries on a winter tree, and I smile.

And then somehow our mouths are doing all the talking for us.

And we don't need to say anything at all.

Nothing.

# Epilogue

## Neesh

It's so hot on the roof of the boat that I can barely breathe in the unbroken air. It's as hot as India. Sammy comes up the ladder to where I'm standing looking out to the horizon, where I see nothing but an empty lake and a line of trees backed by a cloudless blue sky.

'I love you,' says Sammy.

I don't say anything. I think of all the things we've found out. I think of my great-aunt. I think of the way she sank her arms into a boat full of flowers before spraying them into the air. I think of her lying broken and alone after the boys who raped her had all gone. I think of Sammy spinning around with his arms outstretched, taking in all that oxygen – and I think of me.

I am not like them. I'm scared. Scared that the more I talk, the less I see the colours above Sammy's head. I look at the empty horizon and I blink. Blink. Blink, blink. But it all stays exactly the same. There are no more pictures.

'Hey!' says Sammy. 'You hardly ever do that these days!'

And he smiles at me, reaches for my hand, my scarred left hand, stretching it out and linking fingers. He steps up to the edge of the roof of the boat, pulls me towards him until we're standing on the exact spot where my great-aunt once decided to die.

'Look down,' he says. I look, but it's impossible to see beyond the surface of the deep brown water. The lake's as still as glass. All I can see is the shape of the boat lying on the water, and our own silhouetted shadows, staring back at us.

'Doesn't look as though the water's even there, does it?' he whispers. And then, as I watch, I see his reflection move. His shadow shimmers on the water, and when I turn he's standing on the railings, perfectly balanced, and for a split second it's like the whole world is still. The birds don't sing, the wind doesn't lift; only the sun shines, and Sammy stands up in it beautiful and straight and shining ... like a slim column of air ... a pale haze ...

And then he does the thing I fear most – he steps forward.

He falls like a stone, soundlessly, towards his own reflection. He falls until the two meet on the still water and the glassy surface of the lake explodes, sending the silent, heat-exhausted birds flying up out of the trees. The shattered water echoes around the lake before dying away in the heat-deadening air. The water closes over his head. Its glassy surface recovers, and I see the reflection of myself slowly re-form on the rippling water.

For a split second I'm standing alone and then Sammy comes up for air, shaking his head, letting loose droplets of fractured sunlight all around him.

I can't speak.

He climbs back up on to the boat.

He takes my hand.

He takes me a step closer to the railings of the boat and he looks at me.

I'm scared.

'I know,' he answers, even though I haven't spoken, 'C'mon.'

I slip my feet out of my new flip-flops. I feel the railings beneath the soles of my feet. I feel my heart beat wild with fear and excitement, like a caged bird frightened that the door might open. I feel Sammy's hand holding mine.

'Whenever you're ready,' he says, and he steps up onto the rails and waits.

I take a deep breath. I think I'm going to die, that I will never come up for air.

Somewhere outside of me I think I hear a distant rumble

of thunder.

I rest one foot on the rails and his hand tightens. I take another step and I'm balancing beside him. I glance at the world around me, at the trees and the lake and the still-green leaves of the fading rhododendrons. I see it all clearer than ever before.

And I want to be alive and part of it.

I feel Sammy's hand holding me and I turn to him and smile . . . and he smiles back . . . and then we both face forward and we take a step . . . and we fall . . . and the water hits our feet and rushes over our bodies, closes over our heads and shuts out the world.

There is silence.

I open my eyes. I see the bubbles of our breath rising round and clear in the water, and for a terrifying moment I think I'll die. That I'm drowning like my aunt. Then I feel Sammy's hand still holding mine and he looks at me. Our eyes hold as he releases my hand. He lets it go and I turn my face up to the light . . . and realise.

I'm rising.

## The End

# Acknowledgements

Every book or story has its journey to the shelves, not only in the mind of its writer, but through all those who work with and love reading.

Thanks to Sarah Starbuck for plucking WAVES out of a towering slush pile.

To Rosemary Canter for thinking I had a special 'voice'.

Thanks to Barry Cunningham and everyone at Chicken House for turning a long-held dream into a reality. For believing I had more than one book in me. For giving me the time to write each book in my own way.

To Barbara Bradshaw who hears the voice beneath the words.

To Daphne Briggs and Julia Sleeper, who listened and so taught me how to learn.

To Philip Pullman for suggesting I try writing in the third person.

To Rosemary Turan who reads every word of each baby story, and then tells me the difficult truth, that sometimes it's not working.

To every reader who takes a chance and picks me up.

Last, and definitely most, to Adder, Jem, Xa and Ella, who actually have to live with me living through each story – and yet are still there when I wake up in the morning.

Thank you.